IF WE HAD KNOWN

ARLENE LOMAZOFF-MARRON

To my grandchildren, who have begun to discover that reading can take them anywhere they want to go, without leaving their homes.

Chapter 1

It should have been no surprise to Paul Brown that Carly didn't hear him call to her from the living room. She rarely did, although they disagreed on the reasons. She said the sound of his voice did not carry well through the acoustics of the wooden banister and the plush carpeted stairs. Paul thought the problem was with her auditory system—her inner ears could not completely and correctly process the tones and inflections of his baritone voice. It was better than assuming she was ignoring him, as happened so often with marriages of over three decades like theirs.

Over two or three years, Paul had realized that Carly liked the television louder than before. She occasionally misheard lines in the stories, and couldn't reconcile why the storylines took the turns they did. She blamed the problem on modern actors, who often spoke softly and mumbled. Carly had read that in previous times, the actors and actresses in films and television shows spoke in uniform tones and enunciated better, so the difficulty deciphering more recent dialogue was not entirely her fault. When she and Paul watched television together, the increased volume made his ears hurt and his head spin, and after repeated arguments she turned on the closed captioning option instead. While he agreed the volume was now more suited to his auditory system, he hated the language scrolled across the bottom of the screen. He could see and process the words quickly, often before the actors had spoken them, which eliminated the element of surprise when he read a character's confession before its utterance. Carly was happier though, and Paul supposed it was worth some minor discomfort to pacify his wife.

Now, feeling a bit unsteady climbing the stairway to the second floor, his right hand reached for the banister. He surmised the feeling of lightheadedness was related to lack of food. He and Carly had skipped their usual full lunch, settling for apples and yogurt. Carly had reasoned that they didn't want to arrive at the Grangers' party with full bellies. The party, to celebrate Nancy and Brad's wedding anniversary, was also a chance for the Grangers to unveil their new patio, which had taken contractors three months to construct.

Paul crossed the hallway and entered the master bedroom. He caught a glimpse of his wife admiring herself in the full-length mirror which framed her walk-in closet in the far corner of the room. Carly, clad in a black knee-length dress and black pumps, and wearing the onyx necklace they had purchased on a trip to Italy, turned to face him when his reflection appeared in the mirror. Her hair was still the same color of wheat as when he had first laid eyes on her decades before—although now the color was courtesy of a bottle. The skin around her eyes and mouth bore small wrinkles, a small price to pay for more than five decades of life. Carly smiled, pleased to see Paul had worn the clothing she had suggested. Although he had gained about twenty pounds in his torso and a few wrinkles in his face, she still considered her husband handsome. Perhaps not in the same way as love struck twenty-somethings, but marriage had a way of blurring the lines between internal and external beauty.

"I called you from the living room. But I guess you didn't hear me."

Carly's body tensed, and her smile fell. "You used to tell me how beautiful I looked. Now you insult me first."

"I did not insult you. I simply made a statement." Paul sighed, not wanting to revisit Carly's denial of her hearing difficulties now. It was best to ignore her comment, or it would mar their entire evening. "You do look beautiful." He kissed her on the cheek and gingerly lifted the onyx from her neck. "I remember when you bought this necklace, on our trip to Italy. What a wonderful trip that was."

Carly's face brightened. "Yes, it was a fabulous trip. Perhaps the best one we've taken." She adjusted the collar on Paul's gray pinstriped shirt, paired with black linen trousers and a gray sports coat. "I see you are wearing the shoes you bought last week. They look much better than the battered ones you've been wearing for several years."

Paul glanced at his black leather Oxfords, purchased in a men's store where he rarely even window-shopped. He and Carly had been in a rut, sniping at each other over petty matters for reasons they could not explain. Neither had been in a mood to cook, and as often happened with empty nesters like themselves, they had dinner out. He and Carly had dined at a neighborhood restaurant, and she had berated him for wearing the same shoes nearly every day. He had held his tongue and didn't argue, hoping that the car ride home would mellow her mood. When she suggested perusing the selection of shoes in the shop visible from their table in the restaurant, he had nodded. Thirty years of marriage had taught him it was usually better to compromise than to risk further marital discord. He tried on the pricey shoes as a peace offering and had reluctantly handed over his credit card for a purchase he suspected he would regret. But he was more concerned with maintaining a harmonious marriage than spending an extra fifty dollars.

"Yes, I suppose you're right. I wore the shoes a few times this week to break them in. But they aren't stiff at all. They don't pinch my toes or my heel. They feel great. I guess it's better to buy more expensive shoes."

Carly nodded. "For most of her life, my mother wore cheap clothing that rarely fit well. That's the way she was raised. Her father's job barely provided for the basics, so much of the family's clothing came from the local Goodwill. Even when my father earned more money, my mother didn't shop anywhere else."

"Yes. I remember the argument you had with your mother about a dress for Greer."

"I remember that well. She couldn't fathom that I allowed Greer to spend two hundred dollars on a dress for the prom. She said she could buy her entire wardrobe for a year with two hundred dollars."

Carly was pensive. Memories of her mother were always bittersweet. Although they had disagreements like most mothers and daughters, even during their worst arguments, Carly would never have wished her mother a massive stroke. Luckily, Lucia Casperella had succumbed within a day of the cerebral hemorrhage, her physicians in agreement that she felt no pain during her last hours.

The ping of her cell phone interrupted Carly's remembrances. She glanced at the phone and turned towards Paul.

"Thank goodness for alarms. We have to go. Nancy will be angry if we're late. I offered to help her set up the hors d'oeuvres. She's counting on me. It takes precise planning to get everything heated and arrayed at the same time. Nancy would never let the caterers manage this feat themselves." She smiled and wondered why Nancy couldn't let go of a bit of autonomy and structure. Carly had hired the same catering company for their parties and events, and the staff always did a terrific job, without the constant nagging they got from Nancy.

"Then I'd better keep Brad company. I'm sure he needs help to set up the liquor and the other beverages. Besides, I'm thirsty. Perhaps I didn't drink enough today." Paul kissed Carly lightly on the lips and headed towards the stairs.

"Do you want to get something to drink now? We can take it in the car."

"No, it's fine. I'll grab something to drink as soon as we get there. I'm hungry too. But I know they will have plenty of food and drink. Let's go eat and drink ourselves silly."

Paul checked his reflection in the mirror in the foyer, set the house's alarm system, and opened the front door, motioning for Carly to proceed first. As he exited the house, his left foot brushed the Persian rug lining the hardwood floor. He lurched forward and grabbed the door frame to prevent falling. He glanced at Carly, who was descending the four outside stairs and hadn't noticed his misstep. Paul exited the house and pulled the sculpted wooden door behind him. He pulled on the doorknob, and assured he had locked the door, turned towards the stairs.

As he approached his car in the driveway, Paul was unaware that this would be the last time he would meander on his property independently, and on his own feet.

Chapter 2

Traffic was light, and the drive to the Grangers took ten minutes. Paul maneuvered the Acura into the last parking spot on the property; the latecomers would deal with the on-street parking. He and Carly exited the car and proceeded along the cobblestone pathway to the front door of the stately house. Before they had reached the doorway, Brad Granger threw open the door and embraced Paul in a bear hug. He planted a kiss on Carly's cheek.

"Welcome! I'm so glad you two got here early. Nancy is in her usual manic state, afraid that the caterers will drop a tray of food on the ceramic tile, or that our guests will ask for a type of alcohol that we don't have."

At six feet four and weighing over two fifty, his stature was not the only thing incompatible with his wife. Nancy took every opportunity afforded her to announce that she wore the same size dress as on their wedding day—size six. At five feet five and a hundred and twenty-five pounds, with fashionably frosted blonde hair and few wrinkles, she still turned heads, even from men a generation younger. Their friends reconciled the Grangers' personality differences—her constant panic and his calm and unhurried demeanor—with the well known saying about the attraction between opposites. How else could they live together harmoniously?

"Thank goodness you're here! I need your help!" Nancy grabbed onto Carly's arm, eyes large and pleading. "I don't know if we have enough cocktail shrimp. Please tell me I didn't mess up!"

Carly gave the men a wry smile, and the women disappeared into the kitchen. Brad, who no longer reacted to his wife's outbursts, walked nonchalantly towards the bar.

"Paul, help yourself to a drink. We have more than enough for an army," Brad chuckled.

Paul strolled to the bar and perused the bottles of specialty beer and high-end liquor. He chose a craft beer from a local brewery, popped off the lid, found a seat in a chair at the periphery of the room, and took several gulps of the sudsy brew. A young woman wearing a white apron tied around a simple black dress placed a tray of antipasto on the breakfront several feet away.

"Food. Thank goodness," said Paul, as the woman returned to the kitchen. He stood from the chair. His head felt woozy, and he grabbed onto the edge of the table. He knew he needed to eat. Locating the plates and utensils, he piled strips of red and green and yellow peppers onto his plate, and dipped chunks of Italian bread into a bowl of olive oil and pesto. He shoveled the food in his mouth hurriedly, grateful no one could see him behaving like a starving man. A din sprang from the vestibule, and Paul peered towards the foyer where two beaming couples stood: the Millmans and the Larrimores, greeting Brad with outstretched arms and toothy smiles. Paul glanced at his empty plate, chewed and swallowed the food in his mouth, and ambled into the adjoining room to greet the couples.

"Hello," he called, reaching the foursome as the last of the appetizers cleared his mouth. He shook hands with Jack Larrimore and kissed Brenda Larrimore on the cheek. "It's good to see you. Carly is in the kitchen with Nancy."

Grace Millman gave Paul a quick hug and strolled towards the kitchen with Brenda.

"How are you, Paul?" asked Stan Millman, as he reached in and shook Paul's hand. Although nearly six feet in height, he often appeared shorter because of his slim build. He reportedly hadn't gained more than a few pounds since his high school days. He stood back and surveyed Paul. "You look like you lost a little weight. Don't tell me Carly isn't cooking her delicious meals anymore."

Paul chuckled. "No, she's still cooking." He patted his abdomen, which protruded slightly above his belt buckle. "I lost a few pounds, though. And I dropped a pants size." He stepped back and struck a model's pose, right arm in the air. "Carly decided I needed some new clothes." He leaned towards Stan and whispered, "And she made me wear them tonight!"

"I know what that feels like," replied Stan, slapping Paul on the shoulder. "We can't live with our wives, but we can't live without them either!"

"Just don't let the women hear that!" added Jack Larrimore. He cast an imposing figure. A former college linebacker, he had once hoped to play professional football. After an initial disappointing draft, ignored by teams in the National Football League, he opted for a career in the corporate field instead of a football field, despite encouragement from his peers to consider playing football in other lesser-known professional leagues.

A cacophony of aromas wafted through the room. The noise had increased twofold, and as Paul surveyed the room, he noticed people spilling throughout the foyer and into the dining room and the formal living room. His eyes locked on the breakfront and surrounding tables now piled with an array of food. He motioned to Stan and Jack. "The food looks great. It smells delicious. I'm going to grab a plate. Will you join me?"

"Sure," replied Jack, as he rubbed his ample belly. "You know me. I never pass up good food."

"Me neither," added Stan.

The men strolled to the dining room and wasted no time in piling their plates with mounds of lasagne, enormous pieces of chicken parmesan, and strips of braised beef, cooked to perfection. As they neared the end of the food display, Stan and Jack passed on the bread, but Paul piled two pieces of warm Italian bread atop the mounds of food weighing down his plate.

Stan eyed Paul's plate. "I bet tonight you'll gain back the few pounds you lost. Your plate looks bigger than Jack's."

"I'm famished today. And thirsty too. I'm going to get another beer. Can I bring back something for you?"

"A dark beer would be great. Thanks."

Paul grabbed two bottles of stout beer from the bar and strolled back to Jack and Stan, who had found chairs in a corner of the living room and settled in to enjoy the generous spread. Jazz music blared from the speakers suspended from the corners of the ceiling. Paul settled into his chair and shoveled the gourmet food into his mouth. He felt as if he couldn't eat or drink fast enough. The pasta, laden with several types of meat and cheese, was delicious. He used a slab of bread to scoop the food remnants from his plate into his mouth. He exhaled and repositioned himself in the chair. Feeling sated, but odd, he couldn't discern what was different. His body signaled a full bladder, and he rose from his chair.

"I'll be right back," he called to the men. "Got to relieve myself." Paul stood and was overcome with dizziness. The food in his esophagus and stomach threatened a regurgitation, and his vision blurred. He grabbed onto the back of his chair and stumbled backwards, missing the chair and landing on his right hip on the floor. Jack and Stan jumped from their chairs, the food from their plates spilling onto the peach carpet.

"Paul! Are you okay? Did you hurt yourself?" cried Jack, while Stan reached for Paul's arms and tried to right him, and another partygoer sped off to look for Carly.

"I...uh...," mumbled Paul, who seemed unable to articulate further.

"Is anyone here a doctor? Or a nurse?" bellowed Stan. "We need help here."

"Rebecca is a physician. Where is she?" called someone nearby. "Someone get Rebecca."

A fiftyish woman clad in a navy pantsuit ran into the room, straightening her clothing as she neared Paul. "I'm Rebecca Victor. I'm a physician. I was in the bathroom. What happened?" she asked, as she kneeled beside Paul on the carpet. She loosened his tie and unbuttoned the collar of his shirt. She checked the pulse at his wrist. His heart was beating fast. She glanced at his wedding ring. "Is his wife here?" she asked, as Carly ran into the room.

"Let me through. I'm his wife." Carly's face was flushed and her hair askew. "What happened? I was gone for only a few minutes. I left my calcium supplements in our car and went to get them. I heard yelling. Someone said Paul collapsed." Carly kneeled beside Paul on the carpet. "Paul. Paul. Honey, are you okay?" she implored, gingerly touching his cheeks and shaking his shoulders. It was then that she noticed Rebecca Victor beside Paul.

"Who are you?"

"I'm Rebecca Victor. I'm a physician. I moved into the house next door a few months ago."

"I'm Carly. Pleased to meet you."

"Carly. Tell me. Does your husband have any medical problems? High blood pressure? Cardiac issues? A stroke? Diabetes? Has he seen a doctor lately?"

Carly shook her head. "No problems like that. He's a little overweight. He lost a few pounds recently. But he hasn't seen a physician in a while. He was scheduled for a physical earlier this year, but he had a business trip at the last minute and canceled the appointment. I don't think he ever rescheduled it."

"He needs immediate medical attention," responded Rebecca. "Testing. Monitoring. Probably medications."

"The hospital is ten minutes away. I can take him right now. In my car. Of course, I'll need help to get him into the car." Carly scanned the room. There were enough able-bodied men to carry Paul to her car.

Paul moaned and uttered a few unintelligible syllables. His arms and legs twitched, and beads of perspiration formed on his face and neck.

Rebecca checked Paul's pulse again. She shook her head. "His heart rate is increasing. He should go by ambulance. This is a medical emergency."

As Stan dialed 9-1-1 and spoke to the emergency personnel, the other partygoers dispersed into the adjacent rooms, and Carly rested her head on Paul's chest and prayed he would be okay.

Chapter 3

The ambulance driver pulled into the area reserved for emergency vehicles, shut off the engine, and hopped down from the seat. He hurried to the back of the vehicle and opened the doors. He helped Carly descend the two steps to the curb, while Martin, his coworker and recently certified paramedic, gathered the bag of fluids infusing into Paul's veins and placed it on the stretcher beside him. Then the two men wheeled their patient into the emergency department, with Carly running behind, barely able to match their strides.

Martin spoke from memory as the men moved Paul onto a bed in the emergency department. "Caucasian male. Age 54. Collapsed at a party after drinking a couple of bottles of beer. He also ate a variety of foods. Quite a bit of food, according to witnesses. No one else at the party reported feeling ill. Wife reports no medical problems. A physician at the party reported a heart rate in the 150s. 120s en route. Skin cool and clammy. Electrolytes drawn at the scene revealed sodium level 130 and glucose 685."

Carly's eyes were focused on Paul, but the glucose level of 685 caught her by surprise. *That sounds like diabetes. Really bad diabetes.* She lacked a medical background, but recalled a childhood friend, Marla, who had diabetes. Carly remembered Marla tried to keep her blood sugar—glucose—below 150. So a glucose of 685 was truly serious. *How has this happened? Does Paul have diabetes? How long had his blood sugar been elevated?*

As soon as the ambulance crew departed, a group of hospital staff, most clad in navy scrubs, surrounded Paul. They scurried around him, performing specific duties. They attached wires to the round pads the ambulance crew had secured to Paul's chest and upper abdomen. Oxygen flowed into Paul's nostrils, and a cuff attached to a machine on the wall behind the bed checked his blood pressure.

Carly stood to the side, eager for answers but wanting to avoid an interruption or interference. She was thankful to have ridden in the ambulance with Paul, grateful she could hold his hand and provide assurance. Now, isolated from her friends and family, and possessing sparse medical knowledge, her anxiety multiplied quickly. She recalled her mother's sudden illness and rapid demise. Carly searched for a chair, fearful of losing control. Glancing to her right, she saw a set of chairs outside of the room, and gingerly crept around the medical staff to the periphery of the room, then stepped outside into the hallway.

She thought of Greer and David. *Should I call our children? Do they need to know their father has been brought by ambulance to the hospital?* She didn't want to bother them needlessly, especially since Paul was still being evaluated and hadn't been examined by a doctor yet. She would wait until she had more information. That would spare the children from asking questions she could not answer, and free her from making multiple phone calls, providing information piecemeal.

A woman with closely cropped blonde hair and carrying a clipboard, approached Carly. Beverly, according to her name tag, worked in the billing department.

"Excuse me. Are you Mrs. Brown?" she asked, sporting a smile and a mouthful of crooked teeth.

Carly paused. "Well, my husband is Paul Brown. But my name isn't Brown. I mean, I didn't take his name when we married. My last name is Casper. I'm Carly Casper."

"Oh. Sorry for the assumption," Beverly replied. "Well, Mrs. Casper...I guess you might be Miss Casper..."

Carly had no patience for this woman's blabbering. "Do you need some information from me? Are there papers to sign? Just tell me. I want to get back to my husband."

Beverly handed Carly a pen and the clipboard. "I need your husband's insurance information."

Hands shaking, Carly retrieved the insurance card from her wallet and handed it to Beverly, who ambled down the hallway towards the copy machine. Carly perused the papers on the clipboard. At least a dozen forms to complete and sign. *How do they expect people to have sufficient concentration to complete these forms? Don't they know families' first thoughts are of their loved ones, not who will pay the bill? Can't mundane matters like this wait?*

Beverly returned with the insurance cards, looked through the forms Carly had completed, and strolled down the hallway towards the elevator. Carly returned to her vantage point, in view of Paul and the nurses and physicians at his bedside. Paul was more alert, cooperative with the examination, and answering simple questions. She approached his bed.

"I'm his wife. Are there questions I can answer?" she asked the group.

"Hello, Mrs. Brown." The greeting came from a stocky middle-aged man dressed in a lab coat over a black turtleneck and khaki pants. "I'm Dr. Josephs. I'll be managing your husband's case while he is here in the emergency department."

"Hi." *But my last name is Casper. Oh. Never mind.* "What can you tell me about my husband's condition?" she implored. *I sound like a reporter now.*

"We're waiting for the lab results. But his blood glucose...his blood sugar...was very elevated, according to the labs the ambulance crew did. Your husband said he has never been diagnosed with diabetes. Is this true?" Dr. Josephs inquired.

"Yes. That's correct. He's never been told his blood sugar was high. At least he never told me it was high." Carly wondered whether he had kept any information from her. *But why would he keep such important things to himself?* "Actually, he missed his physical this year. He planned to reschedule it. But I don't think he did."

"He said he was at a party. And he ate and drank quite a bit. A fair amount of alcohol."

"Yes. We were at a party. There was a lot of food. And of course alcohol. For most of the time we were there, I was in another room. I didn't actually see what he ate. Or drank," replied Carly. "I didn't see him collapse either."

"Well, we'll wait for our results, but blood sugar as high as what was reported...the crew said almost seven hundred...could certainly cause him to pass out. I don't see any major abnormalities on the electrocardiogram. Nothing with his heart that would have caused him to collapse. I've ordered a chest x-ray. We're giving him some fluids intravenously. We should get his lab results back shortly. I'll hold off on any further medications or testing until the labs come back."

"Thank you, Doctor." Carly approached Paul's bed, took his

hand in hers, and kissed him on the cheek. His color had returned to normal, and his skin was much warmer. He was no longer sweaty.

"Hi, honey. You look so much better," she murmured. "I was so scared when you collapsed. But the ambulance crew was great. I'm grateful a physician was at the party."

"I don't know what happened. I remember falling...and being on the floor with everyone gathered around me." He sighed. "I guess I caused a scene. In front of all of our friends. I'm sorry."

Carly clutched Paul's hand. "There's nothing to be sorry for. I'm sure everyone will be glad you're okay. I'll email everyone later. Or perhaps a text is better. That's quicker."

A young female, her badge identifying her as Nadine, Physician Assistant, approached the bed, while simultaneously entering information into a laptop on a cart.

She faced Carly. "Hello, I'm Nadine. Can I ask you something?"

"Certainly."

Nadine pulled back the sheet to expose Paul's feet. "Have you seen his foot lately? Did you know it looks like this?"

Carly felt the color drain from her face, and dizziness enveloped her. The sole of Paul's left foot was blackened near the third and fourth toes, and there was a large blister at the base of the third toe.

"Oh my gosh! No! I had no idea! I mean, I know he was wearing new shoes. But he said they felt great."

"I didn't have any pain. And I already told the doctors I didn't see it was black," Paul said. "My shoes didn't hurt at all. I don't know how this happened."

"I'm concerned about his circulation. I've spoken with Dr.

Josephs," interjected Nadine. "He's asked for a consultation by a vascular physician."

"Thank you," replied Paul and Carly, in unison.

Nadine's laptop emitted a ping, and she glanced at the display. "Mr. Brown, your lab results are here. I'll notify Dr. Josephs. I'll be right back." She pushed the cart in front of her and hurried away from the bedside.

Carly couldn't determine if the physician assistant's speed was a good or bad sign. She sighed. "I guess we'll know soon what the labs showed," she said to Paul.

Barely five minutes passed before Nadine and Dr. Josephs ambled across the room to Paul's bedside. "Mr. Brown. We got the lab results back," announced Dr. Josephs. "The labs confirmed that you have diabetes. You've probably had it for a while."

"Wow! I had no idea," said Paul. "I didn't have any symptoms." He paused and reconsidered his answer. "Well, I didn't feel bad enough to visit my doctor."

Carly's eyes widened. "What do you mean...bad enough? You never told me you felt sick."

"Well, not sick exactly. Just not myself. Off a little. Hard to explain."

Dr. Josephs spoke. "It's possible you were thirsty a lot. Your mouth might have been dry. You might have urinated more. Maybe your vision was blurry."

Paul nodded. "Yes, I was thirstier than usual. But I thought it was the heat. I complained that the air conditioning in my office wasn't working well. So I drank more." His face reddened. "I had a few bottles of beer today. But usually I drink other things...water or iced tea or coffee."

"I understand," replied Dr. Josephs. "People often dismiss the symptoms of diabetes at first. Of course, the issue with your foot is likely related to diabetes." A ring sounded from the pager on his lab coat pocket. He glanced at it and frowned.

"I have to see another patient. I plan to admit you to Dr. Goldberg's service. You'll stay until we get your diabetes under control. The vascular team will make recommendations about your foot." His pager rang again, and he checked the message and motioned to Nadine to follow him. "I have to go. It's urgent," he cried. He was ten feet away before Nadine caught his words, and she ran to catch up with him.

Carly pulled a chair to Paul's bedside. "I'll send a brief text to Greer and David. I'll tell them you are being admitted to the hospital because you were diagnosed with diabetes. I won't tell them all the details. Just that you're in good hands here."

Paul nodded. "Yes, I guess our children should know. We should tell them the basics. We don't want them to worry." He chuckled. "Of course, we won't remind them of the dozens of times we paced the floor with them when they were sick. Or the times we worried about them driving in the rain...with their friends in the car...doing who knows what."

Carly patted his hand. "No, dear. Greer will learn about that when she has children of her own. Perhaps someday. But I suspect David and Heidi have spent some sleepless nights with Matthew and Emily."

After retrieving her cell phone, she sent a few sentences of text to their son and daughter. As she pressed the button to send the texts, a staff member arrived to transport Paul to his room. As they exited the emergency department, Paul was pensive, and Carly wondered what changes this new chapter of their lives would bring.

Chapter 4

At home, Carly trod on the same patch of carpet for perhaps the hundredth time that night. She had stayed at the hospital until Paul was settled in his room. Now, although physically and mentally exhausted, she hadn't even attempted to sleep, knowing that her body was too restless and her mind too awake to succumb to slumber.

While some of their friends had chronic medical issues and frequent doctor visits, medication bottles on the kitchen counter arrayed like spices, she and Paul had been blessed with good health for so many years. They had each gained about a dozen pounds over the course of their marriage—perhaps two dozen, in Paul's case—but they had not needed to restrict their activities or buy accident or illness insurance for upcoming trips like most others their age. Most days they had only minor complaints. Paul had occasional indigestion when he ate too many fried foods. His left knee ached occasionally when it rained—probably some arthritis settling in, according to his doctor. Paul had spent a weekend in bed a few years before when he tripped on a toy truck Matthew hadn't put away, and fell on the stairs. The muscle relaxants had worked well, and he went to work that Monday, albeit with mild back pain. He had undergone a minor surgery a few years prior and had recovered in a day.

Carly had sailed through menopause with relatively mild symptoms, and although she had occasional migraine headaches, they weren't severe enough to interfere with her job or their social activities. She took no prescribed medications, only a daily multivitamin and calcium supplements to prevent osteoporosis. Lately, she had noticed her hearing wasn't as sharp as it should be, but it did not interfere with conversations or affect her ability to write for the newspaper. Paul had grown weary of her asking him to repeat some dialogue from television shows they watched together, but that had resolved when she turned on the closed captioning option. But those were minor issues, which didn't require recurring medical treatment with specialists, or frequent monitoring, or daily medications.

Carly stopped the incessant pacing and rested on the chest at the foot of their king-sized bed. She said the words aloud. "Paul has diabetes. He is a diabetic. He has a serious medical problem."

In the texts sent to Greer and David from the emergency department, she had downplayed the seriousness of Paul's condition. She professed an ignorance of his actual blood glucose levels—claiming the physicians had only said his levels were elevated and he needed observation and monitoring. David had suggested that Paul would require oral medications and be spared insulin injections, and Carly took the straightforward route and didn't disagree. She had withheld from their children the horrible state of Paul's foot. She shuddered at the image of the blackened tissue she had seen. *How could he not have known it was so bad?*

Then the guilt hit her head on. *Have the new shoes I pressured him to buy constricted and harmed his feet?* He had recently bought new pants, a size smaller than his usual. She had complimented him on the weight loss, although he denied dieting. They hadn't communicated well lately, so perhaps that was why he decided not to tell her he didn't feel well. Their sex life had been fair. *I wonder when it declined from good to fair.* Of course, the lag in their intimacy could affect their communication, and vice versa. *How many signs have I missed?*

Carly reached for a photo in a silver frame on her nightstand. Earlier that year, she and Paul had attended the wedding of the daughter of her close friends, Marjorie and Ken. The photographer had captured Carly and Paul at their finest moment, on the dance floor, heads back, smiling, and seemingly without a care in the world. But she recalled things weren't as rosy that day as the photo suggested. They had engaged in a petty argument on the drive home from the reception. She had taken offense with an utterance from a party guest, a man she knew from other social events, an outspoken man with political views that differed from her own. When she heard him spew a word that horrified her—a word offensive to many people—she wondered why no one else in earshot cringed. Perhaps, being a journalist made her more sensitive to words. Since her most recent newspaper article explored new minority-owned businesses, she felt a civic and moral obligation to support those featured in her story. She had burst into the group of men gathered around the speaker of the remark and opined that she found the use of the word disrespectful and offensive. She recalled mentioning the word's link to slavery and oppression.

It was Paul who found her outburst embarrassing, Paul who was adamant she had misheard the word in question, Paul who forcefully pulled her away and apologized to the group. "He said *niggled*," Paul had said. "The man niggled him. Not the word you thought he said. Not related to it."

Carly, horrified at her error, wanted to apologize to the speaker, but Paul had implored her to avoid any further conversation with the men. Luckily, their designated seats were on the opposite side of the large banquet room, so she only had to avoid the group at the buffet line and on the dance floor. On the way home, Paul started his familiar refrain of frustration with her degrading hearing and her refusal to get a hearing test, while Carly, attempting to control her disgust at making a fool of herself, protected her ego by denying a hearing problem. She rationalized that the newspaper article, published two days before, was fresh in her mind, and therefore at the forefront of her brain. She had simply misinterpreted the comment.

Before that day, she had thought her hearing difficulties only hindered watching the television. The actors' lack of articulation and varied accents justified her difficulty at interpreting their remarks. Now she wondered if she had misheard the statement that caused her outburst. *Do I have a hearing difficulty that extends into everyday life? Perhaps I should contact an audiologist. Will I need hearing aids? I hope not.* Carly remembered her grandmother, wires hanging from each ear, connected to boxes nearly the size of some modern cell phones. Even with the contraptions, the family still needed to shout for her to hear them. No way would Carly wear them. Not even if Paul insisted. She refused to be defined or burdened by such gangly devices.

But this wasn't an urgent issue or a major problem; it could wait. Paul's problems were pressing. She hadn't misheard or misinterpreted the doctor's words. Paul had diabetes—a serious medical problem. Treatment was crucial and couldn't be withheld or delayed. She and Paul likely needed to make lifestyle changes. She wondered how difficult that would be. Uncertainties swirled in her brain. *Will Paul still be able to work? Can I continue to work, or will he need me at home? Can we still take the trip to Scotland we planned for next year?*

Carly replaced the photo on her nightstand and sighed. Their marriage hadn't been perfect, but no marriage was, especially one as long as theirs. She and Paul had been tested before —and passed. She was confident they would come through this episode in their lives intact.

Chapter 5

The cacophony of voices had subsided, the medical personnel had left his bedside, and Paul was finally alone. Traveling on a stretcher onto an elevator, wearing a hospital gown and covered by standard-issue white linens, he had passed other patients wearing the same garb and the same sad expressions. Paul mused that patients lost their individuality when entering the hospital. An observer couldn't discern the chief executive officer from the sanitation worker, or the uninsured from the affluent, when they were draped in identical linens and wore similar hospital-issued armbands.

He surveyed his hospital room. An electronic gadget regulated a plastic bag filled with fluids, which infused into a vein at his left wrist. Saline, to regulate his blood sugar, according to the nurses. Staff removed a few drops of blood every hour from a port at his right wrist to check his glucose. The nurses said his glucose was stabilizing, but when Paul asked when he could go home, no one seemed to know. Stuck to his chest were a series of electrodes which monitored his heart rate; he tried not to focus on the monitor above his head which emitted a steady flow of numbers. A tube delivering oxygen rested in his nostrils, and a velcro strap attached to his right index finger monitored his oxygen levels.

Paul sighed. This was his first hospitalization. He had suffered minor injuries: ankle sprains and an arm laceration. A few years prior, his doctor performed a repair of a hernia that had been nagging him for years. Paul went home within hours, spent his two-day recuperation resting on the couch in the living room, watching sports and National Geographic shows, and returned to his job on Monday. He wasn't permitted to drive for a week, but Carly had taken him to the office in the morning and returned in the afternoon to drive him home. That was the way they did things now, not like a quarter-century before, when his father's hernia operation led to a three-day hospitalization and a recovery period of two weeks. So many of his friends and acquaintances had endured serious medical problems, using precious time away from work for physician appointments, testing, treatments, and therapy sessions. Paul had often voiced how fortunate he was to have avoided serious medical problems or life-altering injuries. *Has my luck run out?*

It was upsetting to think he might have ignored the signs of diabetes: the increased thirst and the weight loss, even though he hadn't cut back on his food intake. The most disturbing thing was the problem with his left foot. The nurses and physicians said there was a blackened area. Carly had seen it too. *How can the sole of my foot be black? How have I not noticed this, or felt something was wrong?* There had been no pain. With all the machinery he had connected to him, he couldn't reach far enough to visualize the problem himself.

Paul wondered if his new medical problems would affect his

career. He was fortunate his job in the insurance industry involved little travel or strenuous physical activity. He supposed he would have to watch his diet and monitor his blood sugars while at work. That shouldn't be too difficult. He could even take off his shoes if they restricted the circulation to his feet. While he occasionally visited clients at their homes, he could schedule the appointments to avoid exhausting himself.

He and Carly had saved a fair amount of money since David moved out a decade ago. When Greer had shocked them with her sudden move the previous year, they had predicted their food bills would decrease, but hadn't expected the other cost savings: a much smaller water bill because of fewer showers and loads of laundry, and a smaller cable television bill since he had revamped their cable service. He and Carly didn't watch most of the nearly 400 channels the premium service had offered. Perhaps in a few years he would consider an early retirement. His branch of the company didn't do financial planning, but he would arrange a consultation with a financial planner in another division. He had corresponded with many of them over his dozen years in the company, and would contact someone to review their financial portfolio. Paul wasn't certain how much money he and Carly had accumulated in their retirement accounts, but he was sure he couldn't afford to retire yet. They each made a decent salary, but it would be difficult to maintain their standard of living if one of them stopped working now.

Paul thought about his coworker, John; his father forced to use a wheelchair since a leg amputation caused by diabetes. John was the primary caregiver for his father, who needed help with nearly all of his activities. John's father called him several times a day, and Paul could sense John's frustration with the myriad of his father's complaints and unceasing cries for help.

While John had built a successful career selling insurance via the internet and speaking with potential clients on the telephone, the frequent calls from his father disrupted the flow of conversations with his customers. Although he had no proof, John's failure to dedicate himself solely to his work while in the office had likely contributed to his failure to get a promotion to supervisor he had coveted for years.

Glancing at the large wall clock, Paul was surprised that it was nearly midnight. He knew he should get some sleep, but he couldn't get comfortable. The mattress was much stiffer than the bed he shared with Carly, and the pillow was too soft; the room wasn't nearly as dark, the lights from the machinery cast shadows across the bed; and the machines and monitors spewed discordant melodies, but he closed his eyes, and was soon asleep.

Chapter 6

S eated at her laptop, Greer searched through dozens of articles on diabetes. She had almost ignored the text from her mother, but a message from a parent after nine o'clock in the evening was usually important, so when her mother's name flashed on the phone screen, she had asked Mickey to pause the video they were watching. The text caught her by surprise: her father had gotten sick at a party and was being monitored in the hospital for an elevated blood sugar. Did that mean he had diabetes? That was a serious medical problem. She didn't recall any history of diabetes in the family. Greer had replied to the text with a few of her own. Of course, her mother either didn't have the answers or deliberately withheld the information. Greer wasn't surprised. Her parents treated her like an uneducated teenager, incapable of understanding complex issues. In the past, when she didn't respond the way they had expected, they claimed she was childish and immature. *How can I respond maturely if they keep vital information from me, as if I was in grade school?*

She was glad she had gotten her own place, even though it was in a dilapidated area of town. She surveyed the tiny studio apartment with barely enough space for a futon, a table and two chairs, a thin mattress on a metal frame, and her books and clothing. The 14-speed bicycle she used for transportation hung from two large hooks on the wall next to her bed. A tiny bathroom with a stall shower, and a kitchen area with a microwave, toaster oven, small refrigerator, and a few mismatched plates and glasses and utensils barely fit in the converted garage. It was all she could afford; she spent more than half of her salary from the three part-time jobs on the rent and utilities.

Of course, her parents claimed she could afford to live in a larger place, in a better part of the town, if she had stayed in college. They repeatedly reminded her she would be a year closer to her degree. They failed to understand that she was so unhappy taking courses she didn't enjoy, studying for a degree in journalism she didn't want. She wondered what she would have been encouraged to study if her mother, Carly Casper, didn't write for the biggest newspaper in the metropolitan area. Greer had been told hundreds of times by her teachers and advisers and her friends' parents that she had inherited the writing gene and could be as good as her mother, if she buckled down and concentrated on her studies. Greer had a good command of grammar and spelling, and she could express herself well. She had written for the high-school newspaper and had won first place and second place prizes in the two local writing contests she had entered. But she hated the college literature classes, and many of the writing assignments bored her. Greer had finally admitted to her mother that she didn't want to follow in her footsteps, which led to a declaration of disappointment so severe that one would think she had announced intentions to marry a mass murderer or join a religious cult and move to a jungle. Shortly after Greer dropped out of college and got a part-time job answering phones at an ambulance company, a coworker announced he was moving from his studio apartment into a larger place with his girl-friend. Within days, Greer had gathered her necessary belong-ings and moved into the space.

Mickey worked as a mechanic at the garage where Greer had sold her ten-year-old Mazda; she needed money for the security deposit and down payment for the apartment. Her parents had purchased the Mazda from the same garage her senior year of high school, before Mickey worked there. Greer and Mickey had been dating for about four months. Greer hadn't spoken of Mickey to her family, for she knew their preju-dices would prevent them from seeing that he was a good and caring person. She feared they would be unable to look beyond his education, his upbringing, and his family's stature in society. Mickey had recently completed an automotive repair program at the local community college and was hoping to own his own garage in the future. Unlike Greer, he was the first in his family to attend a training program or college after high school. His mother had been a server at a local diner since before Mickey was born, and his father was a bus driver. Mickey's sister Robin worked in retail until she and her boyfriend became parents of Dakota; now Robin cared for their daughter while Dakota's father, Oliver, delivered groceries for a local supermarket. Mickey still lived with his parents, but once he had saved enough money, he hoped to get his own place. Greer had briefly considered asking him to share her space, but the apartment was barely big enough for a single occupant. Two months remained on the original lease, and if their relationship continued to blossom, perhaps she and Mickey would get a place together.

Greer enjoyed working at the ambulance company, but she worked no more than thirty hours per week, and the salary wasn't much above minimum wage. Desperate for money and unwilling to ask her parents for help, she had taken an additional job cleaning offices two evenings per week in a building a half mile away. One of the other women cleaning the offices told Greer about a restaurant needing delivery people, so Greer applied there too. She worked at her third job a few hours a week, using a basket attached to her bike to transport the pizzas and sandwiches. She earned more money in tips than in salary, and it was nice to have cash in her pocket after every shift, to hold her over until payday. Eating food the restaurant cooked but didn't sell was an added benefit. Sometimes there was enough food left over that she took home a pizza or salad or sandwich for the following day.

She missed some aspects of college—the camaraderie, the culture, the socialization, the ability to gratify an urge for food or drink at any hour of the day or night. Greer still communicated via social media with her former roommate, Becca, but their interactions had dropped, as Becca's life headed towards a professional career in journalism—she was interning at a local newspaper and networking—while Greer juggled part-time jobs, spent time with Mickey, reheated leftovers from her refrigerator, and decided which bills she could delay paying.

Sometimes she felt stuck in a rut, unable to see the proverbial light at the end of the tunnel. She had considered admitting defeat and returning to college, but Greer would not give her parents the satisfaction of being right, so she soldiered on, hoping for a way forward in the life she had chosen. She had been told many times she would find a career that suited her, that she would know it was right for her. Greer didn't know how she would discover what she wanted to do with the rest of her life. Abby, one of her high school friends, had a dream that she communicated with another person using sign language. When she awoke, she remembered the dream. Although she didn't know sign language, after researching the topic, she enrolled in a school an hour away. On schedule to finish the following year, Abby was now applying to graduate schools, with a goal of working for a company that provided sign language translation in the court system. Greer awoke every morning trying to remember her dreams, but could only recall weird things, like being naked at a party or walking a dog that she didn't own. At night, she had tried reading biographies or books about historical events, instead of the romance novels she favored, hoping that inspiration would strike her during slumber, but she awoke every morning thinking only about what day it was, and whether she was working two jobs or three.

Chapter 7

Paul awoke to the sounds of monitors beeping and phones ringing, as a trail of footsteps neared his hospital bed. He opened his eyes.

"Good morning, Mr. Brown. My name is Dr. Rodriguez," announced a thin, curly-haired male of about thirty, wheeling a cart containing a laptop. "I'm a resident working with Dr. Goldberg."

"Good morning."

"How are you feeling today?"

"Better than I have in a while," Paul said. "I was feeling a little off before. Not myself. A little different. I couldn't put my finger on what was wrong."

"Your blood sugar has probably been elevated for quite some time," replied Dr. Rodriguez. "I understand you missed your physical exam this year."

Paul sighed. "Yes, I did. I had a business trip. I planned to reschedule. But I forgot. Every other year my labs were okay. I guess not going for my exam this year was a terrible decision."

Dr. Rodriguez nodded as he viewed some information on the laptop. "Your labs are definitely better. The intravenous fluids have brought your blood sugars down closer to normal."

Paul smiled. "That's good. Will that be enough? Do I just have to drink more? More water? Or will I need medications?"

"I'll be back in a little while...with Dr. Goldberg. We'll discuss your options after he examines you."

The resident physician smiled and slowly exited the room as a dietary aide entered with Paul's breakfast tray. Paul removed the lid and frowned. Besides weak coffee, so pale he could see to the bottom of the cup, his breakfast included scrambled eggs resembling the plastic play food his grandchildren had loved, two triangles of limp, dry toast, and a slightly overripe banana. In a clear skinny bag, along with a miniscule serving of pepper, Paul found two packets each of sugar-free strawberry jelly and sugar substitute. No salt. No sugar. He sighed. *I guess I won't be eating breakfast like I did before.*

His usual breakfast was more substantial—an omelet with a hunk of bread or sometimes a croissant, waffles with syrup, or sometimes a toasted muffin—and a super-sized coffee with minimally processed sugar. He and Carly were fortunate that their work schedules usually allowed them the flexibility to eat breakfast together. It was a time to talk about the meetings and events planned for the day, whether they would have dinner together—sometimes Carly had an evening deadline for an article or a late meeting—and to discuss mundane matters such as who would retrieve the dry cleaning or drop off a package at the post office.

As Paul followed the tasteless eggs and soft toast with the worst coffee he had ever tasted, Dr. Goldberg entered his room, with Dr. Rodriguez closely behind. About a dozen women and men, wearing lab coats or scrubs, trailed behind the two physicians, like baby ducklings with their mother. Dr. Rodriguez summarized Paul's condition, as the others listened intently, some taking notes on electronic devices.

"Your blood sugars have been decreasing nicely, Mr. Brown," said Dr. Goldberg. "Although not quite normal, we can work on getting the levels lower. You'll need to take medication. Possibly insulin. We'll keep you here a couple of days while we figure out what will work best. The vascular team will see you today. They will decide how to treat your foot. The dietitian will see you too. You will need to change your dietary habits to control your blood sugar."

"I understand. Thank you, Dr. Goldberg." Paul nodded and shook the senior physician's hand.

The men and women filed out of the room and strolled down the hallway. Paul glanced at the remnants of his breakfast. He looked forward to speaking with the dietitian. He would accept using a sugar substitute, but there had to be a way to make food more palatable. Eating was more than just food ingestion; it was a social activity, too. Paul thought back to the party at the Grangers'. *I know I overdid it. I shouldn't have eaten so much. If I can eat some of the food at these parties, even if I have to choose, I'll accept that. Please don't ask me to give it all up.*

Although he didn't realize it then, Paul had just made the first of many bargains.

Chapter 8

David Brown hated the traffic in San Francisco. He spent hours every day driving in congestion, to and from work, or picking up Matthew or Emily from an after-school activity or from a play date with their friends. When his acceptance letter from the Massachusetts Institute of Technology had arrived during his senior year of high school, he had aspirations of a career as a computer programmer or software developer, living the dream life, spending his days soaking up the sun's rays on a Malibu beach and designing software from the deck of his beachfront home in the evenings. He hoped to have his own company, earn at least a half million dollars per year, and retire by age fifty.

But things didn't happen exactly that way. After excelling at MIT, he had fielded several job offers before graduation. He followed his dreams and accepted a position at a start-up technology firm in California. His parents had paid the security deposit and first month's rent for a tiny one-bedroom apartment. He bade the east coast goodbye and swore he would never return to winters of snow and sleet and summers of heat and humidity.

The years had passed quickly. A software developer, he had moved to a higher position at a better known firm several years before. He was well-organized and had a reputation for details. He had not received a promotion recently, but his boss had asked him to manage an upcoming project. David knew that managing a project successfully usually opened the door to a promotion and a significant pay increase.

He and Heidi lived a pretty good life in San Francisco. She was a paralegal in a small law firm, and although she didn't make the quarter of a million dollar salary he did, their combined incomes placed them in the upper echelon of earners. They could easily afford to send Matthew, age eight, for violin lessons and to soccer camp. Emily, age five, studied ballet and had recently asked to take piano lessons. Of course, neither he nor Heidi could transport the children to the activities, which were mostly in the afternoons, so they hired a part-time nanny, a college student named Deborah, who coordinated the clothing changes and snacks and transportation between school and home and activities. They often joked that their expenses could support two or three families in another part of the country. The mortgage payments on their four-bedroom house totaled nearly a hundred thousand a year, plus lofty taxes. But that was the tradeoff for living on the west coast, in a temperate climate, and earning huge salaries. Some of his college buddies had stayed on the east coast and lived in semi-detached homes in walkable communities. Their wives worked part-time or were stay-at-home moms. David thought about them frequently and wondered if they were happier than he and Heidi.

There were other reasons David preferred to live on the

west coast, thousands of miles away from his parents and sister. He and Greer had a decent relationship; they communicated by text or a messenger app, and occasionally they video chatted—she wanted her niece and nephew to know her—but his relationship with his parents was strained. He didn't consider them estranged, but their calls and video chats were usually arranged and stiff. He knew this was because they had expected him to stay close to home after he graduated. It had shocked his parents when he accepted a position in California. They had promised to help him set up his first apartment, and although he expected they would renege on the deal when he moved west and into an apartment with a monthly rent that exceeded their mortgage, they had given him a check as promised. After he had worked at the start-up company for a year, his parents had begun sending him links to computer jobs in their area. At first, the emails were informational: "Just in case you're interested, my friend Bob's company is hiring" but the messages became more direct: "Why don't you come back here? We would love to see you more."

The issue that really divided them was Heidi. When they met, she was working as an escort to pay for school, and Lacy, an acquaintance who was the daughter of his father's colleague, found a picture of Heidi and him on social media. Lacy mentioned, perhaps innocently, that Heidi worked as an escort. With a wink of his eye, Lacy's father commented to Paul that David must be a great lover to land a woman like Heidi. His parents had gone ballistic. Despite David's assurance that Heidi never crossed the line into sexual activity while working as an escort, and his pleas to withhold judgment until they met her—he was certain they would like her—Paul and Carly had decided that a woman working as an escort was socially and intellectually below their upper-echelon educated offspring.

They refused any further discussions. After completing a paralegal course, Heidi quit the escort job and obtained a position at the law firm where she currently worked. To his parents' dismay, David had proposed to Heidi within six months, and they were married four months later. Carly and Paul recited a myriad of excuses that prevented them from meeting Heidi or her parents prior to the wedding. David was concerned they wouldn't show up for his nuptials, but they kept their promise to attend. Carly and Paul flew to California for the wedding, but arrived too late for the pre-wedding dinner and left on the first flight home the morning after the ceremony.

As David and Heidi adapted to marriage and their careers, his parents kept their geographic and emotional distance, phoning on birthdays and holidays. They were thrilled when Heidi gave birth to a son and a daughter, and David hoped that having grandchildren would inspire a renewed relationship with Heidi. But although the phone and video calls became more frequent, they now centered almost exclusively on the grandchildren; their inquiries about their son and daughter-in-law seemed mere afterthoughts.

David's thoughts turned to several texts from his mother the previous evening. His father had passed out at a party and was being observed at their local hospital, where doctors said his blood sugar was elevated. His condition didn't sound too serious, but since his mother rarely shared much information with him, he couldn't be certain. This was the first time she had said his father was sick. The previous winter, David was unaware Paul had missed a week of work due to the flu, until his father's residual cough interrupted the video call with the children. David wondered how serious his father's current condition was. *Will I need to make an urgent trip back east?* He checked the calendar on his phone. His schedule was booked solid for the next few weeks. Between the business meetings, social events, and activities for Matthew and Emily, there was barely time to relax. A flight to see his parents would be difficult to squeeze into his schedule. An extended stay would be catastrophic. *I hope my father's condition isn't that serious.*

Many of his friends were grappling with aging parents and their ever-increasing list of medical conditions. He hoped his father wasn't one of them. He didn't want involvement from afar, or to make frequent trips to their home, and he didn't plan to move back to the east coast, not with things going so well in California. Heidi would never agree to move. Months before, a colleague had left his firm to join a company near Washington, DC. When David had mentioned his coworker's move, Heidi said she would never leave California, even if David was offered more money. David considered the entire issue a moot point. He hadn't searched for other jobs or received employment offers from headhunters. But if the next call he got was a job offer from the east coast, David would refuse it. Even if the offer was substantial, he knew Heidi would never move.

Chapter 9

C arly arrived at the hospital and maneuvered her car into a spot in the visitors' parking lot. Entering the building, she signed in at the information desk in the lobby. Visiting hours didn't officially start for ten minutes, but the guard didn't stop her from strolling to the elevators. She rode the elevator to the fourth floor and exited across from the nursing station. Divergent sounds greeted her: the beeping of electronic monitors, the ringing of telephones, the staff members' voices mingling with the patients' calls for help. It all overwhelmed Carly; she was glad Paul's room was halfway down the hallway, the discordant sounds muffled.

"Hi honey," she said to Paul, as she entered his room. "How are you feeling? You look so much better today." She leaned over and placed a kiss on his cheek. His skin was warm and his cheeks bore their usual ruddy hue.

"I'm feeling better. The doctors were here a while ago. My blood sugar is coming down. They think I'll need some medication to control it. And the dietitian will come by to talk about my diet."

"I can also benefit from eating healthier," replied Carly. "I'm not getting any younger, either."

Paul sighed. "The breakfast they served me was awful. My eggs were tasteless and rubbery. The coffee was brown water. I didn't even get real sugar. Or real jelly for the toast. Everything was sugar-free. It tasted terrible."

Carly patted his hand. "Hospital food is usually bad. Let's wait to talk to the dietitian. I'm sure we can figure out how to make the food more palatable."

"I sure hope so. I want to enjoy my food."

Just then, a burly physician strode into the room, peering at his electronic device. Balding and bespectacled, a few days out from his last shave, wearing ill-fitting scrubs, his appearance belied a professional demeanor.

"Hello, I'm Dr. Radisson," he announced. "I'm a vascular specialist. I understand you have a blackened area on your foot. Can I take a look?"

"Of course, Doctor," replied Paul, as he pulled the sheet back from his left foot, exposing the blackened sole and reddened toes.

After Dr. Radisson completed his examination, he addressed Paul and Carly. "I'll be honest. I'm very concerned about the circulation to this foot. I believe the blood flow has been compromised for some time. The tissue on the sole died in spots. That's why it's black."

Paul was stunned. His lower lip quivered. "How could this have happened? I had no pain. It hardly hurts. Even now, I forget that I have a problem with my foot. That is, until I look at it."

"Your blood glucose was quite high, likely for a significant period of time. Probably not as high as when you were brought in. But probably high for weeks. Or perhaps months. It affected your circulation. And your sensation. That's why you didn't have pain. A person with normal sensation feels pain and looks to see what is wrong. You didn't do that."

Carly cleared her throat. "Um...Doctor. Can I ask something?"

"Of course."

Carly was wracked with feelings of guilt. If she and Paul had communicated better, if he hadn't felt the need to appease her to keep the peace, he wouldn't have bought the new shoes, and perhaps this physician wouldn't be standing before them.

"My husband got new shoes a few weeks ago. A different brand than he usually buys. Much stiffer leather. He wore them a few times. Do you think they pinched his foot? Could the shoes have caused this problem?"

Dr. Radisson was quick to respond. "I can't say for certain. If your husband's circulation had been normal, he would have felt a pinching or rubbing. But with his impaired circulation, the shoes may have contributed to the problem." He swiped the screen on the device and peered at information. "Mr. Brown, I'd like to schedule some tests to check your circulation. Based on the results, we may consider a procedure to improve the blood flow. I likely can do the procedure this afternoon. One of my residents will bring the paperwork by for you to sign."

"Okay."

Paul and Carly exchanged glances. It seemed unlikely that Paul would be released from the hospital that day. That knowledge did nothing to appease Carly's guilt.

Chapter 10

C arly hated to call her editor on a weekend, but she had little choice. Paul's health came first.

"Hi Carly. What's up?" Stephanie asked. "Is everything okay?"

"Yes...well...actually no," Carly replied. "It's Paul. He's in the hospital."

"Oh, my gosh! It's nothing serious, I hope."

"He collapsed at a party. The doctors said he has diabetes. The circulation to his foot isn't good. There's an area that's black. On his left foot. It might be my fault. I insisted he buy new shoes. They were expensive. They may have pinched his foot. He bought them to appease me." The words sputtered from Carly's mouth. She had hidden the worst of Paul's condition from Greer and David. This was the first time she had uttered the truth.

"Oh Carly. I'm so sorry. Please send Paul my best wishes."

"Thank you, Steph. I hate to call you like this, but I need to take a few days off. Hopefully not more than that. I know my article is due. I'll write something up and send it to you."

"Of course! Take care of your husband. Don't worry about the paper. If you can get an article to me in the next few days, that's fine. But don't worry about it too much. I can put some filler in your space instead. That write-up about the new primates at the zoo. Or the bistro that opened nearby. Your family comes first."

Carly exhaled, grateful the conversation had gone well. "Thank you for being so empathetic. It means so much to me."

"You're welcome. I'm ending this conversation so you can focus on Paul. Don't forget to take care of yourself too."

Carly pressed the button on her cell phone and ended the call. She had always loved to write. The editor of her high school newspaper, her essay on human rights was the unanimous winner of a statewide literary competition, which earned her a partial scholarship to college. She flourished in college, excelling in her courses, and was known for her intelligence, hard work, and perseverance, which won her accolades from her professors.

A week before she graduated with honors, a local newspaper hired her as an investigative reporter. The work was grueling—knocking on doors, flashing her badge, and pleading for someone to speak with her—but she worked hard and was successful. Carly had won awards for her work and developed a following. Four years later, a position opened in the Lifestyles Department. Although she initially planned to turn it down, she and Paul had married and wanted to start a family, so she accepted the offer. Writing about art gallery exhibits or boutique openings wasn't as intellectually stimulating as locating and interviewing witnesses to a grizzly crime, but her articles were interesting, well-written, and well-received. As a bonus, Carly was one of the first newspaper employees permitted to write her articles at home, which was especially wonderful with a newborn who required frequent feeding or cuddling, or a toddler who took afternoon naps. The flexibility allowed her uninterrupted time to write her articles, make phone calls, or call in to meetings.

As young children, David and Greer often played at Carly's feet while she sat at the computer in her office at home. When they grew older and asked questions, she shared her work with them. They learned to read by age four, and they understood sentence structure years before its introduction in school. Carly hoped at least one of her offspring followed her career path and was thrilled when Greer expressed an interest in journalism. Carly played both sides—cheerleader and critic—while Greer wrote articles for the school newspaper and joined the yearbook staff. Greer's acceptance at a top-notch writing program resulted in a celebratory dinner at an upscale restaurant. Carly knew she and Paul had done well raising their children. But life threw them a few curveballs—or the children did.

At first, David was the consummate college student; his parents celebrated his success as if it was their own. He completed college in four years and graduated magna cum laude. Then he shocked them by accepting a position in the Bay area of California. She and Paul agreed David could command a much higher salary out west, but the area was home to ridiculously expensive rents. They surmised that David would be on their doorstep with his tail between his legs within a year, admitting defeat. But to their surprise—and privately, their dismay—he built a career and a life for himself on the other side of the country. He could have had his choice of many intelligent, well-bred, and successful young women, but had chosen Heidi, who worked as an escort for wealthy men, doing things not usually discussed in public. But it was no secret that escorts satisfied the whims of the men who paid them handsomely. Heidi had used the money to get an education in the legal field, although Carly was skeptical about Heidi's acceptance to the school solely on her brains. Their daughter-in-law barely spoke to her or to Paul when they called, or on their occasional visits. She didn't seem to tend to the children very much, either. David had agreed to a nanny to transport the children from school and to their activities. Carly sighed. Another expense on top of the exorbitant prices they paid for everything in California. *I can't imagine why they live there.*

Carly was even more disappointed with Greer's decision to drop out of school. *How could she have done that—because of a few literature classes she didn't like? To throw away two years of a college education and a promising career as a writer? Possibly a journalist? What was Greer thinking when she wrote a letter to the dean saying she was leaving school?* Greer had made an impulsive decision, which she would likely regret for her lifetime. Now she worked three part-time jobs just to pay the rent on a dumpy garage apartment in a shady neighborhood. She had even sold her car, and now traveled by bicycle. Carly was still so upset thinking about how Greer had messed up her life that she often lay awake at night, ruminating on her parenting skills. Their son was employed in the rapidly growing computer field, but their daughter had discarded her education and likely a career in writing. Carly agonized that she and Paul had failed to instill the importance of education in Greer. With a degree from a reputable university and a mother in the field, her future would have been set. How could Greer throw it all away? And for what? Perhaps they should have allowed Greer to take the gap year between high school and college that she had wanted. Several studies suggested that young people of seventeen and eighteen didn't really know what they wanted to do with their lives. Perhaps Greer was taking her gap year late. It was nearly a year since she had dropped out of college. Maybe she would tire of working so hard for so little and decide to return to school. She had lost nothing; she could pick up her studies where she had left off, a year later. Carly hoped her daughter didn't delay much longer.

Chapter 11

Alone in Paul's hospital room, Carly alternated between pacing the small area between the bed and the bevy of medical equipment, and perching on the edge of the chair by the bed. She opened an app on her tablet and located a magazine about the lives of television and screen stars. Mindless reading. That's what she needed. Nothing too difficult; just something to distract her from worrying about how Paul was doing downstairs.

Paul had been transported to the interventional radiology department to undergo testing of the blood vessels of his lower body. Dr. Radisson had said that depending on the results, Paul might need placement of a tube—a stent—to keep the vessel open for the blood to flow. He had explained the basics of procedure to them, but Carly didn't want to waste his time by asking loads of questions. Years of research meant she could get answers to almost anything in under a minute on the internet. She scoured medical websites and learned that most people had satisfactory results and the procedure was generally safe.

There was always a chance of a complication, but she put her trust in the physicians.

Carly heard footsteps approaching and looked up from her reading as Dr. Radisson strolled towards her. He wore a blue surgical gown, and a surgical mask hung from his ears and rested near his chin. He approached her, mouth set in a straight line, and she could discern the news wasn't good.

She stood from her seat. "Dr. Radisson. How is Paul doing?" she asked, hoping his words bore more optimism than his facial expression.

"Paul is stable," he replied, his speech precise and practiced. "But there's been a development we need to discuss." He motioned to a group of armchairs nearby. "Let's take a seat here."

Carly's eyes did not leave Dr. Radisson's face. She felt for a chair with her hand and stepped backward before taking a seat. "Tell me, Doctor. What is the development?" she asked, eager for news but afraid of what he would say.

Dr. Radisson sighed. Carly sensed he was trying to phrase his remarks in the best possible way, but she wanted him to speak honestly.

"Please. Just tell me what you are thinking. I need to know," she pleaded.

"We attempted to place the stent into his vessel like we had planned. But the blood clotted around it. We injected a medication to dissolve the clot. But it didn't work."

"Okay. I understand. What does that mean? Can you dissolve the clot another way? Is there another medication you can try? Or another procedure?"

His eyes met hers. He hated to bring bad news to families. "I'm afraid the clot has worsened the circulation to his leg. The leg is cool. The perfusion...the blood circulating through...is no better. It's actually worse than before. There's always a risk when we do any procedure. This procedure was the best chance to improve his circulation. But it didn't work. I'm sorry. My team did everything right. But sometimes things don't turn out the way we planned."

"What will happen? Will he lose the use of his leg?"

It was when Dr. Radisson turned his body to face hers that she panicked. He probably wasn't a card player. His eyes didn't lie. His face revealed sorrow. Carly's heart raced and her palms were sweaty.

Dr. Radisson reached for Carly's hand. "We will monitor him overnight. I'm concerned about the temperature and color of his leg. I'm going to transfer him to the intensive care unit. He will have more frequent monitoring. The nurses there will call me immediately if there is a change in his circulation."

Carly nodded. "Thank you, Dr. Radisson. I appreciate everything you are doing for Paul."

As the physician slowly strolled from the room, Carly trembled, and she lowered her body onto the seat behind her, and uttered a silent prayer for Paul's recovery.

PAUL OPENED HIS EYES AND SURVEYED HIS SURROUNDINGS. THE lights on the nearby equipment blinked and flashed discordantly. The machines emitted a din of sounds, beeps, chimes, and rings of varying intensities and ranges, overwhelming his auditory system. His torso stiffened, more from anxiety at his surroundings than from the mild throbbing in his foot. Paul felt as if the walls were closing in around him. He hadn't felt this claustrophobic since junior high, when a gang of bullies had thrown him into a hole at a construction site and piled dirt on his head. Amid the sounds came a man's voice.

"Help me! Help me!"

As a half dozen nurses and technicians ran towards him, he realized the voice calling out was his. "The noise...the lights...it's too much!" Paul's body thrashed and his arms flailed, loosening the sheets, as two nurses held his shoulders to the bed.

"Mr. Brown! It's okay. We'll help you. Please calm down." The words from the tall blonde nurse soothed him, and he felt the tension release from his upper body. "Take some deep breaths. You will be okay," she whispered in his ear. "Just concentrate on your breathing. Close your eyes and focus on good times in your life."

Paul obeyed the nurse's commands, and his breathing and heart rate slowed, although the lights and sounds around him continued to barrage his senses. He closed his eyes and thought of happier times. His parents. Playing in the backyard with his brother John and sister Susan. His marriage to Carly. The birth of his children.

He thought now of Carly and of their long marriage. They had been blissfully happy for the first several years. He recalled how happy they were when they had purchased their first house. The births of David and Greer made their family complete. But like many couples, the elation dimmed over time, as the realities of daily life pushed through. The long workdays, trying to get ahead in their jobs and further their careers. The vacations and weekend getaways canceled because of a work obligation. Soothing a teething toddler or pacing the floor with a sick child instead of sleeping lent itself to being ill-tempered and prone to petty arguments. He and Carly had often argued about little things: no milk for breakfast because he forgot to stop on the way home from work, her desire to replace the gently used couch because of the color.

As their son and daughter reached the teenage years, he

and Carly had seemed more agreeable to compromise. Their children flourished. David sailed through adolescence and high school and college with little adversity or turmoil. There were no indications he was considering a move to the west coast, so when David had announced he had accepted a position in California at a start-up company specializing in computer programming services and applications, Paul and Carly wondered why he had kept his plans a secret. But David refused to engage his parents in a discussion of his motives. They tried to dissuade him, to convince him he was acting impulsively, but he had received a great job offer and was planning to drive his car across the country and stay with a friend until he found his own apartment. Once he announced his plans, he cleared out his bedroom, packed his belongings in his eight-year-old Honda hatchback, and left within a week. Although they were proud he had graduated with honors from college and had gotten a good-paying position a week before he finished school, they couldn't hide their disappointment that he fled the family home as soon as his college diploma was in hand. Friends assumed they were thrilled their son had done so well, so Carly and Paul hid their genuine feelings from everyone but each other.

Greer's rebellion struck earlier than David's. She didn't wait to finish college to break from her parents' ideas and ideals. Shortly after the beginning of the first semester of her junior year, she had informed them at dinner that she had dropped out of school. At Greer's announcement, Carly had dropped the salad bowl, an anniversary gift from her mother twenty years before, the crystal shattering in a million pieces on the kitchen's ceramic floor. Paul and Carly knew Greer wasn't dating anyone seriously, so they were relieved when she denied she was quitting school because of a relationship or pregnancy. But like her sibling, she had surprised Paul and Carly with unpleasant news and refused to give in to their requests to reconsider her decision or to provide more clarity of the situation.

When Greer had first quit school, Paul wanted to offer her the opportunity to continue to live with him and Carly. But Carly was so disappointed, hurt, and angry that she refused to discuss the issue. Paul wanted to block the door and prevent his little girl from leaving the house, but he knew he would not win the battle, and he refused to risk Carly's wrath in addition to Greer's. Greer would not accept the cash he tried to give her, and insisted she had a plan. He watched her retrieve her bicycle from the garage and secure it to the back of her car, but didn't know her plan included selling the car and using the bicycle for transportation.

The first time Paul had driven past the garage apartment Greer worked three part-time jobs to afford, his breath caught and he fought back tears. Her bicycle leaned against a brick wall that threatened to crumble, perhaps taking a chunk of the foundation with it. Weeds sprouted haphazardly from a mound of dirt between the wall and the garage. A half dozen boys were playing basketball in an abandoned lot a few car lengths away. He heard one of them utter profanities upon missing an easy lay-up. Paul had done his research. The neighborhood was home to few homeowners; most residents were renters. Paul was heartened to read that the area wasn't crime-riddled, but his daughter deserved better. There was no shame in living in an apartment; many were upscale and nicer than his house. But he couldn't fathom how she could have walked away from life in a house in a decent area, with cable television and a free washer and dryer, and moved into a dilapidated garage. She had sold the car they had purchased for her. Paul remembered Greer beaming when she returned from school and found the car in the driveway. "It's yours," he had said. It was the last time he had seen her so happy. Paul didn't understand the choices his daughter had made. He had wondered what would become of her dreams and her aspirations, and wondered what a crystal ball would show about her future.

PAUL WAS AWAKENED BY A CLAMOR AT THE FOOT OF HIS BED. He opened his eyes to find several members of Dr. Radisson's team gathered at his bedside, poking and prodding his left foot.

"The foot has clearly deteriorated," announced one physician. "The toes are cold and mottled."

"I've already beeped Dr. Radisson," replied a young female, barely out of her teens.

Dr. Radisson hurried to the bedside and gave a barrage of orders. "Let's get some labs. Hematology, coagulation, a chemistry panel. I think we'll be going to surgery within a few hours." He turned to Paul. "I've already called your wife."

"Surgery! Are you going to remove the black area from my foot? Then I can go home. Right?"

"Mr. Brown. I wish it was that simple. But it's not. Your circulation is worse than we thought," replied Dr. Radisson.

"Worse? What do you mean? You can fix it. Right?"

Carly hurried to Paul's bedside. "I'm here." Her face was flushed, her hair askew, and her eyes moist. "I came as fast as I could."

Dr. Radisson nodded to Carly. "I was just telling your husband what I told you on the phone."

Carly took Paul's hand in hers. "I'm sorry that the procedure didn't work. But you'll be okay. We'll get through this together."

"Mr. Brown. The circulation in your foot has clearly deteriorated. The skin is now discolored. I can't feel pulses in the foot.

We need to operate as soon as possible. I'm planning to take you to surgery this afternoon," added Dr. Radisson.

"What will you do? Can you restore the circulation to my foot? Can you open up the blood vessels? You can save my foot, can't you?" Paul's eyes locked with Dr. Radisson's. "Please tell me I won't lose my foot."

The physician paused a few seconds too long for Paul's comfort.

"Oh, no! Please don't amputate my foot. Please tell me that's not true!" cried Paul, as Carly hugged him, tears streaming down her cheeks and onto Paul's hospital gown.

"I love you, Paul. You'll be okay. We'll get through this."

Carly knew the right words to say. She just had to convince herself she meant them.

Chapter 12

The call from her mother in the early morning hours upended Greer's world. When her cell phone rang as she stepped out of the shower, her initial response was to ignore it and listen to the voicemail. But, as if prodded by an alternative force, she had wrapped the skimpy bath towel around her torso and trod across the kitchen area to retrieve her phone. Greer wiped the droplets of water that had fallen from her hair onto the phone. She saw with relief that it was her mother calling.

"Hi Mom. Do you have any news about Dad? Is he going home?" Greer asked, as her heart raced and her breathing quickened, awaiting what she hoped would be good news.

The silence from her mother told her the report wasn't good.

"Mom! What has happened? Tell me about Dad."

"Your father...the circulation...in his foot...is worse. I'm so sorry." Carly's sobs were soft and barely audible at first, but within seconds she was bawling.

Greer had never heard her mother lose control like this.

"Mom! Please tell me!" she ordered. "Just tell me what is going on!"

"Dr. Radisson...the vascular specialist. He performed a procedure that he hoped would improve the blood flow to your father's foot."

"What is wrong with his foot? You never said there was something wrong with his foot!" Even though they rarely saw eye to eye, Greer seldom raised her voice to her mother.

"I am so...sorry. I hoped...I could spare you the bad news. Just tell you everything was fine. But it's not fine. Your father has diabetes. He probably has had it for a while. He didn't know it."

Greer clenched her fists and struggled to maintain control. "Okay. I understand. What does that have to do with his foot?"

"The untreated diabetes resulted in diminished circulation to his feet. There was an area on the bottom of his left foot where the tissue went bad. He didn't feel it. The tissue began to die. It was black when they brought him to the emergency department."

"His foot was black? How could you have kept this from me? Did you keep it from David too?"

"No! Not the whole foot. An area the size of...a half dollar...was black. On the sole of the foot. The doctors wanted to fix his circulation first. Then they would work on the blackened skin. But the procedure they tried didn't work. A clot formed and the blood flow to his foot is worse. They...are going to have to...amputate." Carly's mouth and vocal cords were in tandem, but her brain played no part in the utterance. Her mind hadn't processed the information yet.

"Oh my God! Amputate." Greer slid to the floor, unable to articulate more, as her brain fought to comprehend her mother's words. "I'm coming right now. What room is he in? I'll be there as soon as I get dressed."

"He's in the operating room. I'm in his room. In the ICU. The intensive care unit."

Twenty minutes later, Greer secured her bicycle to the designated post in the parking lot, grabbed her messenger bag from the back of the bicycle, and ran through the entrance doors at the hospital. Nearly knocking over a young man pushing an empty wheelchair, she stumbled into the lobby. Gathering herself, she proceeded to the information desk, where a young woman, a hospital volunteer, provided directions.

"Fourth floor," she announced. "Take a right off the elevator."

Greer caught sight of herself in a mirror across from the row of elevators. Tendrils of blonde hair had fallen from the bun she had hurriedly piled atop her head, forsaking the hairdryer to save time. She normally used only mascara and a touch of eye shadow, but today she had applied neither. She had spent three minutes of precious time sending two texts: the first to her supervisor Kevin about needing some time off because of a family emergency, the second to Mickey about her father's condition and her trip to the hospital. For the first time, she was aware of her own foul breath, and realized she had failed to perform basic oral hygiene. She searched her messenger bag, and finding a bit of lint-caked foil in the corner, was relieved it contained a breath mint. Her right foot pounded the floor. All the elevators seemed stuck on the upper floors, wasting more precious time. Unaccustomed to waiting, her impatience grew, and she looked for stairs instead, just as the doors to an elevator opened. She sent a text to her mother: "I'm on my way up."

Greer fought the urge to push past the string of people

exiting the elevator. The last person had barely crossed the threshold to the hospital lobby when Greer rushed into the vestibule and pushed the button for the elevator doors to close. It seemed like an eternity for the elevator to ascend each floor. Greer thought the hospital elevators were unusually slow moving, so as not to exacerbate the symptoms of the patients who might ride them. When the doors finally opened, she exited and saw the sign for the intensive care unit to her right.

As she sped towards the unit where the sickest patients lay, Greer saw Carly exit the bathroom. Mother and daughter embraced, their estrangements and prior disagreements momentarily cast aside.

"Oh Mom," Greer cried, "I am so sorry you and Dad have to deal with this. I wish I had known earlier. I would have been here for you."

Carly wiped her tears with a crumpled tissue as the women located a lounge near the elevators. Luckily, the room was vacant. They huddled together on an orange vinyl couch.

"I had no idea he was so sick. He never said anything to me. He went to work every day. He admitted he didn't feel great for a while. But he never told me, and he didn't think he was sick enough to get medical attention. I would have insisted he see a doctor. To think he might have been able to prevent this awful mess. If he had just gone to see a doctor." Carly hid her eyes in her hands and sobbed.

"Mom, I should have been there. Perhaps if I hadn't moved out. If I was there every day...maybe I would have seen the changes."

"Do you think I wasn't paying attention? Our marriage isn't perfect, but do you think I ignored his symptoms? That I just didn't care?" She glared at her daughter. "What are you saying?"

Greer opened her mouth to spew some hateful words her

mother's way. But anger and vitriol had created a partial estrangement from her parents, a state she didn't want to revisit. "Mom. I'm sorry. I didn't mean it that way. I'm not blaming you." She pressed her mother's body to her own. "If anything, I blame myself. I know I dropped out of school. But I didn't have to drop out of your life."

"Oh, honey." Carly managed a weak smile. "No! This is not your fault. Not at all. Please do not think that. It happened. That's all. But your father is going to need our support. Having diabetes was already a shock to him. Losing his leg is a catastrophe."

"I'll do what I can. I'll move back home. I mean, if you want me to do that."

"Please don't do anything yet. Your father will be in the hospital for a while. We'll see what he needs."

"Okay. Uh...Mom. Does David know yet?"

"I left him a voicemail that I wanted to talk about your father's condition. I didn't want to leave bad news in a recording. I want to tell him myself. But he hasn't called back yet."

"I could text him. He might answer me."

"I'd rather he answer my voicemail. I don't want to involve you. The news should come from me. Not you," said Carly.

"Okay. Let me know if you need me to call him. Maybe he'll respond if he gets messages from both of us."

Greer thought of her childhood, being the recipient of her brother's protection from the older and bigger children, first in the playground, later in social situations, warning his classmates and acquaintances not to use foul language or make suggestive comments in earshot of his sister. He had remained devoted to her throughout his college years. When he moved to California, he promised Greer they would remain close, but his attention drifted away from Greer and onto Heidi. Greer still spoke to David occasionally, but their recent conversations lacked intimacy. Instead, the siblings discussed more mundane topics: the cost of living in California, the snowstorm pummeling the east coast, the political climate. Greer missed their personal conversations, and wondered if their father's illness would bridge the divide.

Chapter 13

David pulled his silver Audi into the parking lot, below the multi-story office building that housed his company's central office. His anger had abated somewhat, but was still simmering behind the outward appearance of calm he was working so hard to perfect. He couldn't comprehend why Heidi had picked today to tell him she wanted to go to law school. As if her declaration wasn't enough of a surprise, she had announced it as he exited the bathroom, his mind focused on a new project at work: an electronic dictionary that interacted with every document. His supervisor Ben was impressed with the proposal and asked David to oversee its development. David had selected the employees to work on his team and was eager to get started that day. Although he liked his job and earned a good salary, he had been increasingly bored at work. He hoped this project would break the malaise and tedium.

He had barely been listening and thought Heidi was referring to a colleague going to law school. Angry that he responded to her announcement with indifference, she accused him of ignoring her. That started an argument about his lack of attention to her; his reply that she must have forgotten what a big day this was for him fanned their simmering anger. From her briefcase she pulled an envelope of law school applications. She threw the papers at him, kissed the children goodbye, and left him holding not only the envelope, but the responsibility for getting the children to school—something he had assumed she would do on a day so important to him.

Now, as he removed his cell phone from the cradle in his car, he noticed a missed call and a voicemail from his mother. The time stamp coordinated with the moment he was showering. He surmised it was an update about his father's medical condition. He checked the time. It was nearly noon there. His mother had likely called to say the doctors had gotten his father's blood sugar under control and he was being discharged. David tucked his cell phone in his pocket and hurried up three flights of stairs to his office. He was already later than he wanted to be; waiting for an elevator would waste more time. He would listen to his mother's message later. Now was his time to lead, his time to shine.

WHISTLING, DAVID RETURNED TO HIS CAR JUST BEFORE SEVEN o'clock. Starting his work day later than he had desired or expected had undermined his sense of order, but he had maintained his placid demeanor. On arrival, he asked his assistant to order brunch for the team. The gourmet muffins and pastries and fresh fruit projected a welcoming message to the employees and set the tone for the rest of the day, and hopefully, for the entire project. In addition, there was ample food for snacking and munching throughout the day, so that although the team paused for breaks, there was no work stoppage for lunch. The team members were engaged and enthusiastic about the new project, especially since concern about a work slowdown and layoffs had been rampant. Their selection for this project had allayed those fears.

David's cell phone remained in his jacket pocket, initially as an example to the team that work matters were of far more importance than personal ones, and later because he was so invested in the team's cohesion that he no longer recalled his mother's voicemail. Now, as he opened the car door and placed the jacket over the passenger seat in the car, he noticed the bulge of the phone. He retrieved the cell phone and found several texts from Heidi, questioning what time he would be home for dinner. There were several additional voicemails from his mother. He surmised the doctors had discharged his father from the hospital. David started his car and drove out of the parking lot and onto the ramp to the highway, musing about the argument with Heidi that morning. He wanted to find out more about her desire to go to law school.

He would try to find the time to call his mother that evening, although with the time change to the east coast, perhaps tomorrow morning was a better idea.

Chapter 14

The sounds of monitors beeping and voices around him jolted Paul awake. He felt a pressure on his right hand and opened his eyes. Carly was holding his hand. He gave a weak smile.

"Hi honey," she whispered. "I'm glad you're awake."

As his vision cleared and his eyes focused, he saw tears in her eyes. *Why is she crying?* Then the memory of the earlier conversation returned, and he shuddered.

"Did they do it? Did they cut off my leg?" He attempted to sit up. His hands reached to check for his leg. The alarms on the monitors reacted to his increased heart rate, and a nurse ran to the bedside.

"Please lie still, Mr. Brown," called Mandy, a nurse of about twenty-five, her long auburn hair in a single braid, as she hurried to the bedside. "Are you having pain?"

"Just tell me. Did they take my leg off?" pleaded Paul. "That's all I want to know."

Carly stood, and her eyes locked with Paul's. For hours, she had rehearsed the answer to the question she knew was coming. They were the hardest words she ever expected to utter to her husband.

"Yes, honey. I'm afraid the doctors had to amputate your leg below the knee. But now you can heal."

"Oh my God!" he cried, his body thrashing about. "No! No!"

Mandy left the bedside, retrieved a syringe, and injected a small amount of fluid into Paul's intravenous line. "It's a sedative," she said to Carly. "It will help him relax. He'll have less pain, too."

Carly sat at Paul's bedside and held his hand while the sedative lulled him to sleep. Her cell phone buzzed, and she glanced at it just long enough to see another text from Nancy Granger. Carly sighed. She had revealed very little of Paul's condition to any of their friends. She had sent Nancy a text the previous day saying Paul had diabetes and was being monitored. So much had happened in two days. *Has it really only been two days since the party at the Grangers' home? How can weeks drag on with little fanfare, and suddenly our lives are upended in two days?*

Although Dr. Radisson had explained the procedure thoroughly and Paul had signed the permit for the surgery, a part of her had hoped that the procedure wasn't necessary. Perhaps only on television did the physician decide at the last second, with a scalpel in hand, that the patient had made a miraculous improvement and wouldn't require drastic measures. But sadly, life rarely mirrored a television show, and Dr. Radisson and his team had performed the procedure as planned. Carly wished she was reading a book of their lives, one she could return to the library without finishing. She knew the beginning and the middle. She didn't want to read the second half, and the ending terrified her. But their life wasn't a television show or a book. It was real.

Mandy strolled to Paul's bedside, checked the printout of his vital signs, and lifted the blanket to check his surgical site. She leaned closer to Carly. "Your husband is stable," she whispered. "He seems comfortable. He'll sleep for a while. I know you've been here for hours. Now might be a good time to go home and take care of yourself."

"If you think he's going to be out for a while, then I think I'll go home. I definitely could use a shower. Or a bath. Definitely some clean clothes."

"Make sure you eat something too," added Mandy. "Even if you're not hungry."

"Good idea. Thanks."

AFTER POURING A GENEROUS SUPPLY OF BATH SALTS INTO THE water, Carly eased herself into the tub. She enjoyed soaking in the water; the aroma settled her sinuses and the silky water soothed her joints and softened her skin. While she had undertaken the practice of soaking her body regularly for years, in the past year she had rarely taken a bath, although she couldn't explain why. Now, with her body tense, her mind tortured, her emotions in turmoil, she was grateful for the release the bathing afforded.

Although they expected some misfortune in life, Carly and Paul had been fortunate to have survived so far with only minor challenges. They had experienced the usual pitfalls of unemployment, albeit short-term, illness that canceled vacations, and minor auto accidents that injured their wallets more than their bodies. The adversities passed in a few days or weeks or months, and their lives continued as before. Their disagreements with David's decision to move to California and Greer dropping out of college resulted in the most turmoil the family had ever dealt with—until now.

Faced with Paul's new and mounting medical problems and the prospect of a protracted recovery period and likely disability, Carly had called Stephanie and asked for a leave of absence. Although she could replace some of her hours in the newspaper's primary office with time in her home office, Carly knew she could not involve herself in the lifestyles of the community, and rejoice in their general good fortunes and celebrations, while grappling with her family's catastrophe. Her brain preoccupied, she would be unable to match the eloquent writing style for which she was widely known. The future would be uncharted and rough, so she had called Stephanie two hours before and asked for a leave of absence of at least three months. Stephanie had agreed—Carly knew she couldn't refuse the request—and as Carly had expected, she was more concerned with Paul's condition and Carly's well-being than a newspaper assignment. She would reassign another reporter to cover Carly's assignment.

As Carly soaked in the tub, calm hindered by her muscles' refusal to relax and her continuing emotional gravitation towards the moribund, her cell phone rang. *I guess a bath won't help me today.* She eased herself out of the tub, wrapped her body in one of the oversized towels she loved so much, and trod into the bedroom. Glancing at the phone, she saw it was Stephanie calling. *What could she want?*

"Hi, Stephanie."

"Hi, Carly. I don't want to disturb you. I was planning to leave a voicemail. But since you answered, do you have a few minutes to talk?"

"Uh...Okay." Carly lowered her body onto the bed. "I'm home. I have a few minutes. What do you want to talk about?"

"I was thinking about you. About Paul and your situation. I have an idea. I know you asked for a leave of absence. I'm not calling to change your mind. Well, not exactly." Stephanie was always deliberate and poised with her speech. It was unlike her to fumble for words. "Carly. I have no business asking. But since you are home, can I stop by for a few minutes? I don't care what you look like. I want to give you an enormous hug. And I want to talk to you about my idea."

Stephanie was one of the few people Carly would allow to see her in this state, at her worst, so she relented. "Okay, Steph. I just got out of the tub. If you can overlook seeing me in my pajamas and bathrobe and without makeup, then you can come."

"I'll be there in twenty minutes. Bye."

Carly dressed in lounge wear and slippers and dried her hair with a towel. There was no need for airs. Stephanie had seen her during bad times before—although worrying about her children's issues paled in comparison to Paul's problems. Although she knew Stephanie wouldn't expect nourishment, Carly trod to the kitchen and perused the refrigerator for something to serve. She found an unopened container of hummus and an opened wedge of brie. She thought back to a few days ago, when she and Paul, sharing a bottle of wine, had topped a pile of crackers with the brie. Four days ago. For decades, their lives had been stable, sometimes exciting, more often mundane and boring. How had their world toppled in just four days?

As expected, Stephanie arrived at Carly's doorstep in twenty minutes. As she parked in the driveway and reached the top step, hand in midair above the doorbell, Carly opened the door. Stephanie stepped into the foyer and grabbed Carly in a bear hug. It was as if Stephanie held the key that opened Carly's bank of emotions. Once in Stephanie's arms, Carly's tears flowed freely, and she sobbed.

"Oh, my God. Steph...I can't believe this happened...to Paul." Tears flowed like rivers down Carly's cheeks, accumulating in a pile and soaking the top of her robe.

Stephanie met Carly's eyes with her own. "I am so sorry. I wish I could make your heartache go away. I know I'm your editor. Your boss. But we've been more than that. More like friends. I wouldn't wish this misfortune on anyone, but especially you. You don't deserve this. Neither does Paul."

Carly wiped her eyes with the belt of her bathrobe. Once she started speaking, as if a faucet had opened, the words flowed from her mouth.

"Thank you. I really appreciate that. I haven't told many people about what happened. I told a few of our friends that he has diabetes. The ones at the party. When Paul collapsed, I thought he was dehydrated. He had complained of thirst. When the doctors said his blood sugar was elevated and he had diabetes, I thought we could manage the disease by changing his diet. Maybe taking a pill. Then they said he needed to take insulin. I figured we could learn together. We could manage that. But now...I don't know how we are going to get through this. How is Paul going to learn to live as an amputee?"

Stephanie awkwardly thrust a grocery bag into Carly's hands. "I brought some pastries. Food is always good. Cake is even better."

Carly forced a weak smile. "Thanks. I really appreciate it. I hardly ate anything today. Do you want coffee? I can make a pot."

"That would be great. But I don't want you to entertain me. I can help you."

Carly pointed to the cabinet containing the cups and plates, and while Stephanie set the table, Carly added coffee and water and set the coffee maker to brew. Once the coffee was ready, the women sat silently, sipping the brew and nibbling on a pastry.

"This chocolate cruller is delicious," murmured Carly. "I don't eat pastries often, but this tastes especially good now." She reached across the table and took Stephanie's hands in hers. "Thank you for coming. For knowing I would need company. Even though I didn't know I needed it. And for being there for me. You've always been there for me. Thank you."

Stephanie smiled. "I'd say it's my pleasure. But this isn't a pleasure call. But I want to talk to you about something. I had an idea. Something for you to do."

"For me? I thought I was on a leave of absence. You approved it!"

"Yes. Of course I did. But just hear me out. Please."

"Okay. I owe you that."

"Thank you, Carly. My idea would involve you getting personal with your readers. But, I think it could work well. Chronicle Paul's illness. How it started, his setbacks, the struggles you have already been through. The ones that are forthcoming. It would be a way to have your own column. It's probably not the column you expected or wanted. But it will put you front and center."

Carly was stunned. "Wow. I don't know what to say." She shook her head. "Look Steph, I am so grateful for the opportunity. I just don't know if I can handle this. I mean emotionally it's a real stretch. Can I find the time to do the writing? I don't know."

Stephanie smiled. "Please, just think about it. I realize I am asking you to lay yourself bare. Of course I'd want Paul to give his okay. But our readers love to see us as more than writers or reporters. They like to see us as human beings. People with emotions and feelings. People who are real. Paul is real. You are real. Readers would see you as one of them. That opens the door for people to commiserate with you. It gives them an opportunity to talk about themselves, and how they have handled similar situations. I expect the feedback will be tremendous. And in a good way."

"I have to admit that the idea of a column is intriguing. After years as a reporter, I had given up hopes of having one. I just don't know. I don't want to increase my audience off of the back of Paul's illness. I would have to show us at our worst. I don't know if I can do that."

"I understand. Take a few days to think about it."

"Okay. I have a few questions. I'm surprised I can think clearly enough to have questions."

Stephanie chuckled. "You are a writer. You possess some ability to compartmentalize."

"Yes. I suppose writers do. But how many columns do you want me to write? How often?"

"Well, I think an introductory column would be a perfect way to start. Your readers can meet Paul in a few days. Introduce your son and daughter too. I guess you should discuss this idea with them to get their approval. Then perhaps a new column every couple of weeks. Maybe a month. Give updates as the situation changes."

"I guess this would cancel my leave of absence?"

"Yes. If you agree with my proposal, your salary and benefits would continue. It could work well. I know you want time off to be with Paul. You won't need to come to the office. Just think about it. But not too long. I need to take it to Steve Collins."

"You mean you didn't get the managing editor's approval yet? How do I know he will be okay with this? What if I decide to do this and he doesn't agree?"

"Don't worry. I'll have him eating out of my hand. He'll be on board. I promise you."

Chapter 15

David pulled his automobile into the driveway and exited the car, nearly tripping on Matthew's scooter laying haphazardly on the concrete. He entered the house and found Heidi in the kitchen, bent over her computer, reading a recipe. He placed a cursory kiss on her cheek. She smiled.

"Hi. How was your day?" he inquired.

"My day was good. How was yours?" Opening the refrigerator, she grabbed a package of beef strips, two green peppers, and an onion. It was then that her smile fell. "Oh. I'm sorry about this morning. I know today was a really important day for you. I shouldn't have picked this morning to talk about my plans."

David sighed. "Thanks. I was really upset this morning. I felt like you had forgotten about my plans. Then you started talking about yourself. It was bad timing. That's all."

"And I behaved badly. I shouldn't have left you in the lurch. I'm sure you were late. And on such an important day." She retrieved a polished wooden cutting board and a Wusthof knife from the matching set perched on the counter. "Matthew and Emily are on their way home. We're having a stir-fry for dinner. And there's a bottle of Moscato chilling."

"Sounds good," David replied. "You are correct. I wasn't happy that I got to the office late. But I made up for it. The team was thrilled with the brunch I ordered. There was enough food for everyone to eat all day. We didn't have to break for lunch. So it was a brilliant move on my part. It cost me a few dollars, but my team got a considerable amount of work done in less time. That should go a long way towards proving I can handle an important project."

"I'm glad it worked out. I wanted to call you...to apologize. But I didn't want to disrupt your day even more than I already had," Heidi murmured.

"I appreciate that. Although my phone was in my jacket pocket on vibrate and I didn't check it until I left the office."

"So my calls would have gone to voicemail. Glad I didn't call."

"Yes. I suppose you're right. But I got a few voicemails from my mother."

"Is your father okay? Was he discharged?"

"I didn't listen to the voicemails. But the doctors had hoped to send him home yesterday. I guess my mom called to say he went home today."

"You should listen to the voicemails. Or call your mother. Just to be sure."

"I will," David replied. "And we should have a serious talk about law school. You mentioned it before, but perhaps I didn't take it seriously enough. But I'll do whatever I can to support you. You'll make a wonderful lawyer."

He looped his arms around her waist and nuzzled his face

in her blonde locks. He thought of his parents' concern that David had married Heidi for her looks and her body, but he had always known she was the complete package. She was a wonderful wife and a devoted mother—and she had brains. David extricated himself from Heidi's arms and retrieved the mail from the basket on the counter. He ignored the advertisements and catalogs and perused the contents of the three envelopes. A letter from their physician announcing a new partner in the practice. A local political action group asking for volunteers to make phone calls. It was the contents of the third envelope that made him cringe.

"Really? I can't believe our property taxes are going up again! Heidi! Our taxes are going up another eight percent. The county reduced our trash collection from three times a week to two. The library cut its hours. And our house taxes are increasing! We're getting fewer services and we're expected to pay more. It's not right." David felt the warmth spread into his neck and face. A glance in the mirror wasn't necessary. He was certain his face was beet red.

Heidi was less disturbed by the news. "Wow! I don't like it either. But what can we do? We choose to live here."

As usual, Heidi was the calmer of the couple. Their friends often said they could read David like a book, but Heidi's cool demeanor masked even the most serious problems. David was certain this would be beneficial as an attorney. Her response calmed him; he could visualize his blood pressure and heart rate decreasing. He felt the tension ease from his shoulders. *Yes, we pay a hefty price to live here, but I can't imagine living anywhere else.*

Then Matthew and Emily came bounding through the front door, breathless and eager to talk about their day. Their laughter was infectious; it spread like a wildfire to their parents.

An outsider spying on them would observe a quintessential American family: two successful parents and a happy and good-looking son and daughter, living in an expensive house in California, planning their weekend activities. A carefree family, living in a beautiful home. In paradise.

Chapter 16

Having finally convinced Carly to go home for some
much needed rest, Paul lay in his hospital bed, alone
with his thoughts. He pressed the control which raised the head
of the bed, until he was upright. He pulled on the blanket and
sheet which covered his lower body, tossing the remnants
towards the foot of the bed, until he could wrestle his left leg
free.

For a brief second, he forced himself to look at what the
surgeons had done. It was all he could bear. The gauze wrapped
around the end of his shortened leg—a stump, they called it—
didn't seem like it belonged to his body. Although he had imagined how his leg would appear, minus the foot and ankle and
shin, he hadn't been fully prepared for what he would see. This
wasn't a picture in a newspaper or magazine. This was his leg, a
part of him since he occupied his mother's womb. A part of his
body disposed of, gone. This was unlike removal of an
appendix or a gallbladder or a prostate. Except for the hidden
scars, no one would know the surgeons had removed those

body organs. A part of a leg was obvious; one didn't need to see the scar. Paul wondered how he could function without his lower leg or foot. He had seen other amputees; some in wheelchairs and some with crutches or a fake foot on a metal rod. People either stared at them or looked away in pity. He didn't want pity, not from strangers, and certainly not from his coworkers or friends.

His coworkers. *Will I ever refer to them as my coworkers again? Will I be able to work again? Will I contribute to the upkeep of the household?* He knew people who received disability checks from the government every month. Some of them were his clients. Although he wasn't directly involved in coordinating the disability insurance, he knew that many of the payments went to those with a physical disability, but some had psychiatric or medical illnesses. Paul wasn't sure which was worse, a physical disability everyone could see, or an invisible one. People with more severe psychiatric diagnoses were often easy to spot; their glassy eyes and involuntary tics characteristic of schizophrenia or psychoses, the side effects of their medications often worse than the symptoms of the disease themselves. Of course, those with anxiety or depression weren't as easy to spot, for they blended in with the rest of society, many of whom had their own afflictions which were untreated.

Paul thought about his house. *Will adaptations be necessary? Will I be able to climb the steps from the driveway? Will contractors need to install a ramp? Will I be able to drive my car?* Perhaps he could, since he drove with his right leg, not his left. A special license plate would be warranted, which would announce to the world that he was handicapped and needed coddling and special attention. Parking in a designated spot closer to the store, others would take notice of his condition when he exited the car. He knew how it worked—he had scrutinized the drivers in these spots, as if a cursory glance could reveal all physical ailments. He vowed never to second-guess the cars' occupants again.

He pictured the inside of his house now. A long staircase from the first to the second floor. The powder room on the first floor meant that he could spend long stretches of time downstairs. *How difficult will it be for me to access the second floor? Will I need one of those machines with a seat attached to the stairs? I hope not.* He didn't want to debase their home with a contraption like that. It wouldn't be fair to Carly, having to look at such a monstrosity every day.

Carly. His thoughts focused on her now. Their wedding vows: *For better or for worse.* This certainly qualified as worse. A few days ago, he had ruminated on following a diet to manage his diabetes. He knew Carly would research how to adapt her cooking and their diet to accommodate his dietary needs. At home, she would likely follow a similar diet to his, both for ease in cooking and for solidarity. He had considered whether he would need to take insulin. The thought of sticking a needle into his body every day terrified him. The image of the needle pricking his skin caused him to tremble. *What if I can't do it?*

It would be difficult for Carly, too. Adjusting to life with an amputee, with a cripple, was different. This wasn't a minor change; it could be a deal breaker. A major change like this would stress all relationships and marriages. Many would break. He wasn't sure theirs could withstand the strain. He couldn't imagine she would walk away, ask for a separation or a divorce. She wasn't like that. He loved her and knew she loved him. Their marriage had lasted more than thirty years, and they had been together for a few before that. *She won't leave me. Will she?* They were good together. He and Carly had their own interests, and their careers, but they got along well, and had raised two children. They laughed at the same movies and usually agreed which dramas or sitcoms or action shows to watch or stream on their television.

Intimacy had waned as expected, although they still engaged in sexual relations, but far less frequently than a decade before. He surmised their age was a factor. In the early years of their marriage, they had made love nearly every day, sometimes more than once. He recalled the lazy weekend mornings, drinking cups of freshly ground coffee in bed, sometimes enjoying a toasted croissant and fresh fruit. After finishing breakfast, they sometimes engaged again in coupling. As the years passed, the job responsibilities and children's social activities cut into their free time and their sleep time, so they spent less time in the bed, and most of it sleeping.

Paul thought of their recent attempts at intimacy and wanted to cry. He could not perform—twice, perhaps—and recalled apologizing to Carly, citing fatigue or too much alcohol. Perhaps he had fabricated another measly excuse. He assured her he hadn't lost his desire for her, but he didn't know if she believed him. Now he wondered if his manhood wouldn't cooperate because of diabetes. Perhaps, instead of offering an apology, he should have sought help. But he would have felt silly going to his family doctor—a woman—and telling her he needed help because he couldn't get an erection twice in a month. He suspected many men of his age had similar problems. That's why there was medication, the advertisements in magazines and on television peppered with images of men in the arms of smiling, attractive women. *Will I need medication? Will it help me? Will regulating my blood sugar help my ability to perform?* A sickening thought numbed him. *Will Carly want to be intimate with an amputee?*

Paul's shoulders heaved, and he sobbed. His body shuddered, and his heart rate rose in response, triggering the monitors to react. The alarms brought a nurse to his bed, who gave Paul a mild sedative, sending him into dreamland, where he saw himself and Carly strolling along a pristine beach arm in arm, on their honeymoon, without a care in the world.

Chapter 17

As they sat in the hospital cafeteria, Carly was grateful for her daughter's support during these trying times. Their relationship had bordered on estrangement, but after the call about Paul's medical condition, Greer had reacted responsibly, prioritizing her father's illness and rushing to comfort her mother. Mother and daughter had tried to keep the conversation upbeat. Carly inquired about Greer's apartment and her jobs, and was relieved to learn Greer enjoyed her work at the ambulance company and had received a small salary increase. Carly didn't ask about Greer's finances, afraid of invading her privacy. It was the picture on her cell phone, Greer with her arms around a male, that Carly couldn't ignore. She calmly related how happy Greer looked. Carly refrained from asking questions about the relationship, and after an awkward pause, Greer said she and Mickey had been dating a few months. Despite a laundry list of questions she wanted to ask, Carly willed herself to keep silent, afraid of tipping their fragile relationship in the wrong direction.

The acknowledgement of her relationship with Mickey had apparently given Greer the push she needed to speak openly with her mother. When her cell phone rang, Greer walked to a corner of the room to take the call from Mickey, and when she returned to sit beside her mother, her mood was more upbeat.

"Was that Mickey? I saw his picture pop up on your phone."

"Yes. That was him."

Carly exhaled. A stilted conversation was better than no communication. "Does he...uh...live close to you?" Carly mumbled.

"He's about ten minutes away."

"That's good. Where did you meet?"

"He's a mechanic at the garage where I sold my car."

"A mechanic. That's a good profession. We all need someone to look after our cars. There must be a lot a mechanic needs to know about cars nowadays. And the newer cars have so many electronics and computers."

Carly detected an almost imperceptible rise in the corners of Greer's mouth.

"Yeah," replied Greer. "Mickey is really talented. He's very mechanically inclined. He can fix anything. He's hoping to open his own garage one day."

"That's ambitious. Good to have goals." *A mechanic is a good trade. But couldn't she find a professional to date?*

"Yes. He's trying to save as much money as he can. His friend Rick works in a bank, and Mickey's been talking to him about the procedure for getting a mortgage. How much he would need. What the rules are. Stuff like that."

Greer paused and exhaled. Carly knew her daughter was preparing to utter something of a serious nature, and willed herself to stay calm.

"Mom. I wasn't planning to say anything yet. But I might as

well tell you now. Mickey and I are kind of serious. I mean, we haven't talked about getting married. But we're probably going to move in together. We can split the rent. We'll both save money."

"Wow! I know your apartment is tiny. Are you going to live there?"

"Possibly. Neither of us has much stuff, so we don't need much space. But Mickey's friend Theo knows a few places that may have openings."

"Okay. Sounds like a good idea. And I suppose there are lots of advantages to living together." *Besides the obvious—sharing a bed.*

"Yes. There are a lot of them, in addition to the money we'll save on rent. We will save time too. Instead of us both going to the laundromat, or to the grocery store, only one of us will need to go. And cook. Stuff like that. And he has a car. It isn't in great shape on the outside, but it runs well. It's dependable."

"Sometimes living alone isn't great." *Perhaps together they can afford a decent place.*

"Mom...I know that you and Dad were disappointed when I quit school. But I was wasting my time there. I don't mean the classes weren't good. Most of them were. But I wasn't satisfied. Everyone says how well I write. I know I can't get a good writing job without a college degree. And honestly, some classes I took were boring. I needed a break. Maybe I'm not cut out to write. That's why I dropped out. I have to decide what I want to do."

"I understand. Well...maybe I don't. I loved every bit of my college education." *Well, most of it.* "I loved everything about writing. And you are an excellent writer. But you're not me."

"No. I know you wanted a clone of yourself. I guess that's what every mother wants."

"Oh, Greer. I don't know that I wanted a clone. But I guess I figured that since you are such a wonderful writer—"

"It's not enough, Mom. Maybe I'm not cut out to sit and write all day."

Carly sighed. "Yes. I am disappointed. I've had dreams of us working in the same field. But I know in my heart that it's more important for you to do something that you want to do. Something that you're passionate about."

"That's what I want too. I want to feel passionate about a career."

"Oh, honey." Carly hugged her daughter. "I just want you to be happy. And feel fulfilled." She smiled. "And of course to support yourself."

"I will, Mom. It might take me a little longer to find what I want to do. But I'll find it."

"I know you will. I'll try to be patient."

Chapter 18

The sun was high in the sky, and David was strolling across the beach, arm in arm with a young woman whose name he couldn't recall. Tall and shapely, her ample breasts were barely contained in the bra of her skimpy red bikini. Her skin was a deep golden color, courtesy of hours basking in the sun, and her long blonde hair lay haphazardly in a ponytail. Every twenty feet, the couple stopped and enjoyed a passionate kiss. David was beaming; he didn't remember ever being so happy.

A shrill noise pounded his ears, and he broke away from the bikini-clad woman. She vanished, as another woman spoke to him. It took him a few seconds to realize it was Heidi's voice.

"Your phone is ringing," she groaned, irritated at the noise and David's failure to make it stop.

David opened his eyes and saw the glow of his cell phone in the bedroom's darkness. He grabbed the phone and swung his legs over the side of the bed.

"Hello," he said, as he rose from the bed. "Who is this? What do you want?"

"David. It's Mom. I'm sorry to wake you."

"Mom! Are you okay? What time is it?" he sputtered, rubbing his eyes.

"It's eight o'clock here. I guess it's five where you are."

He strode down the hallway and turned on the light in his home office. "Five o'clock? What's wrong? Why are you calling me so early?"

"It's your father. I...um...left you several voice mails."

"Yes. Oh. Sorry. I had a long day. I meant to listen to the messages. I suppose the hospital discharged Dad."

"David. We need to talk."

Her utterance jolted his brain to awaken. "What's going on? You wouldn't be calling me so early if he was fine."

"Your father is sicker than we thought. He has diabetes. He needs to stay in the hospital for a while."

"Oh, my gosh. Diabetes. Wow. That means his blood sugar is too high, right? Are they having trouble bringing it down?"

"David. Your father has had diabetes for a while. The doctors aren't sure how long. But it was long enough to damage his circulation and his sensation. He had a sore on the sole of his left foot that he didn't feel. It got worse. It turned black."

"Oh my God!"

"The doctors performed a procedure they hoped would improve his circulation and save his leg. But it failed. They had to amputate his leg below the knee."

As his ears and brain processed the words his mother uttered, he fell to the floor and screamed. Heidi heard his wails and came bounding from the bedroom. She kneeled beside her husband on the carpet, and he buried his face in her chest and howled.

. . .

IN THE TIME IT TOOK DAVID TO BOOK AN AIRLINE TICKET, RENT A car, and call into his boss, he had finished three cups of coffee and packed his suitcase with ample clothing for several days. Now, as the plane lifted off, he found himself unable to concentrate on any of the news journals, books, podcasts, or videos downloaded to his laptop. Anxiety ran rampant through his body. It was difficult to maintain comfort in the skimpy airplane seats, and his shoulders and back were stiff and painful. His digestive system had already regurgitated what it could; his bowels were working overtime, too. Whenever the anxiety abated enough to think rationally, David was overcome with guilt over dismissing his mother's voicemails as mundane, his neglect of his parents' general well-being, and the estrangement he had felt for years.

As a fresh college graduate, a technology company in California had wooed and wowed him so effectively that he felt justified leaving his parents and sister and friends behind. It was an answer to his dreams—to break free of his family's restrictions and beliefs and make his way in the world. He dove into his work with momentum that his bosses interpreted as passion—but it was really covering his homesickness, loneliness, and fears of failure. He accepted nearly all invitations for dinners, parties, and other social gatherings, and it was at a retirement party for a colleague he had met only once that a coworker introduced him to Heidi.

It was an enormous boost to his ego and libido when she agreed to a date. While he thought of her initially as eye candy, he found she was intelligent, funny, and caring. She had taken a job as an escort to make a substantial amount of money in a short time; funds she planned to use for her education. Their relationship flourished, and she had moved into his compact apartment. He had posed for pictures with Heidi at a friend's wedding, and it was those pictures, posted on social media, that led to his parents discovering Heidi worked as an escort. As he and Heidi discussed marriage, he thought his parents were sufficiently open-minded to put aside their prejudices, stereotypes, and rules. But he had been wrong. His parents never said his partner disappointed them, but they were less than welcoming when he and Heidi spent their first Thanksgiving visiting on the east coast instead of celebrating together in California. It disappointed him that his parents' flight to California for their wedding allowed little time for anything except the ceremony and the reception. Storms at home had delayed their flight's departure, and their plane landed in San Francisco with barely enough time for a shower and clothing change. They left on the first flight home the next day.

Heidi had done well in school, and was working as a paralegal at a small, but reputable, law firm on the other side of town. He had downplayed her previous remarks about advancing in the legal profession and was sorry they hadn't discussed it in more detail the previous day. He knew she had the intelligence and fortitude to be a lawyer. Perhaps his parents could erase the image of her in escort clothing if she had a Juris Doctor after her name. He smiled. He was proud of her, and of her work in the legal field. She had worked hard and was respected by her bosses and coworkers. It surprised him that people, blind to the training and knowledge about the legal field needed to become a paralegal, often thought they were glorified secretaries, unaware that they worked in tandem with the attorneys, researching legal terms and case studies. It was the attorneys who got the fame and fortune, not the support staff. Since Heidi already had a solid legal background, it should be easier for her to take the leap and go to law school. Besides the prestige of being an attorney, she would earn more money, which would certainly ease the burden on him, the primary breadwinner, although her current income was far more than some of her friends earned, especially those in social sciences fields. When he returned home, he and Heidi would discuss her plans for law school.

David hoped he wouldn't spend more than a few days away from California. He had worked hard to land this project and didn't want to miss more time from work than was absolutely necessary. He worried about his father, and felt uneasiness that once he saw his father was in stable condition and mentally intact, the vast emptiness of their estrangement would take center stage again. He wished he and his father could discuss a mundane topic like sports, or play a card game. A mindless game of gin rummy would suffice. Anything to pass the time.

Although he was eager to see his father, he hated everything about hospitals. Hours before his arrival, his palms were sweaty and beads of perspiration pooled on his neck and upper back. He had pressured Heidi to have home births, but she insisted on delivering Matthew and Emily in a hospital, concerned about extended and difficult labors or additional medical care the newborns might need. Luckily, Heidi had uneventful deliveries, and their son and daughter predictable nursery stays. Heidi compromised by asking for discharge from the hospital when Matthew was a day old. She spent an extra day in the hospital after Emily's birth, but David left the hospital shortly after the delivery to care for Matthew.

A flight attendant approached, offering beverages, and bags of pretzels smaller than his palm. David requested a gin and tonic. He needed something to calm his nerves in anticipation of the turmoil ahead.

Chapter 19

A melamine coffee cup whizzed so close to Madeline Townsend's head that she nearly dropped the syringe she held. The blonde nurse glared toward its origin. It couldn't be. Paul Brown? She hurriedly injected the medication from the syringe into Gail Mackey's intravenous line, then ran to Paul's bedside.

"Mr. Brown! Are you okay? Why did you throw the cup at me? I could have been injured!" she implored. It had taken all of her professional fortitude to stifle her anger. The act was uncharacteristic of him. It was clear something was causing the outburst.

"The coffee here is terrible," he cried, eyes bulging and face contorted in anger. "I can't stand it here! They should have left me on the floor. I should have died at the party. Instead…I'm here drinking this disgusting concoction they call coffee. If I hadn't let the doctors take off my leg, I would have run out of this place a long time ago!"

Madeline checked the monitors and logs, and examined

Paul's surgical site. His heart rate was elevated, but expected with his outburst. He didn't appear to have an infection. "Mr. Brown," she murmured, "I understand you are upset. You've been through a lot in such a short time. It's a lot to endure." She removed the pillow from under his head, fluffed it, and carefully replaced it. She smoothed the linens on his bed and strode to the medication cart. Returning to Paul's bedside, she injected a sedative into his intravenous line. Within minutes, Paul's body relaxed and his eyelids closed.

PAUL AWOKE TO THE SOUND OF FOOTSTEPS. OPENING HIS EYES, HE saw a petite middle-aged woman at the foot of his bed. Hearing him stir, she looked up from her laptop.

"Mr. Brown. I'm Dr. Villanueva. I'm from Psychiatry."

Paul shook his head. "I think you've got the wrong patient, Doc. I'm not crazy. I don't need a shrink," he declared.

The physician smiled, accustomed to the crude synonym. "No one has said you're crazy. But you did throw a coffee cup at a nurse. I want to find out why you did that."

Paul looked away. "I'm sorry," he replied. "I know that was wrong. She's been so nice to me. All the nurses have been. I shouldn't have done that. I'm glad she wasn't hurt."

The physician was vigorously typing on her laptop, and Paul thought perhaps she hadn't heard him. Dr. Villanueva raised her head, scanned the room, walked to the nurses' station, and returned with a narrow wooden chair. Placing the chair within arm's length of Paul, she settled in to speak with her patient. Paul, however, stared at the sheets.

"Mr. Brown. You have been through a trauma," she replied, her voice barely above a whisper. "You've been diagnosed with a serious medical condition. That alone could cause anger. But

94

it's been even harder for you. The surgeons removed your lower leg. You've lost a piece of yourself. It's okay to be angry. In fact, your anger is expected."

Paul raised his head and stared at the psychiatrist. "Expected?"

"You are grieving," Dr. Villanueva explained. "You've had a loss. Not the loss of a loved one. But a loss of a body part." She paused to let Paul comprehend her words. "There are five stages of grief. Five emotions one feels. Denial. Anger. Bargaining. Depression. Acceptance. It appears you're currently in the anger stage."

Paul was stunned. His eyebrows rose and his eyes widened. "Wow! I had no idea. Five stages of grief." He shook his head. "So I'm not crazy. My behavior was expected."

Dr. Villanueva smiled. "Well, I wouldn't say that your nurse came to work today expecting you would throw a coffee cup at her. But your anger is...normal. That doesn't mean you have to experience everything on your own. I can help you with that."

"Okay. What do you suggest?"

"I'll start you on some medication. A small dosage, to see how you do. It can be increased if you need it. How does that sound?"

"As long as people don't think I'm crazy, I'm okay with trying some medication."

After the psychiatrist departed from his bedside, Paul repeated the five stages of grief: Denial. Anger. Bargaining. Depression. Acceptance. *Okay, at least there's hope that I'll accept what happened to me. Eventually.*

Chapter 20

Carly stood at the threshold of the foyer and fought back tears. The last time she and Paul had walked out of their house together was to attend the party at the Grangers' home. It seemed like an eternity had passed, but in reality, it was about four days. While time often seemed to stand still, and tedious weeks stretched into months with no occurrence out of the ordinary, their life had irrevocably changed in an instant.

She surveyed the foyer. A wooden bench, built by hand by Paul's father Malcolm, rested against the wall. A rack containing Paul's shoes stood across from the bench. Visions of Paul seated on the bench, donning his shoes, came into view. Carly wondered whether Paul would ever sit there again. *Will he wear the same shoes?*

His shoes. The shoes she had encouraged him—no, urged him—to buy. Carly remembered how tense she and Paul had been at dinner that night. They rarely argued, choosing to hold their thoughts and their tongues, but sometimes silence was worse. That evening was the culmination of several days of snide remarks, petty comments, and rude behaviors. She recalled marching across the bedroom floor on the way to the bathroom, her foot hitting a creaky spot at the exact angle to rouse Paul as he drifted off to sleep. The next morning, Paul drank the last drops from the bottle of orange juice without asking if she wanted some. Behaviors not serious enough to start a war or file for divorce, but far removed from the niceties they usually showered on each other.

Of the two, Paul was the most likely to cede to Carly's demands or requests. Sometimes it surprised Carly that she wasn't the one who gave in. After all, she had convinced herself decades before that he had saved her. Although not quite a knight in shining armor, he had appeared in her life at just the right time. He hadn't swept her off her feet, but she brushed her torment and worries aside as their relationship deepened. She confessed to prior relationships but hid the details she feared would doom their togetherness. Paul had acknowledged feeling uncomfortable around females. The party girls and cheerleader types weren't interesting, and the studious and knowledgeable women intimidated him. When he and Carly met at a party given by Ethan, a mutual friend, Paul found Carly easy to talk to, but not a know-it-all, and Carly remarked to friends that Paul was easygoing and a good listener.

Years later, Ethan told her how elated Paul was that a woman of Carly's intelligence and class could love him. Carly had never revealed her delight that Paul had such a calm demeanor and wasn't the type to pry into her background or the choices she had made. He had readily accepted the explanation that her name change was necessary for her career advancement, much like Hollywood stars or television personalities adopted a new name to accompany their fledgling personas.

Now sadness enveloped Carly. Uncertain if it stemmed from depression or guilt or basic melancholy, she walked through the rooms on the main floor, something that usually brought her comfort and calm. She and Paul had so much to be thankful for. The living room contained well-made and durable furniture, not museum quality like many of their friends' furnishings. While many of their friends spent little time in the living room, despite the designated name, this room had been the center of their family's lives. Even though they had other options, Carly and Paul still spent much of their free time there. A contractor had constructed a window seat next to the bay window installed twenty years ago. It was the focal point of the room. Carly had loved window seats since her childhood and was delighted when the project was complete. Even now, she loved to cuddle there with a book. With her back resting upon the corner of the window, her feet barely extended halfway across the spacious window seat, the space large enough for two to sit comfortably. Some of Carly's fondest family memories were of her and Greer seated opposite each other on the cushion, engrossed in books, their silence speaking volumes.

Carly's second-favorite part of the room was the baby grand piano she had purchased a few years back, at a price too good to pass up, when a local music store suddenly went out of business. Carly's mother had insisted her daughter learn to play a musical instrument. Lucia promised to purchase the instrument of Carly's choosing, but expected she would desire something small and portable—a flute or a violin or a saxophone. But after hearing students play at the Curtis Institute, Carly chose a piano, so Lucia purchased a gently used one from a second-hand shop. For many years, Maxine, a neighborhood music teacher, gave Carly weekly piano lessons. Carly's musical abilities never rose to the level of the Curtis students, but she exhibited musical aptitude and enjoyed playing. She never needed cajoling to practice, and unlike some of her friends who considered music practice a chore, it brought her joy. Now, decades after the lessons had ended, she still enjoyed playing the piano. Her tastes were eclectic, but she especially loved jazz and show tunes. She strolled to the piano, lowered herself to the bench, and placed her fingers on the keys. The music that resulted was mournful and slow, her fingers in tune with the sorrow in her mind and her heart.

She arose from the piano seat and walked to the bottom of the staircase leading to the second floor. Patterned carpet squares lay atop the hardwood steps, embellished with a wooden banister with large newel posts. Carly wondered if Paul would learn to climb the stairs to the second floor. *Perhaps we'll need to install a motorized chair to transport him between floors. Will he be confined to a wheelchair? If so, how will I move his wheelchair to the second floor, so he can use it there?* The gravity of their situation hit her head on, and she seized the newel post as the room spun. Perhaps Paul would be confined to the first floor, unable to access the rest of the house. Besides the necessary adaptations, she hated to think of the damage to his ego. Although the first floor of their house was physically and aesthetically better than the average home, Carly knew Paul would feel like a prisoner in his own home. In addition, the half bathroom next to the foyer lacked a shower or bathtub.

Reaching the second floor, Carly meandered into their bedroom and surveyed the king-sized bed. The frame, raised about a foot from the floor, would need to be lowered. She located a pad of paper and a pen and started a list of all the changes the house would need to make it more accessible and more comfortable for Paul. *Will we still be able to share a bed? I hope so.* She shuddered to think he might need a hospital bed to better position himself, or that he might find one more comfortable. While they seldom had experienced physical intimacy of late, she hated to dismiss that part of their relationship. They were only in their fifties, an age where, pregnancy no longer a possibility, some of her friends boasted about their newfound sexual freedom.

Above the bed hung a painting of rural Scotland in a glittery gold frame. Although Paul didn't advertise his Scottish background, all it took for him to speak for hours about his parents' birthplace was a comment about the United Kingdom, or British royalty, or the Parliament or Prime Minister. "My parents came to this country from Scotland," he would say, and launch into the tales they had told him about the old country. His parents had settled in the United States shortly after their marriage, before the births of their three children, John, Susan, and Paul. Paul was so enamored with the Scottish culture that he insisted on giving his children traditional Scottish names. Carly refused his choice of Angus for their son, so they compromised on it as a middle name; he was David Angus. When their daughter was born, they agreed to name her Greer Karen. Carly liked the sound of the name Greer, and Paul had been grateful she agreed with his choice.

Visible from the bed was the master bathroom, recently remodeled with a stall shower and extended vanity with a double sink. At the advice of their contractor, they had installed a bench in the shower. He had said that older people liked to sit while showering, and even if she and Paul didn't need it at the time, the bench would almost certainly be useful in the future. Carly was grateful they had heeded the contractor's advice and installed the seat.

After Carly showered and donned her nightgown, she slipped beneath the comforter onto the cool, crisp linens. She turned off the lamp on the table beside the bed and rested her head upon the pillow. The shower had helped soothe her body's exhaustion, but did little to ease her mind. She considered reading a book but knew she lacked the concentration. She reached for her tablet, and scrolling through her playlist of music, settled on a list of smooth jazz favorites. Although the music calmed her and she was asleep within a half hour, she slept fitfully, her sleep peppered with images of Paul held captive behind steel bars, his left leg chained to the wall.

CARLY AWOKE EXHAUSTED AND TEARFUL. HER KNEES ACHED AND her neck was tense. While waiting for her coffee to brew, she retrieved the newspaper from the porch and viewed the headlines. The front page bore news of a turnpike auto accident that claimed a young couple and their three small children, a teenage male shot in a case of mistaken identity, and the increasing number of people losing their jobs, and with it, their health insurance. Nothing to lift Carly's spirits out of the cellar. She had suffered from a mild depression during the period leading to menopause, but the symptoms had eased a few years prior. Seated with her coffee and two slices of wheat toast, Carly recalled an interview with a psychiatrist who counseled women undergoing catastrophic lifestyle changes. Women who became disabled because of illnesses or accidents, penniless mothers left to care for young children abandoned by their fathers, abused women attempting to rebuild their lives. Her problems paled in comparison, but she needed the same professional guidance. Carly searched the contact list on her phone, located the psychiatrist's information, and placed a call to the office.

Chapter 21

David, seated in the back of the plane, retrieved his carry-on bag from the overhead compartment as soon as the airport runway was in sight, but even after the plane had landed and the flight attendants had given permission to exit, the other passengers didn't seem to share his impatience to exit the airliner. Finally, he crossed the threshold and ran up the ramp into the airport, clutching his bag in front of him and maneuvering his lean body between the groups of families hugging and kissing before him. Finding clearance, he sprinted through the airport, past travelers carrying coffee cups and bulky luggage, and barely missed an airport employee pushing an elderly man in a wheelchair. The sight caused David to slow his momentum slightly. He thought of his father, needing a wheelchair to negotiate the long halls of the airport. He wondered if his father would gain the ability and stamina to walk independently, or whether he would need a wheelchair for the remainder of his life.

Sliding into the passenger seat of the rental car, David

shoved his way into the exit lane and nearly sideswiped an SUV whose driver was already entering the single turnstile. He ignored the driver, who honked and swore and gave David a middle finger salute.

"Can't you see I'm in a hurry? My father had his leg amputated! I have to get to the hospital!" David yelled through the open window. Surely his situation was more dire than wherever the driver of the SUV was headed.

David exited the airport and pulled onto the highway. He entered the name of the hospital into the app on his phone and was dismayed to learn that road construction and traffic jams would delay his drive by fifteen minutes. An extra quarter of an hour in traffic in California was a usual occurrence, but now, the reality of the physical and emotional estrangement from his father hit him full force, and impatient and riddled with guilt, fifteen minutes was an eternity.

He thought of his childhood with fondness. He had been an exceptional student who required little prodding to excel academically. His father had been active in his life, encouraging him to participate in social activities: karate and baseball and Boy Scouts. Like most teenagers, he had rebelled against authority and rules that infringed on his burgeoning social life. Quick to test the boundaries of his parents' authority, he had briefly challenged his curfew, but the embarrassment of driving his prom date in his dilapidated coupe with faulty air conditioning instead of his father's new sedan convinced him to toe the line for a few more months. He applied to several colleges throughout the country, and when the acceptance to MIT arrived, his family celebrated as if he was elected President of the United States.

During his college years. David had fantasized about living on the west coast, lured by images of the sun and surf and sand.

A few days after college graduation, he had piled his belongings into the car and traveled westward across the country to California. A membership at an athletic club with branches throughout the United States allowed him to shower and change his clothes, refill his water bottle, and swim a few laps in the pools. He stayed until the building closed, then parked in a far corner of the lot and slept a few hours in his car, unnoticed and undisturbed. Arriving in California after five days on the road, with help from a college friend who had moved there a week before, he secured a tiny, overpriced apartment. He met Heidi a year later, and proposed to her much quicker than he had planned, optimism buoyed by his dreams of them on a pristine beach, a picture-perfect couple glowing in the sun's rays. Heidi graduated at the top of her class and secured an offer from the law firm where she still worked. She had taken care to avoid disclosure of her escort position or to post pictures of herself in skimpy attire or in questionable surroundings. If the law firm knew of her previous work history, they didn't see it as a liability. But his parents viewed it as a problem. Their disappointment in his choice of a mate angered him, and it would have surprised their wedding guests to learn it was he who had hurried the wedding preparations, not Heidi.

Now, as the traffic congestion cleared, David turned his attention to the road. He arrived at the hospital and parked the car in the lot closest to the entrance. Hurrying from the vehicle, he stopped only briefly to allow an elderly woman using a cane to pass. He searched the text from his mother for the number of his father's hospital room. Locating the text, he rushed to the elevator.

"Can I help you, sir?" came a voice from his right. A petite female, long black hair in a neat ponytail, perched at the information desk.

David walked the short distance to the desk and addressed the woman. "Hi. I'm going to see my father. Paul Brown. He is in room 403. I just drove from the airport. I live in California. My father is sick. I need to see him. Now." For someone usually able to bridge the gap between common and technical language, David suddenly could not express himself beyond basic sentences of few words.

"Okay, sir. I'll check his room number. Yes, he's in room 403. You are correct." She pointed to a clipboard secured to the desk. "Please sign in here. Visiting hours are over at nine o'clock."

David glanced at the clock above the desk. "It's already after eight. I came from California. Traffic was awful. There was construction, too. Can't I stay later?"

"That will be at the discretion of the staff on the unit," she replied.

"Thank you. I appreciate your help." An elderly man and woman sauntered from an elevator, and David barreled towards the empty car, barely entering it before the doors closed. He exited at the fourth floor and followed the signs to room 403.

He stopped unexpectedly outside his father's room, impeded by his pounding heart, sour stomach, and sweaty palms. He had traveled thousands of miles by plane, endured crowds at the airport and snarled traffic, but here he was, standing outside—but not inside—his father's hospital room. David exhaled, opened the door, and stepped inside.

His father looked small in the bed, under the linens, surrounded by pillows and blankets. Although a thin cream-colored blanket covered his body, the dip in the blanket disclosed the absence of his left leg. A bag of fluids hung on a pole, attached to an electronic box which regulated the flow of liquids to his father's arm.

Paul, seeing movement, turned his head towards the door. He beamed, and his arms reached towards his son.

"David! What a surprise! Wow! You came all the way from California!"

David crossed the distance separating them, and father and son hugged. David thought it was their first hug since he was a boy, and it surprised him how long it lasted and how good it felt.

"It's good to see you Dad. I'm glad I could get here. I booked a flight at the last minute. Traffic from the airport was terrible. But I'm so glad I got here."

Paul beamed. "It's been...what? A couple of years since your mother and I have seen you?"

The dim lighting prevented Paul from seeing a crimson flush spread from David's neck to his cheeks.

"I...think you might be right. Something like that. Too long. Mostly my fault. Heidi and I are so busy...with the kids and their activities." A lump formed in David's throat. *That's the truth. Isn't it?* He perused the room, removed a pillow from a chair next to his father, and lowered himself to the chair.

"I guess Mom left already."

"About an hour ago. She wanted to wait for you. But she was exhausted. Kept falling asleep in the chair. That pillow you moved was hers. I sent her home. She's been running herself ragged. It's bad enough I'm here. The last thing I need is for her to get sick. Or have an accident driving. So I sent her home and promised she would see you tomorrow." Paul winced.

"Dad, are you in pain? Should I get the nurse?"

Paul grimaced again. "Hold up. Just a second." He pressed a button in his hand, attached to the machinery holding the bag of fluids. "I can take this pain medication every hour. I think it's time."

"I didn't know they had machines to dispense pain medicine that you can control yourself. Does it work okay?"

"Yes. It helps. Of course, there's a limit to how much I can give myself. And a restriction on how often. But it's much better than calling for a nurse every time."

David examined the machine and smiled. "Wow! I'd love to take this apart and see what type of computer is in there."

Paul gave a wry smile. "I bet you would."

David stretched his arms above his head and yawned.

"You aren't going back home tonight. Are you?" Paul asked.

David patted his father's hand. "Relax Dad. No. I'm not leaving yet. I'm just a little stiff from the plane. I'll be here for a couple of days. I want to spend some time with you. I want to make sure you're okay before I go home."

"I'm doing better than when I came here in the ambulance. I didn't know I was sick. I guess your mother told you about my blood sugar?"

"Yes. She said it was very high."

"It was almost 700. The doctors said it was probably high for at least a few months. But I had a few beers at a party at the Grangers'. I ate a lot of carbs there too. The combination likely caused my blood sugar to skyrocket. Then I passed out."

"That's what Mom said."

"Then the doctors and nurses saw my foot. I had no idea there was a problem. They did a procedure to improve the circulation. But it failed. And they had to amputate my leg." Paul's lower lip quivered. "I'm sorry. The tears come often. The psychiatrist said it's normal. Sometimes I get angry, too."

David thought he had misheard his father. *A psychiatrist?* He reached for Paul's hand. *I can't remember the last time I held his hand.* "I'm glad you're getting help. It's a lot to happen at once."

"I know. I didn't want to take any medication, but I after I threw a cup at a nurse—"

"Wait! You threw a cup at a nurse?"

Paul sighed. "Anger is the second stage of grief. I have three more stages to go. And I might go back and forth between them. Who knew? But the nurse accepted my apology. Apparently it wasn't the first time a patient threw something at her."

"I am so sorry, Dad." A solitary teardrop slid down David's right cheek. He brushed it away with his hand. "I'm sorry about everything. Especially that I didn't come until today. Mom left me a voicemail. Actually...a few. But I was busy at work. I'm managing a project. I hand picked my team. I was so caught up in the job that I never listened to the voicemails. I assumed they had discharged you. That you were home."

"That was the plan, to stay overnight or perhaps a second day. But I'm still here."

"Mom called me about five this morning. I called my boss and caught a flight here."

"I appreciate you coming. I'm sorry my illness interrupted your work. And your home life."

David sighed. "Please don't be sorry, Dad. I'm the one who is sorry. I should have been here yesterday. Well, at least I should have returned Mom's phone calls. I have no excuse. My work is important. My wife and children mean the world to me. But I shouldn't have neglected my family here."

An hour later, a nurse making rounds observed Paul asleep in his bed, and his son dozing in a chair beside him, their fingers intertwined, matching smiles on their faces.

Chapter 22

It wasn't until David had left his bedside that the reality of his condition hit Paul head on. Although he knew now that it was a normal response, he had never felt such anger. Anger at everyone who walked on their own two feet. Hostility at his doctors for not being able to improve the circulation in his leg. Even Carly had failed him; she had neglected to notice his discolored foot when he donned or removed his socks. He had never been religiously observant, attending church on Christmas and Easter and for weddings and funerals—but he cursed God, anyway. *Why did you allow this to happen to me?*

Paul realized with chagrin that the person he was most angry with was himself. He had missed his yearly physical. He hadn't seen a blister or signs of infection on his foot. *But who really looks at the underside of their foot? I shouldn't have dismissed my fatigue and thirst. I've also been walking differently. Why did I dismiss that?* He was angry that he hadn't taken good care of himself. He and Carly had money and medical insurance. It shouldn't have taken a catastrophe for him to seek medical care.

I've been a good man. I've been a good husband. I haven't cheated on my wife. Although, like most men, I've had my chances. I've made a decent living. I don't smoke or drink to excess. I don't gamble. I don't cheat. I give money to charities. I'm not perfect, but others have done worse.

Paul thought of friends he knew who had committed adultery. He was certain Stan had sexual relations with Patrice, a former secretary who was young and beautiful, and who received a sizeable severance package when she quietly left the company after a six-month employment. Grace had questioned Stan about the sudden flurry of late evening business meetings; he replied he was trying to save his work project from failure. A few days later, he informed Grace that Patrice was leaving. He didn't say that he paid the severance package from his personal finances instead of the business account. Grace learned of the large withdrawal when she transferred money from their joint account to finance a surprise party for Stan. When confronted, he acknowledged the payment to Patrice, but claimed she threatened him with sexual harassment—which he denied. He insisted he paid her to avoid damaging his reputation. Grace didn't believe Stan; days after dozens of their friends received an invitation, she canceled the party. Stan stuck with his story about the false sexual harassment claim, but few of their acquaintances believed him, especially since Stan and Grace began attending couples' counseling shortly thereafter.

As tears flooded his eyes and spilled onto his cheeks, Paul thought of his former neighbor Izzy, who had owned a local car wash. Few cars passed under the spray of suds and water, but to the surprise of many, the business remained open. Federal agents arrived at the property and carried several ledgers from the building. The ledgers appeared to be duplicates, but although the dates matched, the cash flow did not. A judge sentenced Izzy to ten years in prison for money laundering, but his attorney got the case overturned on appeal, because the federal agent who testified was charged with perjury in another case, so his testimony in Izzy's trial was questionable. Izzy listed his house for sale and left town one night with his belongings in a U-Haul trailer. Paul wondered why Izzy, guilty of a serious crime, got a reprieve and carried on with his life. He had literally driven away from his troubles.

But Paul couldn't walk away from his burdens. He recalled his parents' assertions that life wasn't always easy, or fair. As a boy, with ample food, clothing, and shelter, he didn't think life was tough. Now he understood.

Chapter 23

Carly arrived at the psychiatrist's office, housed in the lower level of an enormous stone edifice. Pristine landscaping and an immaculate driveway devoid of a windblown leaf or stray blade of grass surrounded the building. She exited her car and strolled to the entrance. A bell chimed as she entered the spacious room. Within seconds, a female voice called to her.

"Please have a seat. I'll be with you momentarily."

Carly perused the room. The furnishings belied an office waiting room. Several pots of orchids in rainbows of colors sat atop antique wooden tables of various shapes. Upholstered overstuffed chairs in harmonious flowered prints lined three pale blue walls of the room. An enormous gas fireplace covered the fourth wall; an almost imperceptible flame poked through the imitation gray bricks lining its interior. Carly knew a great deal of thought had gone into the design of this room. It had a homey feel; a calming effect for people seeking help with their problems. She had been seated for less than a minute when a middle-aged woman with a short gray bob and small oval wire-rimmed glasses appeared before her. She extended her right hand in greeting.

"Hi, Carly. I remember you from our interview. Welcome. I'm Dr. Cooke. Hannah Cooke."

Carly stood and lightly shook the psychiatrist's hand. "Yes. I'm Carly. I'm pleased to meet you again. This room is lovely. I've never been in a waiting room so much like home."

Dr. Cooke smiled. "I always said that when I had a practice, I would furnish it like my home," she said, as she led the way through a sculpted wooden door across the room. "Come back to my office."

IF ASKED, CARLY MIGHT HAVE SAID THE THERAPY SESSION EASED her mind a bit, but in reality, it soothed her mind and her body. It wasn't until a driver cut in front of her at an intersection that she realized her reaction was much tamer than the waving her middle finger and shouting obscenities she had adopted of late. She used the extra minute of idling at the traffic light to glance at the storefronts lining the avenue, an eclectic mix of specialty clothing shops, bistros, electronic stores, and other retailers selling flowers, party supplies, and musical instruments.

She thought again of the shoe shop. Carly had voiced her concerns to Dr. Cooke; the fear that the doctors amputated Paul's leg because of her insistence that he buy new shoes. Expensive shoes. Better quality shoes than he usually bought. Footwear constructed of leather that promised to bend and mold and provide a custom fit. But the shoes had pinched his foot and caused a blister to form; a fluid-filled sac that annoyed most people and perhaps made walking difficult. But Paul was ignorant of the degrading skin on the sole of his foot, so he had donned his socks and shoes and proceeded with the events of his days.

Dr. Cooke had listened to Carly as she rambled repeatedly about her guilt over the shoes. Carly acknowledged understanding the physicians' consensus that diabetes caused Paul's impaired sensation, and ultimately, the amputation. Dr. Cooke finally convinced Carly that the shoes were the mechanism that caused the harm—not the reason for it. Carly had nodded in agreement with the assessment. If not those shoes, it would have been another pair of shoes that pinched, or a wrinkled sock that exerted extra pressure on his toes, or a corner of a dresser that caught Paul's bare foot as he walked to the bathroom in the midnight darkness. By the end of the hour-long session, Carly realized the tension in her shoulders had eased, her brain felt less foggy, and her mood had lightened. Dr. Cooke gave her a prescription for a mild sleeping pill and scheduled a follow-up appointment in two weeks. She thought Carly might need a medication for anxiety, but delayed that decision until the next visit.

Carly filled the prescription to prevent another night of tossing and turning, but she wasn't certain if she would keep the follow-up appointment. The psychiatrist had done her job, and Carly had nothing else to discuss with her.

Chapter 24

My Life and Yours- by Carly Casper

To my valued readers: I usually pen articles about community programs and people of interest, but with the approval of my editor Stephanie and my husband and children, I am temporarily authoring a column. The contents are special to me and I hope my words will resonate with you. I rarely share my personal life with my readers, but I have done so now, as camaraderie and as a message to all of you reading this column.

First, a little about myself. My husband Paul and I celebrated our thirty-second anniversary earlier this year. We were together a few years before that. I did not take his last name when we married. We are empty nesters; our son David lives with his wife and children in California. Our daughter Greer lives in the area. Our marriage has been solid, and like most couples either married or living together for a long time, we have had our good times and bad. Recently, we endured a bit of a rough patch, not the type that sends one to a marriage counselor or a divorce attorney, but a malaise or lethargy. Unfortunately, that was just the precursor of what was to come. We had no way of knowing that a wake-up call was lurking in the shadows.

Paul and I had been blessed with good health, with no major medical problems or surgeries like many of our friends —and many of you. We awoke every morning and stepped out of bed, ready to go to work and engage in our daily activities. We prepared our meals or ate out. Sometimes the meals were healthy, but we didn't worry if we occasionally ingested too much fat or calories. All of that changed a few weeks ago.

Paul's collapse at a friend's party was traumatic, but that wasn't the worst of it. Unbeknownst to us, when he canceled his physical exam earlier this year to attend to work matters—he works in the insurance industry—he likely delayed receiving a diagnosis of diabetes. He was unaware of his elevated blood sugar. The high sugar caused damage to his body. The circulation to his lower extremities became compromised. He didn't know that, either. His new shoes may have pinched his feet, but because of his impaired circulation, he experienced no pain. His blood sugar was nearly 700 when he collapsed, and part of the sole of his left foot was black.

Several wonderful and capable physicians attempted a medical intervention, but ultimately, Paul's circulation did not improve, and his foot worsened. Paul, my life partner, the father of our children, grandfather of two, became an amputee when the physicians removed his leg below the knee. Paul is currently stable and will need rehabilitation to regain his independence and hopefully learn to walk again. When he is ready, he will be fitted for a prosthesis.

I invite you, my readers, to stay with me as Paul and I take a journey we never planned and didn't want to travel. Our destination isn't an exotic island or a tourist attraction. We will stay in our home. Our goals are simple but unlike any we have considered previously: control of diabetes, management of diet and exercise, and ultimately, Paul's physical independence.

Chapter 25

Seated in a chair at her father's bedside, Greer stared at the television, which was tuned to a twenty-year-old sitcom. She peered at her father, who gazed at the television, his expression blank. Growing up, Greer had rarely watched sitcoms; her parents eschewed them because of the repeatedly crude humor and the characters' ability to solve any problem in a twenty-two minute—without the commercials—television show. When she visited her father now, the television was always on, tuned to a sitcom, or occasionally, to a cartoon. Greer thought perhaps an infection, anesthesia, or the pain medications had compromised her father's cognitive abilities. The nurses said he knew his name, where he was, the approximate time of day, and that he was in a hospital—and Greer didn't want to press the issue further. She had perused medical articles and blogs on the internet, and learned that people recovering from a major illness needed all of their energies to overcome the medical problems, and therefore couldn't concentrate on a program with multiple characters or plot lines. It made sense. Greer recalled the times she had vegetated in front of a television after a strenuous day in school, or when the pace of her three jobs caught up with her. Those were the times she tuned to a reality show or a mindless program.

As she sipped from a bottle of flavored water, Greer heard a light tap on her father's door. Strolling to the door, she was surprised to see Mickey, dressed in a collared shirt, beige Dockers, and clean brown loafers. He had combed his hair to the side and was clean-shaven. He held a decorative paper bag by the corded handles.

"Hi! Wow! I didn't expect you here!" She hugged him. "What a pleasant surprise. You didn't tell me you were coming."

Redness crept through Mickey's face and ears. Greer had never seen him blush before.

"I...thought...I should come. It's about time I met your parents." He scanned the hospital room. "Okay. Your mother isn't here. Well...your father, anyway."

Paul slowly extended his hand. "Thank you. I appreciate the effort."

Mickey pressed the bag into Paul's hands. "Hello, Mr. Brown. I...uh...brought you something. I mean, I didn't know what to get...since I hadn't met you before. But I wanted to bring something. So I stopped at the bookstore. I got an anthology of stories by comedians. I thought maybe reading one or two at a time would cheer you up."

Greer saw Mickey tremble, and her affection for him increased threefold. *He is really a kind soul. And a good person.*

Paul glanced at the book's cover and scanned the table of contents. "That's very thoughtful of you. I could use a little humor right now. Um...I'm sorry. What did you say your name is?"

"Mickey, sir. Mickey Hollins."

"I'm happy to meet you, Mickey." Paul motioned to the chair next to him, and Mickey moved Greer's jacket aside and took a seat. Paul handed the television remote to Mickey.

"Is there something else you would like to watch? I don't really pay attention to any of these shows. They are really just background noise. Something to keep my mind off of thinking about my troubles."

"No, sir. I'm just happy to be here. With Greer and with you. And I'm... uh...sorry about your troubles."

"Thank you. I appreciate that. I'm glad you came."

Greer was stunned. Her father had rarely conversed with her during the hours she spent at his bedside. But he was perusing the contents of his new book and having an appropriate conversation with Mickey.

Mickey tried to ignore Paul's stares, and his eyes focused on Greer instead. She was smiling for the first time in days.

"What do you do, Mickey? How do you know Greer? Do you work with her?"

"Uh...no, sir. I don't work with her. I'm a mechanic. She sold her car to the owner of the shop where I work. We got to talking. We're um...good friends."

Greer noticed he was blushing again. *I didn't know he was so sensitive. I like that.*

"A mechanic. A good profession. We always need mechanics. Especially with the advances in technology in the cars. More things to go wrong, I suppose," murmured Paul.

"Yes. But the technology works both ways," said Mickey. "It helps us to diagnose problems with the vehicles easier and quicker. We don't have to remove all the working parts of the car to check the things that are underneath."

"How long have you been a mechanic?"

"A few years. I studied the basics in high school. Then I

went to a trade school to learn the rest. I'd like to open my open shop some day. I'm trying to save for that now."

"It's always good to have goals. Gives you something to look forward to. To work towards."

Greer hadn't expected her father and Mickey to converse so easily. That was the main reason she had told Mickey he shouldn't come to the hospital. But he had surprised her by showing up to visit her father and to support her, and by his attire, his gift, and his attitude.

Unexpectedly, her reservations about the permanency of their relationship had drifted away.

Chapter 26

David parked his car in the driveway and strolled through the cobblestone walkway to his house. As he entered the foyer, he saw Heidi in the kitchen. He placed his carry-on bag on the blue silk divan and went to greet his wife, who was scooping avocado into a bowl.

"Hi. I missed you," he murmured, as he held her in his arms.

"Hi, honey. I'm glad to see you're home. Matthew and Emily are at the Warrens' house until eight. I'm making guacamole. I figured you might be hungry. How was the flight?"

"It was fine. I was able to relax a bit. I wasn't nearly as tense as when I flew out there," David replied.

"I'm glad the trip went well. Um...I mean, I'm glad you got to visit with your family. And that your father is doing better than you expected."

"I'm happy his mind is okay." David retrieved a bottle of beer from the refrigerator, popped off the lid, and took a few gulps of the cool brew. "At first, the sight of him lying in the bed, minus part of his leg, really threw me. I nearly lost it right there. At the door to his room."

"That must have been difficult for you, to see part of his leg gone."

"Yes, it was hard. But I felt better once I talked to him. Of course he was upset that the doctors had to take his leg. He and my mom had hoped they could fix his circulation. But overall, he is feeling better. Of course, he has some pain. But he managed it by getting medication through an electronic delivery system connected to an IV. He didn't have to wait for a nurse. Pretty high tech." David plucked a pile of mail from the counter. He perused the contents: mostly bills and advertisements. He held up an envelope.

"Bay Area School of Law," he announced. "Is this an acceptance letter? Were you accepted? Are you planning to go?"

"Relax, David. It's a confirmation that I started the process. I haven't finished the application. I sent some preliminary paperwork and files. But I still have to take the LSAT. It's too early for a decision."

"LSAT. What is that?"

"The Law School Admission Test. I need to take it to get into law school."

"Okay. Did you sign up to take it?"

"I've gotten some information. I've been trying to study when I get home from work. And after Matthew and Emily are settled for the night. But I don't know how I will find enough time to study. With my job and all the commuting. And the kids' activities. Plus preparing dinner, laundry, shopping. I barely get enough sleep now." She wrung her hands on the dish towel. "Perhaps this won't work."

"Of course it will work. Why won't it work?"

"Your work hours can be crazy. You have this new project. I

know how important it is to you."

David's voice rose and his face reddened. "You already know a lot of the legal stuff, don't you? After being a paralegal for years, you shouldn't have to start at the beginning. You can probably learn the stuff in half the time!"

Heidi tossed the dish towel on the counter and glared at David. "Yes, I already have a decent amount of legal knowledge. But I still have to study for the exam. And your reaction proves we have a bigger problem."

"A bigger problem? What kind of problem? It isn't money. The kids are doing fine. We have a fabulous house. We're healthy. So what kind of problem do we have?"

"You can't even see how overwhelmed I am. Even if I do well on the LSAT and get accepted to law school, how am I going to go to school, study, work, take care of the kids, do the laundry, make the meals? I'm already doing as much as I can."

David ran his hands through his chestnut hair. "Okay. Calm down. I didn't mean to upset you. I know how much you do. We already have Deborah helping us. Perhaps she can help more... do other things."

"No! She can't do any more. Deborah is already taking a heavy course load in school. She wasn't certain she could continue working for us. She told me a few weeks ago she might have to quit."

"What? You never told me that!"

"I handled it myself. Deborah agreed to continue with us. But—"

"But what?"

"I offered her more money."

"You didn't tell me. How much more?"

"Two hundred more."

"Per month?"

"No!" Heidi exhaled. "Per week."

A stream of beer spewed from David's mouth. "Two hundred dollars more per week? Are you crazy?"

"No! I had no choice. I couldn't let her walk away. Then we'd have no one."

"Wasn't there another way? We're talking an extra ten thousand dollars per year!"

"I can do the math. I know how to multiply."

David gave a lengthy exhalation. "I'm not saying you can't do math. But it's a lot of money to just agree to give someone. We already pay her a lot."

"So what should I have done? Should I have let her walk away? Should I quit my job? Should I tell Matthew and Emily they need to quit their activities?"

David clutched his forehead with his hands. "I don't know."

"Oh, I know! Our children can be latchkey kids. They can walk home by themselves and play video games until I get home."

"Stop it! You know that's not the answer."

"Why do you think I agreed to pay Deborah the extra money? She's worth every penny."

David sighed. "I'm sure she is. I just wonder why we are working so hard. Trying to earn more money. Then we have to pay more to work more. To earn more."

"I know. I feel like we're stuck. That's one reason I thought that if I go to law school—"

"I agree you will eventually earn more money. But not right away. And after you finish school, you might not earn much more than what you make now."

Heidi clenched her fists and fought the urge to scream. "Are you trying to talk me out of going to law school? Should I forget about taking the LSAT?"

"That's not what I'm saying."

"Then what are you saying? Do you want me to give up my dream of being a lawyer?"

"No! I don't want you to do that. But I'm so frustrated. I know we love it here. But it costs so much to live in this area. Sometimes I wonder if it's worth it."

Heidi glared at David. "Well, where else would we live? We've talked about it before. We want to be near a big city. We don't want to live in the south. We're too liberal to feel comfortable in the middle of the country."

David sighed. "I'm sorry. I didn't mean to get on you. I know you're doing the best you can. I am too. But with the money we make, I thought we would have more."

"We have a wonderful house and expensive cars. The kids go to an excellent school. They have their activities. What more do you want?"

"I don't know. I know we have more than most people. I'm grateful for that. Seeing my dad in the hospital really got to me. I didn't realize how much I missed seeing him."

"David. I'm sure it was a tough trip. To see your father sick. And with his leg amputated."

"It was tough. The plane ride was the worst. But I actually felt better once I saw him and talked to him. He's better than I expected. He looked okay physically. Other than his leg, of course."

"I'm glad to hear that. What a shock it must be. So much happened in a few days."

"I know. I don't know how I would handle something like that," mused David.

"I hope we never have to. Our problems are minor. But your father's are life changing."

Chapter 27

The attendant maneuvered Paul's wheelchair into a space at the corner of the gym. Paul scanned the sizable room and estimated it was the size of the field where David had played Little League baseball. While the center stretch of the room was devoid of equipment, contraptions of various shapes, sizes, and materials lined its periphery. Weights on pulleys brought forth memories of a gym where he had practiced and trained as a twenty-something interested in improving his physique to catch the eyes of females.

Paul had expected stares at the spot where his lower leg should have been, but the other patients had problems of their own and didn't seem to care about his missing body part. About a dozen patients sat or slouched in wheelchairs, some in standard-issue hospital gowns, others clad in sweatsuits or shorts. Some men and women seemed unaware of their surroundings. A few had misshapen extremities visible. A man of about ninety was slumped in a wheelchair; his withered left arm rested on a wooden board positioned across the wheelchair, and spittle oozed from the left side of his mouth. Despite the surrounding clamor, his glassy eyes stared straight ahead. A young male sat ramrod straight in his wheelchair, a steel apparatus protruded from screws placed in his forehead; its circular shape resembled a halo. Paul couldn't imagine being able to hold one's head upright with that contraption in place, but the man was moving his arms and legs, and conversing with a therapist.

A man in his early to mid thirties with short curly brown hair approached Paul. His eyes were an unusual shade of blue; they reminded Paul of the water in the Caribbean. He wore well-fitting khakis and a slim-fit polo shirt which highlighted his muscular arms. At about six feet tall with a solid physique, Paul surmised he was a hit with the ladies.

"Hello Mr. Brown. I'm Brian Snyder. I'm a physical therapist. I'll be working with you today," he announced, extending his right hand to Paul.

"Hi," Paul answered, shaking Brian's hand, but unable to sound as cheery. "You can call me Paul."

"Okay, Paul. Sounds great." Brian wheeled a stool to Paul's chair. He removed a pen from his shirt pocket and wrote Paul's name on the first of a stack of papers on his clipboard. About ten minutes passed as he posed an exhaustive list of questions. Then Brian tested the motion, sensation, and strength in Paul's arms and legs. He carefully and methodically unwrapped the ace bandage from Paul's stump. Paul diverted his eyes, still unable to look at the bare stump. He wondered how he could move forward, take care of himself, be independent, if he considered himself a freak.

"Paul. Please look at me," said Brian. "You turned away when I unwrapped your stump."

Heat rose in Paul's cheeks. "I'm sorry. I really am," he blubbered. "I'm trying to adjust...I really am." His right hand brushed away tears forming in the corners of his eyes. He had cried in the presence of the nurses, but not in front of another man.

"I know it's hard to look at your leg when part of it is gone. Perhaps you consider yourself less than a man now. But you shouldn't."

"Yes! That's exactly how I feel. I can't stand on two feet. I can't do things I used to do...help my wife...carry groceries...fix things in the house." He was powerless to stop the cascade of tears that flooded his cheeks. "I'm sorry," he sobbed, "I don't know what happened. You must think I'm a baby." He looked away again.

Brian's firm hands held Paul's shoulders. "Paul. Please look at me."

Paul studied Brian's kind face and reassuring smile and willed himself to follow his directions.

"I will help you get through this. We'll work together. I promise you," vowed Brian.

Paul nodded. He clutched Brian's hand as if it was a life preserver. "I'm glad you understand," he murmured.

"We need to start with baby steps. I want you to look at your leg...and your stump. Let's try for three seconds," Brian replied. "Just three seconds."

Paul clenched his teeth. His face reddened. He looked at Brian, then at the floor. "I don't know if I can do it."

"I know you can do it. Just three seconds. I'll count with you." Brian took Paul's hands in his own. "Are you ready?"

"I guess so." *I don't want to act like a baby.*

"Take a deep breath."

Paul inhaled sharply.

"Great. Okay. On three. One. Two. Three."

Paul opened his eyes and looked at his leg, as Brian placed Paul's hands on his stump. Paul placed his fingertips at the scar along the bottom. Except for the roughness of the scar, the rest of the skin felt as it always had.

"You are doing great, Paul." Brian shook Paul's hand. "That was a major accomplishment. You should be proud of what you did here today."

"Yeah. I guess I did okay." Paul gave a weak smile. "Better than I expected."

"Let's talk about therapy goals," said Brian, more casually than Paul had expected. "You were independent before your surgery. Where do you see yourself in a few months?"

Paul was somber. His brief smile had faded. He shook his head almost imperceptibly. "I don't want to be a burden to my wife. That's all I ask. She doesn't deserve to care for a cripple."

"We don't use terms like *cripple*," replied Brian. "But I don't expect you'll be a burden either. You're a muscular guy. You were independent and active before. There's no reason to think you won't be independent again."

"Really? You think I'll be able to do everything for myself?"

"I see no reason you won't be," replied Brian. "With the exception of the amputation, you're in fairly good shape. Middle aged. There are no cardiac issues. Your core strength is above average and your arms are strong. You should be able to move around independently."

Paul was pensive. "What I really want to know is...if...you think I will walk again."

"That's a fair question. I expect you will be able to maneuver your body from bed to chair and toilet independently. We'll work on your standing balance and tolerance. You should be able to dress yourself. My goal is to get you ambulatory. Walking with a device. A walker. Maybe less. Your stump is healing nicely. We may fit you for a prosthesis in the near future."

Paul's eyes widened. "You mean an artificial leg? I might walk with an artificial leg?"

"Yes. It's very possible. But we have a lot to work on before we get to that point."

"Can you give me some exercises to do on my own? To get stronger?"

"Yes. Absolutely. I'll grab some instructions for you." Brian stood from his stool. "Paul, I think we'll get along just great. I love working with people who are motivated."

BACK IN HIS HOSPITAL ROOM AFTER THE THERAPY SESSION, THE nurses found a beaming Paul, sitting in a wheelchair, diligently performing arm exercises. "My therapist Brian said I won't be a burden to my wife!" he exclaimed. Paul retrieved his cell phone to call Carly with the wonderful news.

Chapter 28

Greer was seated at her desk at the ambulance company when her phone rang; the caller ID showed it was Morgan, her supervisor. Like many Fridays, the morning had been hectic, as the hospitals often discharged patients before the weekend, resulting in juggling of ambulance crews and dispatches from hospital to home or to rehabilitation facilities. Greer switched the button on her headset to answer the call.

"Hello," she said. "It's Greer."

"Greer," replied Morgan, "can I see you in my office?"

"Uh...okay...sure. I'll be right there." Greer wondered if someone had lodged a complaint. Known for being efficient and detail-oriented, she could manage even the most demanding callers. Greer removed her headset and meandered to Morgan's office.

"Come in Greer," said Morgan, looking up from her computer. "Please take a seat. I'll be just a minute. I need to finish this email."

Greer found an empty chair across from Morgan. Her

sweaty palms matched the waves of anxiety in her body. *What if I'm fired? I need this job.*

"Okay, Greer. Thanks for waiting." Morgan lifted her coffee cup to her lips. "I just made a pot. Would you like some?"

"Thanks. But I just finished a cup."

Morgan turned to face Greer, but Greer could not decipher her boss's body language.

Morgan perused a manila file and spoke. "You've been with us nearly a year."

"Yes, it will be a year soon." *Almost a year since I left school and my parents' house.*

"You've done a superb job for us here. You're extremely organized and a quick learner. And you're great with the callers."

"Thank you. I'm glad to hear you're happy with my work."

"We hired you as a part-time worker. Although you've been working a lot of hours."

"Usually about thirty per week."

"Right. And your evaluations have been excellent."

"Thanks. I've been told I'm doing a good job."

"Well, I have an opening here. For a full-time worker."

Greer's eyes widened. Full-time meant more hours. And benefits.

Morgan paused. "I will tell you that there is a catch."

"Okay..." Greer's enthusiasm fell. What could it be? *I hope the position isn't on the night shift. If it is, I might have to turn it down. The hours would jeopardize my relationship with Mickey.*

"It's a supervisory position," announced Morgan. "Ronnie is leaving. Normally we promote a full-time person to the position, but you have been working nearly full-time. And I can't think of anyone else I would like to have in that position."

"Really? You want me to take Ronnie's position?" *He works the day shift!*

"If you accept the position, then yes, you would replace Ronnie."

"Wow! I mean...I am surprised. That's all."

"So I guess that means you are interested?"

"Well, yes! I'm interested." Greer knew she was blushing; her cheeks were warm and she was certain redness was rising from her neck to her forehead. She had never been good at hiding her emotions. "I didn't know why you wanted to see me. I braced myself for the worst, I guess."

Morgan smiled. "Like when you're called to the principal's office."

"Yes! That's right. I didn't expect you to offer me a promotion."

Morgan grinned. "This is the part of my job I love the most. Unfortunately, it doesn't happen often enough. Many days I feel like a school principal. Telling employees what they did wrong. But I'm thrilled that you are interested in the position."

"Thank you for offering it to me."

"You deserve it. Do you have questions for me?"

"When would the position start?"

"In two weeks." Morgan opened the bottom drawer of her desk and handed a manila envelope to Greer. "The information in here will outline your new salary. And of course your benefits."

"Thank you so much."

"You are quite welcome," replied Morgan.

AFTER HER SHIFT ENDED, GREER STOPPED AT A COFFEE SHOP A half-block away from the ambulance company. She ordered a cappuccino, and after the barista brought her drink to the table, she opened the manila envelope.

Greer scanned the papers and learned that besides a change in title, she would receive a pay raise of about twenty-five percent. *Not bad!* The increased salary would allow her to quit one of the other jobs. Greer wasn't certain which one she would give up, but she would get a little more free time, and more money remaining after she paid her bills.

She recalled feeling a bit embarrassed at her initial interview. Her appearance was fine, and she knew she had expressed herself well. But despite her acknowledgement that she had quit school, and her uncertainty about a career path, she had been offered a position within minutes. Morgan was impressed that Greer had studied English and writing; she expected Greer would be capable of good communication. Greer hadn't expected her first job interview since her high school days to be successful and was delighted to leave the building with a job she would begin the following day.

Besides paying for most of her health insurance premiums, her full-time status and promotion would also allow her paid time off and reimbursement for education in a healthcare field. Greer was grateful she could take a day off with pay. Although happy to see the company valued higher education, she didn't plan to pursue training for a healthcare career. But the promotion had raised her hopes. *Perhaps my parents will see this as a move in the right direction. It will be a step up from answering phones and entering information into a computer. Perhaps I can parlay the promotion into something even better.*

Greer wasn't sure what the future held. But she was moving up the ladder. Hopefully success would follow.

Chapter 29

Paul had learned how to move his wheelchair safely, and he wheeled himself into the gym, maneuvered the wheelchair to Brian's station, and applied the brakes. He gave a brief wave to Gary, a man about eighty years old who was recovering from a recent stroke. Gary had lost his wife Betty to cancer several months before, after a marriage of over fifty years. He had described his marriage as wonderful, flawed only by the couple's inability to have children. Paul thought it was no wonder that Gary's body was giving out after losing the love of his life and having to adapt to living alone, with no family for support. Unless Gary recovered nearly all of his physical independence, it was unlikely he could return to his house. He was trying to remain optimistic, but Gary told Paul that the social workers were contacting nursing homes. Paul felt sorry for Gary, who had lost more in under a year than many people lost in a lifetime. For the first time, Paul thought his life wasn't so bad. He had lost his lower leg, but he had so much more than Gary: a wife able to help physically, emotionally, and financially; a house to meet his needs; and two adult children—although one lived thousands of miles away. Paul was so deep in his thoughts that he didn't immediately notice Brian's arrival at his side.

"Good morning, Paul," said Brian, as he pulled his stool next to Paul's chair. "You look like you're deep in thought. How are you today?"

"I'm doing well," said Paul. "I was just thinking about Gary over there. It doesn't take long to find someone worse off than yourself."

"Yes. That's true. Especially in a place like this. There's always someone who has it worse." Brian covered his mouth with his hand as he yawned. "I'm sorry. Forgive me. I had coffee this morning, but I'm still tired."

Paul noticed dark circles under Brian's eyes. His face lacked its usual glow and he sported faint whiskers on his cheeks and chin.

"What's up? Didn't you sleep well?"

"No. Not really. Well...it's not that I didn't sleep well. I just didn't get enough sleep. Not for at least two nights."

Paul wasn't one to pry into others' lives, but he considered Brian a friend, now that Brian had seen him at his worst.

"Tell me. What's going on that you haven't slept?" He chuckled. "Women problems?"

"No. Not that. Well, actually, there is a woman involved. My mother."

"I'm sorry. Is your mother sick?"

"No!" Brian sighed. "Sorry, but I don't tell many people about my personal affairs."

"But I cried in your midst. One can't get much more personal than that."

"Yes. You are right. You did." Brian paused, took a deep

breath, and continued. "I was adopted as an infant. I've known since I was a kid. My parents were open about it. I never tried to find my birth parents. Not until recently. I was thinking of proposing to my girlfriend." Brian gave a loud sigh.

"I take it you are no longer with your girlfriend. I mean, it sounds like there's a problem."

"You are right. We are no longer together. We broke up recently. I'm not sure what happened. But anyway, I decided to search for my birth parents. I hate referring to my mom and dad as my adoptive parents. They're the only parents I have ever known. I thought it would upset them when I said I wanted to know more about my birth parents. But they expected I would eventually ask about the circumstances of my birth. My mother gave me papers from the agency that handled my adoption. I've contacted the agency to see if they will release the information to me."

"Growing up, did it bother you to know you were adopted?" inquired Paul.

"No. My parents raised me from infancy. I was a few days old when they took me home from the hospital. They raised me as their own. My sister was adopted, too."

"I suppose you don't look like your parents. Does it feel weird that you don't resemble them?"

"Not really. But people ask my father if it bothers him to have a son who doesn't resemble him. I'm a few inches taller. My facial features are much different. My eyes are different. People always talk about my eyes. What an unusual color they are. Not the usual blue shade."

"Yes. Your eyes were one of the first things I noticed about you. The color reminded me of the water in the Caribbean. My wife and I went on a cruise to the Caribbean before our children were born. The water there is amazing."

"I haven't been to the Caribbean. But my eyes were always a hit with the chicks. Especially when I was younger. The women like my eyes...but then they want more. Go figure!" Brian rubbed the stubble on his chin. "But enough about me. Let's get started."

Brian watched as Paul wheeled his chair to the parallel bars, locked the brakes, and used his arms to stand on his right leg. He held the bars, straightened his torso, and stood in position. The activity caused perspiration to pool on his forehead and on his palms. Brian stood by and assisted Paul back into the wheelchair.

"That's great, Paul," called Brian. "You are doing wonderfully."

"I can't believe how hard it is. But I did it. I won't be an invalid." Paul beamed.

"Yes, Paul. You did it. You will get stronger every day. We'll concentrate on increasing your tolerance for standing. Then I'll work with you to take a few steps."

"I'll be so happy if I can walk even a little."

"We'll work together. We're a team."

"Thank you so much," said Paul, as he shook Brian's hand. "I'm so glad you're treating me. I owe you so much. I can't thank you enough. When I get home, my wife and I will invite you over to the house for a meal."

It wasn't the first time Brian had received an invitation to a patient's home. He had graciously refused all the others. He was certain that he would decline this one as well.

Chapter 30

My Life and Yours- by Carly Casper

To my valued readers: Paul and I have been overwhelmed by your prayers, letters of support, and good wishes. I was initially reluctant to share such intimate details of my life, and it took some time for Paul to agree to me doing so. He wanted to keep our struggles private, but I needed an outlet to share my hopes and my fears. So I tested the waters. I dipped my toe in. By your responses, I've agreed to jump in with my entire body.

Paul is progressing as well as we can expect. He performs his exercises to strengthen his body with vigilance and perseverance. Although he was initially horrified, he has accepted that his left leg looks different. He is working with a wonderful physical therapist, Brian, who is teaching him to examine the stump for skin breakdown, and to wrap the ace bandage in a

figure-eight fashion, to aid its shaping for a better fitting prosthesis. Thanks to Brian, Paul can move himself to the toilet or
the bed by pivoting on his remaining foot. We expect he will
need therapy for quite a while, but we are no longer concerned
that he will be confined to a wheelchair. Paul is determined to
walk again. In addition, he has adapted to a diet to keep his
blood sugar more consistent. He can look at a menu and decide
which choices are optimum. A wonderful diabetes educator is
teaching him to test and monitor his blood sugars several times
daily, and to inject himself with insulin. This is a man who was
previously squeamish about removing a splinter from his
finger, and who nearly fainted at the sight of blood. I am so
proud of the progress he has made.

As a journalist, I have interviewed and chronicled grief-
stricken people: victims of crime, accidents, and bad luck. I've
spoken with angry parents whose children were taken from
them too soon, held the hands of people as they sobbed about
the injustices of the world. I am familiar with and have written
about the five stages of grief. What I did not realize was that
Paul will travel through the stages. The death he is mourning is
not a human life, but the life he has known. Accustomed to
bounding from the chair to answer the doorbell or get a bite to
eat, every movement is now calculated and measured. Paul is in
the midst of his journey. We can measure how far he has come,
but not the stretch of road remaining. There is no map detailing
the slowdowns or roadblocks that he may yet face. He has
stumbled on some bumps in the path, and there will be more
falls, but we are confident that he will complete his journey.

Since our son moved to California nearly a decade ago and
our daughter got an apartment last year, Paul and I have rein-
vented ourselves as empty nesters. We focused on our own
needs—and as much as it pains me to say this—we often lost

touch with each other. We spent our days communicating more with our calendars and with our coworkers, and sending or reading emails, than we did speaking with each other. But Paul's illness has shown us that we are a team, and that only by working together, communicating our fears, and celebrating the small successes, can we thrive as a couple.

We communicate with our adult children regularly, but to a significantly lesser degree than when we all shared a living space. Physical distancing encourages estrangement. Paul and I have spoken with our children by phone or texted with important news. We video chatted with the children and grandchildren for birthdays and special occasions. But Paul's illness has shifted all of our priorities. We are more cognizant of the precariousness of life. We embrace the comfort of family. Our son and daughter have spent more time with their father in recent days than in previous months. While they initially may have felt an obligation to do so, the relationship with their father has deepened beyond duty. Paul and David and Greer describe it as a rebirth. I could focus on the whys and wherefores, but I prefer to give thanks and revel in their joy and rejuvenation.

Chapter 31

As visiting hours began, Carly arrived at the hospital and took the elevator to the nursing unit. She strolled to Paul's room, but he wasn't there. Glancing along the corridor, she saw him in his wheelchair, speaking with a tall man with soft brown curls. She ambled to meet him as Paul finished his conversation.

"Hi honey." Carly kissed Paul on the cheek. "How was your day?"

"I had a great day," he replied, tapping Brian on the arm. "Carly, this is Brian, the physical therapist I've been raving about. The man who has helped me so much. Brian, this is my wife Carly."

"Hello," said Brian, extending his right hand. "I'm pleased to meet you."

"It's my pleasure, Brian," replied Carly, softly shaking his hand. "Thank you for all you have done to help Paul." As she studied the man before her, she noticed his lean body, muscular build, and well-fitting clothing. She briefly studied his hairline and his face. She was certain they had never met. *Why does he look familiar? None of our friends have a family member who is a therapist. None they have mentioned.* She peered at him more closely, trying to show nonchalance, afraid he would notice her staring. His chestnut hair was well-cut and neatly combed. His angular chin and broad cheeks and nose gave no clues.

It was his eyes that told her. Those blue eyes. Like the water in the Caribbean. The memories stunned her, and in an instant, before her demeanor raised questions she did not want to answer, she turned and sped away. Seeing a sign for a visitors' bathroom, she hurried inside. Entering the stall, she barely made it to the toilet before regurgitating her lunch.

LATER, AT HOME, CARLY FOUND IT IMPOSSIBLE TO SLEEP. SHE HAD concocted an apology for her quick exit, along with a feeble excuse about an urgent stomach problem. That wasn't a lie. Except it hadn't been short term as she had claimed. Her insides were still in shock. Switching the conversation to his progress, Paul had related in exquisite detail how well his therapy session had gone. He accepted her bathroom excuse and was relieved she had recovered.

Now, more than thirty years and thousands of tears later, Carly was still in shock. There was no mistaking those eyes.

She remembered with extreme clarity the time in her life when it all changed. When she was an innocent, living in a different town, with another name. Before she met Nathaniel. Only her close friends knew about her relationship with the college professor. The professor at the college where Carly was enrolled as an undergraduate; the school she left months later to escape him. She was naive enough to believe his promise to take care of her. Although engaged to be married to Melanie, he said he didn't love her. He claimed he wanted to be with Carly, but desired tenure at the university before they went public with their relationship. She was studying journalism and he taught economics, so it wasn't a professor-student relationship. Carly stayed clear of his department, and the school administrators had no clue. She had been intimate with two boys before him, but they were immature youths. He was a man, respected for his knowledge, with a clear career path. A man she was sure her mother would love.

Carly got a prescription from her doctor for birth control pills, but she neglected to go to the pharmacy for several days. Finally, after Nathaniel reminded her he hated to wear condoms and was glad she was taking responsibility to prevent a pregnancy, she remembered the prescription neatly folded in the corner of her wallet. She started for the pharmacy one Friday evening after her hours working at the dining hall had ended, but her car stalled in the rain, and by the time she got the engine running again, the pharmacy had closed for the weekend. Together in his apartment two days later, Carly did not disclose to Nathaniel that she had not started the prescribed contraception, and after performing a mental calculation of her probable ovulation date, she decided she was likely safe. Except she wasn't.

The following day, she and Nathaniel had a huge argument. The decision about his tenure was fast approaching, and in an attempt to prevent blemishing his stellar record, Nathaniel told Carly he wanted to break off their relationship for a few months. She was crushed. But that wasn't the worst news. Two weeks later, Nathaniel admitted he was planning to marry Melanie. The wedding was to take place in a few weeks. By the time the university decided his academic future, he would be a married man. Carly spent several days locked in her dorm room, crying about her stupidity. She returned to class, made up the missed work, and seemed to have gotten over the affair.

Then she missed her period. A pregnancy test from the pharmacy was positive. Aware that Nathaniel's wedding was a week away, she told him he would be a father in several months. He was an honorable man, and she surmised he would marry her instead of Melanie, even if just to give his child a name. Willing to forgo her dreams of two hundred guests at a large banquet hall, and planning to offer a quickie wedding at the courthouse before his tenure was decided, Carly thought that once they were married, Nathaniel would be happy and forget about Melanie.

But Nathaniel didn't marry Carly. He married Melanie. When Carly told him of her pregnancy, he was furious. When she admitted she hadn't filled the prescription for the birth control pills, he responded with rage. She had never seen him so angry—his face contorted and ugly, spittle spewing from his mouth.

"I never want to see you again!" The force of his words nearly knocked her over. And then he proved he had no honor.

"I don't care what you do with this baby. Get rid of it! Give it away! But if you raise it, never ask me for anything. And I will come after you if Melanie ever finds out!"

She was crushed by Nathaniel's declarations; she had been certain he would marry her. But there would be no wedding to Nathaniel, no celebration of their love. They had made a baby together, but would not raise it as a couple. He would not provide financial support. She was on her own.

Carly knew she couldn't raise a child as a single mother. She would have to drop out of school and settle for a job in retail or food service. That wasn't fair to a child—or to herself. She would not ask her mother to care for a child at this stage in her life. She wouldn't have an abortion; life was too sacred. Raising this child would mean giving up her dreams and getting a job she likely wouldn't want. She didn't want to be an angry mother, or one who needed handouts to support her child. Worse yet, her mother still referred to children raised by single mothers as *illegitimate*. But this baby was *legitimate*, a real person. Carly didn't want to bring shame upon herself or her mother. She looked at the calendar and made a calculation. After a week of sleepless nights and a few calls to a childhood friend who had moved to another state after middle school, Carly called her mother to tell her she was spending her summer break with her friend Amy.

Amy made space for Carly in her one-bedroom apartment, and Carly gave birth to her nearly eight pound son in the early morning hours of August third. Amy whispered words of encouragement during the lengthy labor and delivery; the women gave a collective sigh when the baby cried vigorously seconds after birth. Afraid of changing her mind about the adoption, Carly had allowed herself to hold her newborn once, for a brief time. She signed the adoption paperwork and recuperated at Amy's apartment. Two weeks later, when the new school term began, Carly informed her mother that she had transferred her credits to another school, where she planned to complete her degree. Lucia was unaware that along with a change in colleges, Carly also legally changed her name. She replaced the name her parents chose as an homage to Italy, their country of birth, with her new name, *Carly Casper*. Her mother, already widowed, accepted Carly's explanation that the new name was more modern and better suited for an aspiring journalist. She never knew the primary reason for her daughter's decision, or of the baby Carly relinquished for adoption.

Lucia loved seeing her daughter's name in print, and began to call her by her new name as she glowingly showed Carly's writings to her friends.

Carly thrived after transferring schools; she studied hard and excelled in her classes. She maintained her friendship with Amy, but not with her former classmates. She was disappointed to learn that Nathaniel had gotten tenure a few months after his marriage to Melanie. In her senior year, she attended an off-campus party, where she met Paul. It wasn't quite love at first sight, but she grew to love the young man with a pleasant smile, good manners, and a strong work ethic. They married a year after her college graduation.

In the beginning of their marriage, she was an editorial assistant at the newspaper and Paul worked in the insurance industry. Paul never knew the real reason for her name change, or of the past she worked so hard to hide. Carly never searched for Nathaniel. Gradually, over many years, she thought of him less and less.

When Carly gave birth to David, only her obstetrician knew this wasn't her first pregnancy. Paul had no clue that the newborn boy he held in his arms was Carly's second son. Her firstborn would have been nearly five years old. No one besides Amy knew that Carly celebrated another child's birthday every year—her firstborn son.

Chapter 32

Brian stared at the name on the birth certificate the agency had sent him. He had little chance of finding his father, as the document listed him as *Unknown*. According to the agency, his birth mother either could not identify the man who had fathered her child, or she had hidden his identity. Brian hoped it was the second. He could think of a hundred reasons why a young woman would not want to identify the father of her baby, but he hated to think that at least two men could have been his father. Of course, he knew many men who had been intimate with several women in a single weekend—some in a single day—and he supposed there were women who would admit to the same. But that had never been his style.

Brian thought of Mimi, with whom he had just ended a long-term relationship. Miranda—since childhood, everyone called her Mimi—was an accountant with a good job in a large firm. He and Mimi had been together for two years, and he had thought seriously about proposing to her. In his mid-thirties, he wanted marriage and a family. But the thought of children, of passing on his genes and DNA, made him think about the origin of his own traits. He had experienced a sudden desire to know which parent had passed on his unusual eye color. He wanted to learn what medical issues he might have inherited.

His parents had told him of his adoption at age four, just before they adopted his sister Laura. Brian remembered feeling a little confused at first, wondering if the mother who had given birth to him now wanted him back. Why else would his parents be getting another baby? But they assured him he wasn't leaving; they wanted to share their love with another child. He and Laura had a good relationship, but she never wanted to learn about her birth parents or the reason for her adoption. But Brian's desire to have his own children fueled a hidden longing to know his own background. His adoptive parents were supportive of his decision. They had expected both of their children to search for their birth parents.

He had shared his feelings with Mimi, as couples in serious relationships do. To his surprise, Mimi accused him of being foolish and childish. She adored his parents, and wondered why he wanted to know about the woman who had given him away, why he would chance learning something unflattering or dishonorable about his birth parents. Her response surprised Brian, but he let it pass. But the interaction was the catalyst for a series of arguments that destroyed their relationship within a week. He took offense to her calling him foolish. She said the adoption search left him preoccupied and unable to concentrate on basic things, like watching a movie. He said the movie didn't hold his interest. Mimi said the movie received a 98% on *Rotten Tomatoes;* she questioned if he had also lost interest in her. He waited a millisecond too long to answer. Mimi took the toiletries and clothing she kept at his apartment and bade him goodbye within minutes. She didn't answer her phone when he called her the next day. She had not responded to his texts, and all of his phone calls went to voicemail. He could not fathom what he had done to cause the split. He had not slept with other women, forgotten her birthday, or spoken badly about her.

That evening, he was home alone with no desire to meet friends or bar hop or attend a new employee's party. Brian sat in his kitchen, staring at the writing on his birth certificate. He now knew his mother's name and the hospital where he was born. Although he yearned for Mimi and missed a woman's comfort and compassion, the breakup would allow him time to immerse himself into his search. *A silver lining.*

Chapter 33

The cup of water Brian gave Paul eased his thirst, but beads of perspiration remained on his brow, face, and neck.

"That was a great session." Brian shook Paul's hand. "You are doing wonderfully. And I heard you'll be going home in a few days."

"Yes. That's what the doctors tell me."

Brian handed Paul two sheets of paper. "Here are some things your wife needs to consider. She may need to make some adjustments to your house to prepare for your return home."

Paul scanned the information. "Okay. We have a bathroom on the first floor. Well, a powder room. I'll talk to Carly. Since I can't climb stairs yet, I'll stay on the first floor. But I might need a bed for the living room."

"It might be a good idea. At first, anyway."

Paul tucked the papers into a pocket on his wheelchair. "Say Brian...I keep forgetting to ask you. Have you searched any more for your birth parents?"

"I got a copy of my birth certificate. My father is listed as unknown. A woman at the adoption agency said that it is more likely that my birth mother did not want to disclose his name. He might have been a well-known person. Or perhaps he didn't know she was pregnant."

"That makes sense. Maybe your mother was a professional and didn't want to disclose her situation. Times have changed. Single motherhood is accepted more now."

"I considered that too. But she was nineteen when I was born. So it's more likely she was a student. She might not have wanted to tell her parents who the father was."

Paul smiled. "As a parent, I can understand that. I'm sure my children have kept lots of things from me. As has happened with every generation."

Brian chuckled. "Yeah, I'm sure that's true. Even though I didn't get into much trouble, I didn't reveal everything to my parents."

"But it's great that you have your mother's name. You can start looking for her."

"Yes. And it's an uncommon first name. Carlotta."

"Carlotta. It could be Italian. I wonder if they call her Carly. Like my wife."

"It's possible," replied Brian. "It's time for my next patient. I'll see you tomorrow."

CARLY APPEARED IN PAUL'S HOSPITAL ROOM AS HE WAS FINISHING dinner. She smiled and kissed him on the cheek.

"How was your dinner?"

"Not as bad as some others. But I'll be so glad to get home. And to eat your cooking."

"I'll be so happy when you are home. We can act like an old married couple again."

"Yeah. There's comfort in that."

"How was therapy today?"

"I did great. And the doctors said I'm almost ready to go home." Paul motioned to the papers secured on his bulletin board. "Brian gave me a checklist. We can see what I need before I go home. Brian said…"

"I can tell how much you idolize Brian. You mention him every day." *I can't believe I said his name. How can I stop thinking about whether it is him when Paul talks about him all the time?*

"He's a great guy. I really like him," Paul interjected, as he finished his last spoonful of fruit. "Oh, Carly. Did I mention Brian is adopted?"

It was fortuitous that Carly's back was to Paul. Her face spoke volumes and never hid her feelings. Paul had often used this to his advantage. He would have known in a second that his utterance had touched something inside her.

"Really?" she responded, willing herself to sound nonchalant.

"Yes. He's been looking for his birth parents. He has a copy of his birth certificate too."

The room spun and Carly felt she would faint. She grabbed the head of Paul's hospital bed to steady herself and gain control, and willed herself to stay upright. After all these years of carrying her secret, she could not let down her guard now.

For the first time, Carly wondered if this was the end of the life she had built for herself.

Chapter 34

It had been an exhausting day. Besides his therapy sessions, Paul had attended a class on managing his diabetes. The dietitian had explained how important it was to follow his diet; how a few extra carbohydrates might throw off his blood sugar, and how noncompliance could be detrimental to his body. Paul watched videos and received some material on acceptable diet options. He was grateful that many restaurants now added nutritional information to their menus. Grocery shopping would be easier now too, unlike decades before when one had to cook everything from scratch, or guess the ingredients in restaurant food. Although he would need to regulate his intake and use more care in choosing his meals, Paul was happy to learn that he would have more flexibility with his intake than he had expected. As he perused the pamphlet in his hand, Greer arrived.

"Hi Dad! You're looking good." She planted a kiss on his cheek and glanced at the pamphlet. "*Managing Your Diabetes with Diet and Exercise,*" she read aloud. "Sounds like you will eat much better than you have."

"What do you mean? I've been eating okay."

"Come on, Dad. Really? Three slices of sausage pizza and a beer?"

"Okay. You are right. That's not a great diet. But I only ate like that when your mother was out. When she cooks, or when we eat together, my diet has been healthier."

Greer took a seat in the chair beside her father. "So...um, Dad. I want to talk to you about something. I'm moving out of my apartment. I'm going to move in with Mickey."

Paul had spent years thinking about how he would respond to news that his daughter was no longer an innocent. It all came back to him: the relief at escaping her adolescence without car stops by police, school suspensions, illicit substance use, or teenage pregnancy.

"Okay. I'm not shocked," he admitted. "You're a grown woman. I'm not going to treat you like a teenager. You can make your own decisions."

"I'm relieved to hear that."

"Is his place big enough for you to live there too? Although you two can probably just squeeze together on the couch. Or in the bed."

"Dad! Stop!" Greer giggled like an adolescent caught by her parents kissing a boy. "He's making more money now. He found an apartment big enough for both of us. And I can help pay the rent. I already gave my landlord notice. I'll move out at the end of the month."

"I guess your relationship is serious. I like Mickey. He seems like a good guy. It sounds like he's an excellent mechanic, too. He has a good head on his shoulders. And he treats you well."

"He's not like the other guys I dated. Most of them were

losers. Although of course I would have denied it if those words had come from you and Mom."

Paul chuckled. "Your mother and I agreed that we really didn't like any of the guys you dated before. But we promised not to interfere. You and Mickey seem like you're good together. It might be nice to have a mechanic...in the family."

"Please, Dad. Don't get ahead of yourself. We're not getting married. Not yet. Besides, I know you weren't too fond of him at first."

Paul nodded. "I admit I wasn't. I wanted a professional guy to steal my little girl's heart. But I got to know Mickey...when he came to see me here. I decided I had been too harsh."

"Thanks Dad, for admitting that. So many people look at his family and his job and make judgments before they get to know him. Thank you for raising me to look at the whole person. Not just the outside."

"I've always tried to look at a person's character," replied Paul. "That says a lot about the values instilled by the parents. Before David was born, I never realized how hard it was to parent. It's a tough job. Some people aren't ready to have children. They might be too young, or immature, or have no family or friends for support. I guess that's why babies are sometimes relinquished for adoption. To give them better lives."

Greer hugged her father. "I know I've done some things you and Mom didn't agree with. But I'll make you proud of me. I promise."

Chapter 35

His doctors had agreed he was ready for discharge, and Paul had risen early and dressed with the clothing Carly had brought. He had learned it was easier to wear sweatpants instead of jeans or cotton pants, so she had brought old gray pants from the bottom of his dresser drawer. Usually reserved for days lounging on the couch suffering from a cold or other ailment, Paul was grateful for the clothing's familiarity. The nurses gave Paul instructions for his care and information about his diet and medications, and promised that a nurse and physical therapist would visit him at home.

The ambulance Greer had arranged was prompt and the crew professional. The two men treated Paul as if he were royalty, using extreme care when moving him to the gurney, and apologizing for the bumps on the concrete that caused the gurney to jostle slightly on the way to the ambulance. Since Carly trusted that Greer's crew was competent and professional, she had waited for Paul at home. Paul closed his eyes during the ride home, but could sense the location by the traffic and turns. Finally, the vehicle stopped, the driver turned off the engine, and Paul knew he was home. He opened his eyes. The doors of the ambulance opened, and Paul nearly cried with relief. *I made it home!*

Suddenly, his insides twirled with anxiety. No longer did he have the safety of the hospital, the ability to call a staff member with a question, or report he had pain or anxiety, or needed help. Carly had gotten training to help him, and Greer had rearranged her work schedules to lend some help daily. Paul wondered now how people without family support managed at home; men and women much sicker than himself, many with fewer financial resources. The previous evening, he had heard nurses talking about another patient who was going to a nursing home because he lived alone in a tiny second-floor apartment without an elevator. Paul knew it was the older fellow across the hall who couldn't even get to the toilet by himself.

Now, he was inside the front door. He viewed the living room that he had last seen nearly a month before. The familiar bright colors and comfortable furniture cheered him, but disappointment tempered his joy. Carly had rearranged the furniture for placement of a bed and table, and ample space for maneuvering his new wheelchair, which sat beside the bed. *My welcoming committee.*

Carly ran down the stairs, breathless. "Honey, I'm so sorry! I knew you left the hospital. I was standing by the front door waiting for you. But I guess my insides got a little nervous. I was in the bathroom for a while."

"Oh. You could have used the bathroom down here."

"That's set up for you."

"Excuse me. Mr. Brown. Where do you want to sit? In this

chair? Or should we help you into the bed?" asked James, whose husky build and sturdy hands were reassuring to Paul.

Paul surveyed the room, his new living quarters. "I think I'd like to try the chair."

James and his partner Keith helped Paul stand and pivot to the chair. He lowered himself onto the soft cushion.

Paul's heart was racing. *Suppose I can't get up?* "Can you wait, please? I want to make sure I can get out of it."

"Of course. Take your time." James placed the walker next to Paul.

Paul placed the walker as he had practiced many times with Brian. Then he shifted his buttocks forward, placed his hands on the arms of the chair, and stood, grasping the walker for support. After counting to sixty, he again lowered his body into the chair and exhaled.

Tears flooded Carly's cheeks. "That's wonderful. It's a start. Welcome home, honey."

Paul brushed the mist from his eyes. "I'm so glad to be home. I wasn't sure that I would make it. I thought you'd have to put me in a nursing home. But the nurses and Brian helped me so much. I'm so grateful. Especially to Brian."

Carly silently expressed her gratitude to Brian, but hoped Paul never mentioned him again.

Chapter 36

I t was a message every parent hopes never to receive. When a buzz came from Heidi's desk drawer as she was speaking with clients, she ignored it, expecting that the call or text on her cell phone was spam. Everyone knew of her dedication to her work and disregard of calls and texts during work hours, except on a bathroom or lunch break. Heidi proceeded to explain the legal paperwork to her clients, but her phone continued to buzz. After about a half dozen interruptions, Heidi surmised it was a caller obsessed with spamming her or someone who needed her urgently.

"Excuse me one moment," Heidi said to the husband and wife seated before her. She opened her desk drawer and moved the phone into view. She read the texts and froze. "I'll be right back. I'm so sorry," she cried, as she ran from her office, not caring what the clients thought of her. She burst through the door of the staff lounge, and barely missed hitting a senior partner emerging from the room, a cup of coffee in her hand.

"I'm sorry, Grace," floundered Heidi, waving her cell phone.

"I got some urgent texts about my children. I have to find out what's going on."

"Let me know if you need anything," replied Grace.

Heidi pressed the call button on her cell phone. Her heart throbbed in her chest and the morning's coffee rose in her throat. At last she heard a familiar voice.

"Heidi! I'm so glad I reached you. I was trying David's phone too."

"Deborah! Is everyone okay? Were Matthew and Emily hurt? Are you okay?"

"Matthew and Emily weren't hurt. They're just shaken up. The other driver is okay too."

"I don't really want to know about the other driver. I care about whether my children were hurt in the accident. And...I care about you." Heidi exhaled noisily. "I want to talk to Matthew and Emily."

"Of course. I'll put Emily on first."

Heidi heard Emily sniffling through the phone line. "Mommy," Emily cried, "Deborah drove through the red light. I saw the light was red. I told her she should stop. Everyone knows to stop at a red light. But she kept going. And then a man in a black car hit us. But he had a green light. Isn't that right, Mommy? He was coming from the other street. So if we had a red light then he would have a green light."

"Honey, I'm so sorry Deborah had an accident. But I am so happy that you and Matthew are okay." Heidi wiped the tears on her cheeks with her sleeve. She wanted to ask Deborah to turn on the video chat feature so she could see her children, but she heard her speaking with someone in the background. *The police perhaps? Maybe I'll ask Emily to look for the video button on Deborah's cell phone. But that is probably too much to ask of a five-year-old, especially one traumatized in an automobile collision.*

Emily broke the silence. "I'm okay. Deborah's car is all broken. The side is smashed."

"That's okay, sweetheart. Now can I talk to your brother?"

"Okay, Mommy. I'll get him. Bye."

A half minute elapsed before Matthew came to the phone. "Hi Mom," said Matthew. "Deborah had an accident. But we're all okay."

"I'm so glad. Your dad and I love you and Emily so much. I don't know what we would do if you were hurt."

"Mom. I tried to be brave...when the other car hit us. I was scared. I didn't want to cry. But I did. A little." Heidi heard faint sobs and sniffles. She wanted to reach through the phone and hug her son.

"Sweetheart, I'm going to come get you. I want to talk to Deborah. I need to know exactly where you are."

"I know where we are. We're near that Chinese restaurant that Dad likes. The one with the good egg rolls."

"Okay. I know where that is. I'm leaving work now. It'll take me about twenty minutes."

"Okay, Mom. Emily and I will stay here. But hurry. Emily needs to use the bathroom."

Heidi ended the call and ran through the hallway to Nancy's office. An associate in the firm, Nancy was about twenty years older than Heidi. She had a grown son and daughter, and three grandchildren. If anyone would understand that Heidi needed to get to her children, it would be Nancy. Heidi was panting as she reached Nancy's office. She peered through the rectangle of frosted glass that decorated the center of the office door. Nancy was conversing with someone via speakerphone, but she motioned to Heidi to enter.

Heidi had never been good at hiding her emotions, so it was no surprise that Nancy could ascertain immediately that something was wrong. Nancy pushed the mute button on her phone and addressed Heidi.

"What's wrong? Is it David? The children?" she implored.

"Deborah...the college student who drives Matthew and Emily to their activities...She was in an auto accident. My children are okay. But I have to get to them. I need to hug them. To hold them. There are clients in my office. I was reviewing paperwork with them. I'm not sure I can concentrate—"

"Of course," interrupted Nancy. "Ask Rachel to cover for you with the clients. The Murphys, right? Rachel knows them. Go to your children." Nancy motioned Heidi towards the office door as she pressed the phone button to unmute herself. She addressed her client on the phone. "Bailey, remember what I said. Don't offer any information. Just answer the questions posed to you."

The tires on Heidi's Audi squealed in response to the rapid turn from the parking lot. In the five minutes since her departure from Nancy's office, she had given basic instructions to Rachel and sent a text to David. Now, as she sped down the street towards the highway, Heidi wondered if she and David could continue along the path they had followed for years.

Chapter 37

S eated at the table in his wheelchair, Paul ended the phone call as Carly entered the kitchen.

"Was that a call about your therapy session?" she asked, pouring coffee into a mug.

"Yes! I can't believe it! Brian has been assigned to handle my therapy. I am thrilled he can see me here at home."

Oh, no! Carly dropped a second teaspoonful of sugar into her coffee.

"Since when do you add two sugars to your coffee?" Paul asked.

"What? What did you say?"

"You added two spoons of sugar. You usually drink coffee with one."

Carly sipped the coffee and wrinkled her nose. "You're right. It's too sweet. I guess I wasn't paying attention." She discarded the coffee in the sink and poured a fresh cup. "What time is Brian coming?"

"In about half an hour."

"Okay. That will work with my plans."

"What plans? I didn't know you had plans. You said yesterday that your schedule was free."

"Well...what I meant was that I had nothing scheduled. I always have errands to do. You need some pajamas. And sweat-pants. I'll go to the mall."

"I have enough to last for a while. I haven't checked to see what's available online. Maybe you don't need to go to the mall at all. Besides, I'd like you to meet Brian. Properly. Not like that time in the hospital hallway. And he can give you some tips for the layout of the house. Maybe we should move some furniture. Or he might make some other recommendations."

"You don't need me here for that," she scoffed. "You're a smart guy. You can remember what he says." She opened a drawer, removed a pen and a pad of paper, and placed them beside him. "Or you can write down what he says."

"Maybe you should wait to go to the mall. Brian might make some recommendations for other items to buy. Then you'll have to go back there. You can save yourself a trip. Besides, I just got home."

Carly glared at Paul. "I'm aware you just got home. But now is the best time to go out. You'll have a professional here. Someone who knows more about your care than me. I don't understand what the problem is. You've raved about how good Brian is. You're thrilled that he's still your therapist. So why do I need to be here?"

Paul knew he couldn't win this argument. He wondered why they were arguing at all. Even if he was right, he didn't want to alienate the person he needed most. "Okay. No problem. Leave for the mall when you're ready. Just leave the front door unlocked. I'll send a text to Brian and let him know he can come right in."

Carly ascended the stairs to the bedroom and returned ten minutes later. She kissed Paul on the cheek. "I'll be back in a couple of hours. I haven't been to the mall in months. A lot of new stores opened. Call me if you have a problem. Bye."

BRIAN ARRIVED AT THE HOUSE ABOUT TWENTY MINUTES LATER. HE entered the foyer and glanced at the surroundings. Paul was seated in his wheelchair about ten feet away.

"Hi Paul. This is a great house."

"Thanks. We like it."

"It seems you have everything you need on this level. Are you doing okay?"

"Yeah, pretty well."

"Where's your wife? Carly is her name. Right?"

"Yes. Carly. It's strange, because I expected she would want to be here. Especially since it's my first session at home. But she said she needed to go to the mall. I don't understand why she needed to go now." He shook his head. "Women. We can't live with them and we can't live without them."

Brian chuckled. He wasn't certain which side of the equation was more fitting now. His heart still ached for what he had lost since his breakup from Mimi.

"Yeah. I agree. It's a no-win situation. Now Paul, let's get to work."

TEARS SPILLED DOWN HER CHEEKS AS CARLY ARRIVED AT THE mall and parked near the main entrance. She turned off the engine but remained glued to her seat, unable to convince her body to exit the car. She knew how much Paul enjoyed working with Brian, and was grateful that he was receiving therapy from a capable and trustworthy person. But she couldn't escape the feeling of dread at seeing Brian again. Her mind ran rampant with possibilities.

Perhaps I'm imagining things. Maybe Brian is older or younger than he seems. Perhaps his eyes aren't that shade of blue. Maybe he wears tinted contact lenses. Perhaps Nathaniel isn't the only one with those eyes. He was an only child. But maybe his cousin had a baby.

I can't avoid Brian. I can't leave the house every time he comes to treat Paul. Perhaps I can say a quick hello and not look at his eyes. I can find something to do in the house while he treats Paul. I don't want to tell Paul, because what if I'm wrong? What if he's not Nathaniel's son? Or what if he doesn't know he's adopted? What if he doesn't want to know me? That would be the worst—if I told him and he couldn't handle it. What if he decided he couldn't work with Paul? That would be my fault. No! I can't do it. I can't let either of them know. But I don't know if I can deal with this on my own.

Carly retrieved the phone from her handbag. She scrolled her list of contacts and found the one person who would understand. The only other person on earth who knew her secret. After two rings, a voice answered.

"Hello...Carly. It's been a long time."

"Yes, Amy. It has."

"So how are you?"

Carly wasn't surprised at the strained conversation. It had been many years since she and Amy had been close. Most of their recent interactions had involved holiday or birthday cards, or occasional emails with family pictures or articles of interest. Their relationship had faded since the birth of Carly's son decades ago. Carly considered that friendships were often like books that encompass years or decades in time. Some chapters skipped from one generation to the next, decades gone with a simple turn of the page. Then there were passages that seemed in no hurry to move along; the paragraphs full of exquisite detail: the surroundings and clothing worn by the characters, a conversation over coffee in a cafe. Their friendship had been no different. Amy and Carly were bound emotionally when Carly needed it most. Amy had held Carly's hand during the labor and delivery, when she signed the adoption paperwork, and when Carly suffered through weeks of turmoil: saying goodbye to a child others would raise, her body's hormonal changes, breasts filled with milk her baby would never drink, the knowledge she had deliberately kept the pregnancy and delivery from her mother, and the decision not to list Nathaniel as her newborn's father.

"Amy. I'm sorry our relationship has faltered. That's probably my fault more than yours."

"Carly. We should share the blame for the communication lapses. I understand why you wanted to forget what happened. You wanted to build a life with Paul. I chose to let you. I could have tried harder to stay in touch. I'm sorry I didn't."

"I am so sorry about that. I wanted to pretend I knew you from another life. A life I wouldn't return to. But I need someone to talk to. You're the only one who I can do that with."

"Okay. Something's happened. I get that now."

Carly was somber. "I don't know what to do. I can't talk to Paul. Not now. Not after everything that's happened to him."

"I'm so sorry to hear about his health. And his surgery."

"Thank you. Paul's home. The physical therapist is at our house now. I told Paul I was going to the mall. Well, I got to the mall parking lot. But I haven't gotten out of the car. I know this is a lot to ask. But is there any way we can meet?"

"I have a couple of hours free. But I need a few minutes to get ready. Can we meet in twenty minutes? How about that cafe across from the mall?" replied Amy.

"That would be perfect. Thank you."

Chapter 38

It was during the therapy session that Paul and Brian heard footsteps approaching the door. They turned as the visitor entered the living room.

"Hi Dad!"

"Greer! Sweetheart! What a pleasant surprise. I didn't know you were coming by. Aren't you working today?"

"Not until four. Gary needed the evening off, so I switched shifts with him. I figured I'd come by and see how you are doing. But I see you are in good hands here." She studied Brian's face. *What nice eyes he has.*

"I'm fine. Your mother made sure I was okay before she left about thirty minutes ago. Said she was going to the mall. It's a shame she didn't know you were coming. Perhaps she wouldn't have gone out."

"I spoke to her yesterday. I told her I would come by this morning. Perhaps she forgot," replied Greer.

"That may be true. She certainly has a lot on her mind. She

is responsible for everything now. But anyway, I'm doing great. Now that Brian, my favorite therapist is here."

Brian blushed. "Well, Paul, I think I'm your only therapist. But I'll accept the compliment."

"Hi Brian. I'm Greer. I'm glad to meet you." She extended her hand. "My dad talks about you all the time. By the way, I'm his favorite daughter."

"Ha ha," replied Paul. "Okay, you got me there."

"Great to meet you too," said Brian. "Greer. Unusual name. I like it."

"Her mother and I loved the food at a local restaurant. Greer's. It was named after the owner. We ate there quite a bit during Carly's pregnancies. The name fit with what we wanted, a Scottish background. It's derived from Gregor. If she had been a boy, we would have named her Gregory. Greer means alert. Or watchful."

"Which I am doing now. Watching."

"Pay attention. You might learn something useful."

"Okay, Dad. I'm watching." She observed Paul moving himself from the wheelchair to the hospital bed.

"It's called transferring," he said. "Moving something from one place to another. Although my body is the thing that's being moved."

"I got it." Greer grinned. "I'm happy that you are doing so well."

But it was her father's therapist who commanded the most attention. *Brian is handsome and well-built. He's friendly. If I was looking to date someone, he would fit the bill.* But Greer didn't imagine what he would look like on the cover of a romance novel. She watched his muscles flex, how he held onto her father's arms, how he described the synchronization of the muscles and tendons. Greer thought of her high-school class-

mate Erica, who aspired to be a physician. She had been vale-
dictorian at graduation and studied pre-med at an Ivy League
school. Greer learned via social media that Erica had decided
not to go to medical school. Halfway through her undergraduate course work, she had switched her major from medicine to
physical therapy. The decision had stunned her parents, who
believed their daughter had taken a step backward. But Erica
proclaimed it was very difficult to learn everything necessary to
become a physical therapist. The bones, the muscles, the
tendons, the mechanics, the physiology—of the entire body.
Greer had thought a therapist's job was to show people how to
maneuver a cane or walker. She had never considered there was
more involved.

Now, as she watched Brian and her father working together,
Greer wondered whether she had the intelligence and fortitude
for a physical therapy program. *I like science and enjoy learning
how things work. It might be worth researching.*

Chapter 39

C arly entered the cafe and spoke to the woman at the counter. "I'm waiting for a friend," she said. "There will be two of us."

"Okay. As soon as your friend gets here, I'll seat you," replied the redheaded hostess, as she wiped the laminated menus with a white cloth.

She had arrived a few minutes early, so Carly took a seat on the beige vinyl-covered bench by the door. She scanned the room. The owners had redecorated the restaurant since her last visit, with new wallpaper and modern seating. It was the food, not the ambience, that brought customers to the cafe in a strip-mall a quarter mile off of the highway. Today, her taste buds took a back seat to her personal problems; she had a more pressing matter on her mind. Carly heard the door open behind her and turned in time to see Amy enter. She rose, and the women embraced, albeit somewhat tentatively.

Amy stepped back and surveyed Carly. "You look good. A

little tired, but overall pretty good." She touched Carly's curls. "I like your hair this way. Shorter. It's very becoming."

Carly touched her head as if she had forgotten about her recent hairstyle change. "I asked my hairdresser to cut my hair shorter. I don't need a hairdryer. It's one less thing to worry about."

The hostess showed the women to their table and gave them each a menu. Carly knew what she wanted to order, but biding her time, she continued to read the menu. *Why is it so tough to talk to Amy? The only person who knows my secret; the woman who has seen me at my lowest.*

Amy broke the silence separating the women. "Okay, Carly. Tell me what's up," she implored.

"The thing is...after all these years, I think I saw my son... who I gave up..." Carly's hands trembled as she fought back tears.

"Where did you see him? And how do you know it's him?"

"Paul's therapist. I think it's him."

"His therapist." She cleared her throat more forcefully than she had wanted. "Okay. How do you know it's him?"

"I saw him. I recognized the eyes. They're the same shade of blue. I'll never forget his eyes." Carly shuddered. She hadn't uttered his name in years. "Nathaniel."

"I see. But let's say he's Nathaniel's son. Perhaps it's his son with his wife. That would explain his eyes."

"Paul said that Brian...that's his name...was adopted," Carly blurted.

"Oh! I see."

A server barely out of her teens appeared at the table to take the women's orders. The women ordered salads—Caesar for Carly and Greek for Amy—and two iced teas. As the server departed, Amy continued the conversation.

"I imagine Paul has been working with the therapist... Brian...for a short time. And he already knows Brian is adopted? How did that happen?"

Carly sighed. "I wondered that too. I mean, men rarely talk about stuff like that. But apparently Paul noticed Brian was exhausted one day. They got to chatting. Brian told Paul he had stayed up late to research information on his adoptive parents."

"Wow. Hard to believe that after all these years it might be him. And you didn't live in this area when he was born."

"I know. That's one of the things that is so hard to believe."

"So, you saw him. Did you speak with him? Did you say anything?"

Carly blushed. "Well...actually I ran."

Amy gulped. A stream of iced tea dribbled down her chin. "You ran?"

"Yes. I saw Brian with Paul one day in the hospital. As soon as I saw his eyes, I made a run for the bathroom. I faked a stomach issue, although it wasn't a total lie. I really lost everything in my digestive tract. When I came out of the bathroom, Brian was gone." Carly sighed. "But that's not all. It's worse."

"Worse? How?"

"Brian is treating Paul at home. Paul said it's rare for the therapist from the hospital to follow patients at home. Apparently Brian got special permission to do so, because he has such a good relationship with Paul. Paul has made wonderful progress working with Brian. The home care agency is owned by the hospital. So it was easy for Brian to continue to see Paul."

"Okay. I understand. Have you seen Brian again? Has he come to the house yet?"

"Today. He's there now."

"Oh! It all makes sense now. I bet you left before Brian got there. The trip to the mall was an excuse to avoid seeing him."

"You know me well. Yes. I had to think of something quickly. But I can't leave the house every time Brian comes."

"And you want to tell Paul...and Brian. But you don't know how."

Carly sighed. "I knew you would understand. You're the only one." She leaned forward in her seat, as if what she planned to say next was more of a secret than what she had had already admitted. "I went to see a psychiatrist. I've had trouble sleeping. The guilt about what happened to Paul was really affecting me."

Amy peered at Carly, her eyes questioning. "Why would you feel guilty?"

"He bought new shoes to appease me. They may have pinched his foot."

Amy grinned. "I'm impressed. A psychiatrist. That's a big step for you. You refused to talk with anyone about Nathaniel, or about the adoption, although there was more of a stigma then. Out of wedlock pregnancies were rarely discussed in public. We were young and idealistic. We thought we could handle everything life threw at us. Without professional help."

"I know. We thought we were invincible. At least I did. I thought I could give up my baby and forget about him. I thought I would just move on with my life. Sadly, I was wrong."

"We definitely realize our mistakes as we age. And we learn to accept them. So Carly, do you think you'll go back to the psychiatrist? Spill your secret?"

"I don't know. I thought I'd try having lunch with you first. I don't have to reveal anything to you. You know all about my past. And lunch is cheaper than a therapy session," chuckled Carly.

"Yes. That's true! And we have time to catch up. It's been too long. But let's get back to your problem. The man who might be your son."

"I have spent years trying to forget about the baby. And Nathaniel. Of course, I never forgot about my son. No matter how hard I tried, I couldn't do that. Every year on his birthday..." Carly trembled. "I'm sorry," she sobbed. "I thought I could keep it together."

"Oh, Carly. I'm so sorry. It must have been awful for you. All those years. But you were not alone. I thought of you...and your firstborn, every year, on his birthday."

Carly retrieved a tissue and wiped the tears spilling from her eyes. "You did? I had no idea. I thought I was alone."

"No. So he had two people that he didn't know thinking of him. But what are you going to do? Now that the man who may be your son is coming to your home?"

"I don't know what to do! I haven't gotten a decent night's sleep since Paul's collapse. At first, I was worried about him. Now that he's doing better, I have to deal with this. I'm a wreck."

"Okay. First, confirm he's your son. Perhaps you're getting riled up for nothing."

"Apparently Brian has a copy of his birth certificate."

Amy's bottom lip dropped nearly to her chin. "Oh, my gosh! If you confirm your name is on it—"

"Those eyes. My heart says it's him. I'll see if Paul knows the mother's name from the birth certificate. I don't know how to ask him without rousing suspicion."

The women finished the last bits of their salads, as the server cleared away their dishes. It was then that Amy gathered the courage to ask the toughest question.

"Do you hope your name is on the birth certificate?"

Carly covered her eyes with her hands and sobbed. Gray droplets flooded her face, her tears mixing with the mascara she had applied that morning. "I don't know. I have kept this secret for so long. How can I admit to Paul that I had an affair with a professor? That I got pregnant and had a son who I gave up for adoption? That Brian might be my son? And if he is my son, how do I tell David and Greer that they have a half sibling? It will tear my family apart."

"Carly, listen to me. Nathaniel took advantage of you. The university should have fired him for what he did. If you had pursued a case against him, he probably would have been. His career might have been ruined. But you did the responsible thing. You had the baby and relinquished him for adoption. Your family would understand that."

"I suppose they would forgive me for that. But I kept my past from Paul. I could easily explain the affair with Nathaniel. But how do I explain that I kept a child from him? How can he forgive me? I never told him that David wasn't my first baby. I even changed my name. How do I reconcile all the lying and omissions?"

The server appeared with a dessert menu, but Amy motioned her away.

"Paul knows about your name change, right?"

"He knows that I changed it to make it less ethnic sounding. When we met, he knew of my aspirations to be a journalist. He agreed that *Carly Casper* had a nice ring to it. I told him my birth name shortly after we met. I overheard him telling someone at a party a while ago that my birth name was much longer and Italian. That may be all that he remembers of the conversation. As we talked about marriage, he agreed I should keep my name."

"Okay. So even if Brian told Paul the name on the birth certificate, it might not mean anything to him."

Carly exhaled. "Yes. It's possible. But what if he recognizes it? That could be worse. He would know that I kept the secret of Brian's birth from him since the beginning. I'm struggling with that."

"Okay. Here's what I see. The major issue. It's bigger than keeping this information from Paul, or how he or your children will react."

Carly leaned forward, her face inches from Amy. "What is the issue?"

"If what you say is true, do you want to acknowledge Brian as your son?"

Chapter 40

Although her son and daughter seemed mostly unfazed by their afternoon ordeal, Heidi was an emotional wreck. After rushing to the accident scene, she had enveloped her children in hugs until they begged her to stop. Heidi watched as a tow truck loaded Deborah's battered car onto the flatbed. The striking vehicle had come from the right side of the intersection, and had hit the passenger door, a few feet from where Emily sat restrained in the back seat. A split second later and... Heidi shuddered at the thought.

Driving from the scene, Heidi considered taking Matthew and Emily to an ice cream shop, treating them to their favorite dessert to compensate for the trauma, but she changed her mind before announcing her plan to the children. A stop would mean a detour from the route home, in addition to parking the car. Heidi had always been superstitious. *Who knows what else will happen? Why push our luck by taking a detour when they have already been traumatized?* She chastised herself for not offering

Deborah a ride home, but the welfare of her children had crowded her mind, leaving no space for concern for others.

Now, at home, she found it difficult to concentrate on preparing dinner. David was on his way home; Heidi had called him from the accident scene once she confirmed Matthew and Emily were okay. Heidi had not begun to chop the lettuce or peppers or tomatoes bundled on the counter; she had spent the time watching her children play video games. She couldn't find the words to ask them to start their homework, or muster the energy to chop the fixings for the salad. Instead, Heidi imagined what it must have been like for Matthew and Emily, in the backseat of Deborah's car, as an automobile slammed into its side.

On her arrival at the scene, Heidi had questioned Deborah about the accident. Deborah had begged for forgiveness and claimed she was preoccupied and hadn't seen the red light at the intersection. It was impossible to miss how tired she appeared. On the ride home, Heidi had casually asked the children about Deborah. Matthew said she had yawned a few times during the drive and claimed she had been up late to finish a paper and study for a big exam.

Heidi knew what it was like to lose sleep over school work. She recalled nights as an escort, often returning home in the early morning hours to study; existing many days on coffee and finger foods, scattered over long hours of attending classes, studying, research, and writing papers. *But I didn't have the added responsibility of caring for children.* She couldn't imagine how difficult it would be to care for children and to attend to all the coursework. Add in a job, and it was too much to think about.

The guilt over her decision to offer Deborah more money to tend to her children hit Heidi head on. Deborah had wanted to quit caring for Matthew and Emily. Working twenty-five hours per week was a requirement of her new job on campus, a condition of the grant which helped defray the costs of her college education. Besides her school responsibilities, studying, and transporting Matthew and Emily to activities, Deborah was working at the school. No wonder she was awake when she should have been sleeping, and sluggish while driving. *She told me she was overwhelmed, but I not only dismissed her concerns, I offered her more money.*

Handing over more money was easier than searching for another person to drive the children to their activities. But Heidi had sacrificed her children's safety by her decision. Luckily, she hadn't paid the ultimate price for her foolishness. Although they loved their house and its location, Heidi wondered how long she and David could continue to live their current lifestyle. While she agreed it was paradise, they lived closer to disaster than most outsiders realized. The financial cost to maintain their lifestyle was astronomical. For the first time, Heidi realized there was also an emotional price to pay. Her paralegal job was secure, but she wondered how she could keep the position and attend law school. It was the major reason she had offered Deborah a huge salary increase to stay with them. It was unlikely Deborah would work full time for them after her graduation. Why would she get a college degree and work as a glorified nanny? And Deborah had been so fatigued and preoccupied that she had put Matthew and Emily in harm's way. Perhaps she wasn't the person they should trust to watch their most precious possessions.

Heidi thought of the evenings and nights spent working as an escort. She had never admitted the job caused her embarrassment. She loved dressing in fine clothing and parading on the arms of wealthy men, attending dinners and parties with overpriced and often underwhelming food, and stale entertainment. Her boss had expected few men would hire an escort who refused dalliances, but Heidi had her share of regular clients: single men who pretended they were handsome or oozed sufficient charm to attract a young, beautiful woman, or married men who loathed being seen with their wives or whose wives preferred an evening alone. The two or three evenings a week had paid for her paralegal schooling. Sometimes the men gave her extra money, and occasionally jewelry. When her relationship with David grew serious and they spoke of marriage, she decided the safer route was to pawn the jewelry. She refused to wear another man's gift in David's presence, and she feared hiding the bracelets and earrings and necklaces would backfire. She added the money from the pawn shop to their wedding fund. Better their friends and relatives should rave about the wedding venue than about her jewelry.

Heidi sat alone at the kitchen table and wondered if their finances could survive a law school tuition besides their other expenses. David loved his job, and now that he was managing a new project, a promotion and salary increase might be on the horizon. *Will it be enough?* The children were thriving and happy, and doing well in school. If they had ever considered moving to another area of the country, the time was long past. *Perhaps law school is out of reach. Should I be content to be a paralegal? If David gets a substantial raise, and I stay at my job, we might be okay.*

Even if their financial situation stabilized, Heidi wondered if her emotional state would.

Chapter 41

Alone in the bedroom, Carly ruminated on the conversation with Amy. Since Paul thought she had spent time at the mall, she had stopped at a clothing store after leaving the cafe and purchased two pairs of sweatpants for Paul. They were a designer brand and far more expensive than the ones he usually wore, but she invented a huge sale and a tale about a U-turn across two lanes of traffic to get him the most comfortable and well-made pants she could find. The only accurate part was the U-turn.

Under different circumstances, it would have brought her happiness to have reconnected with Amy. As teenagers, they had spoken of their secrets and aspirations and fears. Amy knew of Carly's shame at engaging in sex with a man she idolized but who cared little for her. She held Carly while she sobbed and howled about hiding her pregnancy from her mother. It was Amy who accompanied Carly to the appointment at the adoption agency, who stayed by her side through a twenty-hour labor, and who held a sobbing Carly as she saw her baby for the last time. Carly had always admired Amy for her ability to cut through the periphery and identify the real issue, and Amy hadn't disappointed her this time. When Carly had asked about telling Paul about her affair and pregnancy, Amy had compartmentalized the situation; she had pushed aside Carly's concerns and raised the real question. *Do I want to acknowledge Brian as my son?*

She knew the answer within seconds. *Yes, if Brian is my son, I want him to know. I want Paul and David and Greer to know. I want us to have a relationship.* The revelation brought forth an unexpected calmness, a peace from within that Carly had never expected. She knew there was one obstacle to overcome before she could approach the man she suspected was her son.

I will have to speak with Paul.

Although their marriage had seen more good times than bad, she and Paul rarely talked about their relationship. A kiss on the lips was their sole public display of affection, but friends knew they cared for each other. With friends at the theater, they overheard a noisy argument between a husband and wife; the spouses threw profanity-laced insults at each other and revealed secrets unknown in their social circle. Paul and Carly refused to air their complaints outside of their home. She had occasionally and deliberately withheld unsavory comments during parties, only to let loose on Paul once they were in their car and away from the others.

The events of the recent weeks had posed the biggest challenge to their marriage. Although their acquaintances and friends weren't privy to the emotional turmoil she and Paul had endured, most knew of his medical emergency and loss of his leg. Paul was still experiencing a physical and emotional recovery. She recalled the stages of grief. The anger over his condition had passed, but it was likely to return. The previous evening, he had spoken of his desire to communicate better with Greer and David. Perhaps it was his time to bargain, to offer something in exchange for walking better or requiring less help. Carly had to determine how to tell him her news without further damaging their already fragile relationship. Over their long marriage, they had responded predictably to most of their problems, but Carly couldn't predict how Paul would respond to her most damaging confession. *Will he forgive me? Will he be so angry that he will want a separation? Or will my news cause him to sink into depression, since he is unable to live on his own, even if he wanted to end our marriage?*

Carly was a person who eschewed purchasing lottery tickets or betting on horse races. She occasionally played card games, but never for money. She rarely took risks. She would not bet on Paul's response to her disclosure. *I might lose.*

Chapter 42

The other employees had left the office, and David was
alone. He wasn't one to imbibe, but just for once he
wished for a bottle of Jack Daniels in his desk drawer. The day
had been awful. He wanted to blame his father for being hospi-
talized, forcing David to hop on a plane and miss three work
days on the project he had worked so hard to secure. But David
couldn't condemn his father for getting sick. It wasn't his fault.
There was never an opportune time to have a serious illness, or
undergo a life-changing, emergent surgery. He couldn't blame
the members of his team, who continued the project when
David was away. He had chosen them because of their work
principles, and he was proud they had continued to work on
intricate details although he wasn't physically present to guide
them. His father hadn't disappointed him. Neither had his team
members. It was his boss Ben who had pulled the rug out from
under him, who had thrown him under the bus. He had
behaved unfairly, changing the rules and blocking David's path
to success.

After agreeing to the proposal David submitted, Ben had announced in a meeting that morning that David's team was going in the wrong direction, that their work ran counter to the company's ideas and ideals. Ben had replaced David with Daphne, who although barely finished with her orientation, had been assigned to lead the project. David had trained Daphne when she began working for the company the previous year. The announcement stunned David, who stormed into Ben's office after the meeting and demanded an explanation. Ben had refused to discuss the issue and threatened a security escort from the building if David continued his tirade of criticism. David returned to his office, anger raging within him, unable to comprehend what had happened. He knew Ben's signature was on the project proposal. He searched his computer for the documents and emails about the project. The hunt took only a few minutes.

David's breath caught, and he cried out in agony. The signature of Stuart, the CEO, was missing from David's proposal. He searched the files on the firm's server and found the answer—a document he had never seen. His heart sank. The previous day, Stuart had disagreed with David's proposal. He wanted to move in a different direction. In addition, he had requested Daphne Wilkinson lead the project. David couldn't imagine why Stuart chose Daphne. She was capable, but not a superstar, and far from a leader.

But Daphne led the firm in one area—appearance. At five-eight and about a hundred and thirty pounds, with a shapely body, unblemished skin and pearly white teeth, she was stunning. During her initial orientation with David, she acknowledged her previous modeling jobs. David had casually replied that she might earn less money at his company than she did as a model. She answered that she had posed for brochures and magazine covers to pay for her degree in computer science. David's thoughts of Heidi helped to calm his burgeoning libido. He told Daphne about his wife—but omitted her previous escort jobs—and showed Daphne pictures of Heidi and his children. His tactic worked modestly—for him, anyway. During the weeks spent training Daphne, David had thought her computer programming skills were adequate. He hadn't considered her proficient enough to work on his team. *Why is she leading such an important project? Why was I replaced?*

Now, David reviewed dozens of pages of project documentation and emails. Ben had initially informed Stuart that he had approved the project and assigned David to lead the team. But suddenly, Ben had switched course and said he agreed with Stuart's recommendation, that David's proposal was weak and the team should proceed in a different direction and with a new leader. *We've always worked well together. Why would he betray me?*

He felt his insides rumble, another barrage to his system. Deborah's auto accident had upended their peaceful existence. He and Heidi were thankful the accident wasn't more serious, that the children were spared injury—or worse. But Emily still clung to her parents, and the previous night Matthew slept with a teddy bear stored for years in his closet. Heidi had taken a few days off from work in the interim, to spend more time with the children and search for alternative child care. David didn't believe in omens or predictions or signs from above, but now he wondered if outside forces were conspiring against him. *Is this a message? Perhaps it's a suggestion to change our lifestyle now. Before further disaster strikes my family.*

Chapter 43

Paul was thrilled to learn he was ready to receive therapy as an outpatient. He had been working hard on maneuvering the four concrete stairs from his front door to the driveway. Paul had declared that after home confinement, leaving the house twice a week would seem like a vacation, even if he traveled to a therapy appointment instead of a beachfront resort. Now, as he sat in the chair waiting for Brian to greet him, he recalled the first time he had been in this gym, a few days after the surgery that had cost him his lower leg. He remembered thinking his livelihood was over, that he would be an invalid, a cripple, faced with a lifelong disability. *How things have changed!* He looked at the other men and women in the gym. Many others were receiving therapy as outpatients. They were the graduates of inpatient and home therapy, the ones who, although perhaps not completely independent, were no longer homebound. Paul saw Brian stroll across the gym towards him.

"Hi Brian." Paul extended his right hand and shook Brian's.

"Hi Paul. Good to see you. Did you have any difficulties getting here today?"

"Nope." He paused. "Okay, I admit I was a little anxious. But I got down the stairs on my own. I needed a little help to get into the car. But Carly was very patient."

Brian keyed in some information on a laptop. "That's great. Is she here?"

"No. She went to the supermarket a few blocks away. But she'll be back soon."

"I'm really glad that I met with Carly during our last session at your house. She returned from the pharmacy just in time for me to show her how well you are doing. She was interested in the details, and how to help you. I can tell you really care about each other."

"Yeah. I don't know what I would do without her. She's been a rock."

"It's great that you have her to help you through this. I know so many people who have no one to lean on. They would be grateful to have a marriage such as yours. Lasting decades. Stable."

"I'm a lucky guy. I appreciate her more than ever. We've had our problems over the years. But we can talk about things. We don't keep secrets. We've been faithful to each other. I know so many guys who've had affairs. They hide the hotel receipts from their wives. And who knows what else they hide. But Carly and I can talk about anything. I guess that's how we have stayed together so long."

"That's great." Brian stood from his stool. "Okay, Paul. I'd love to sit and chat, but we have work to do. Now let's get you walking."

Paul spent the next half hour walking on the set of stairs in the gym and strengthening the muscles of his upper and lower body. As he returned to the chair, he viewed Greer at the far corner of the gym. She saw him, smiled, and crossed the gym to greet him.

"Dad! I saw how well you did. You're looking great!"

"Thanks! I didn't expect to see you here. Did you come to see me?"

"Well, yes. But I also came to talk to Brian about some things." Paul glimpsed a sparkle in her eyes. He recalled a similar look when as a child, she received a new toy.

"Paul. I'll be right back. Sit here and do your exercises. I want to show Greer something," said Brian, as he sprung from his stool.

That was when Paul fit the pieces together. It was an easy puzzle to solve. Greer was an attractive young woman who lacked direction and purpose. Brian was handsome, unattached, and professional. An attraction between them made perfect sense. But Greer was living with Mickey. Paul realized he had grown fond of Mickey, who was more caring than Paul would have imagined. It was obvious he loved Greer. Mickey had intimated to Paul that he wanted to propose to Greer, so he was picking up extra hours at the garage and working on friends' and neighbors' cars in his spare time, to earn enough money to buy her a ring, as well as setting aside money to purchase a garage of his own. *I wonder if Greer's feelings for Mickey have faded. Perhaps she has reevaluated their relationship, reassessed the life she would have with him. Mickey is a hard worker, but it might be several years until he saves enough money to purchase his own business.* Then he would need enough customers to pay the mortgage, hire workers, and advertise.

Maybe Greer was growing impatient and thought she could do better with Brian. But Brian was more than a decade older than Greer. If Brian found the right companion, he would likely want to settle down and start a family. *Is that what Greer wants?* She still seemed like a lost soul, working varied hours and three jobs. Paul often thought of asking about her plans, especially since their relationship seemed less delicate since his illness, but he didn't want to risk fracturing their bond. He had faith that his daughter would decide on a career choice and find stability. Whether she chose Mickey or Brian or someone else, he vowed to support her decision. *But Brian would be a wonderful choice.*

Chapter 44

When Heidi heard the front door slam, she ran from the kitchen. David's appearance announced his mood: tie loose and askew, his dress shirt, normally tucked neatly into his pants, hung haphazardly, the shirttails wrinkled. His eyes lacked their usual luster and his face was joyless. She knew he had slept well the previous night, but his demeanor suggested otherwise. She thought immediately of his father.

"What's the matter? Did something happen to your father?" she cried.

"No! Ben double-crossed me."

Heidi exhaled. *At least it isn't his father. We can fix anything else.* "What happened? What do you mean he double-crossed you?"

"I'm off the project. The company is going in a different direction. They want someone else to lead the team. And no one even had the decency to tell me. Or explain why."

"That's awful!"

"Get this! They gave the job to Daphne. Remember her?"

Heidi couldn't forget the model who had turned the head of every male over age twelve at the firm's holiday party. Heidi had been insecure for weeks after the party and wondered if David had been involved with Daphne aside from work. She had searched his eyes every day for a betrayal. She wasn't surprised when David acknowledged Daphne was beautiful. What shocked her was David's announcement that he had rebuffed Daphne when she propositioned him months before. Heidi questioned him for days on how he had resisted the beauty and charms of such an attractive woman, while secretly delighted he had done so. But David insisted he told Heidi about Daphne's actions because he and Heidi trusted each other; he did not want to risk remarks from his coworkers, or Daphne's attempts to blackmail David with a lie. Their marriage was valuable, and both were committed to its success. Heidi knew that countless men would have jumped at the chance to bed someone as stunning and sexy as Daphne, regardless of the consequences.

"I'm sorry. I know you didn't think Daphne was capable."

"She isn't! And I can't imagine she can lead a team...get the job done. I wonder why she was chosen. But I suppose it's because of other attributes. Not her brains or her abilities," he scoffed.

"Do you think she is involved with someone in the company? Is that what you mean?" Heidi hoped David didn't see her exhale, grateful it wasn't David who was unfaithful.

"I'm sure her involvement is with someone high up in the company. Ben. Perhaps Stuart. And the worst part is that I found out in a company meeting that I was being replaced. No one mentioned my name. Just that the company is going in a different direction than they originally thought. I nearly lost my breakfast right there."

"I'm sorry, honey. Did you speak with Ben?"

David ran his fingers through his tousled hair. "I tried to. But he wouldn't see me. Ben actually threatened to call security if I didn't leave his office. Perhaps he wants me to quit. Or he intends to fire me if I don't. I don't know why. He was supportive about my father. He told me to take off as much time as I needed. Perhaps that's when he conspired to remove me from the project."

Heidi caressed David's cheek. "Honey, I'm so sorry. You deserved better. Especially after how hard you've worked. But perhaps it's a sign of things to come. An omen. Maybe you should look for another job."

"I hope things don't get that bad. But I suppose I might have to go somewhere else. I hate to start over. I thought my job was stable. That I'd be in line for a promotion. And I was hoping for the extra money too. Especially if you want to go to law school."

"I'll postpone that. If I have to." The words flew from Heidi's mouth, but she wasn't sure her heart agreed.

"I don't want you to do that. My career is important. But so is yours. It wouldn't be fair to you."

Hours later, after David had gone to bed early with a headache, Heidi wondered how much she would compromise for David's career. Their lives would be difficult if she went to school and he kept his current job and salary. Loss of his job would wreck her dreams of law school. Heidi thought of her friends who lived in other parts of the country, most with careers and families. Living in variable climates and earning less money, she knew they were jealous—while she and David lived in the proverbial sunshine and warmth of California. *If they only knew that our lives aren't free of clouds and worry.*

Chapter 45

For several days, Greer had found it increasingly difficult to arrange the ambulance transports. Her promotion to supervisor would occur in three days, but now she wondered if she was up to the task. For the fourth time that day she had asked a caller to repeat the information. It wasn't as if she had slept poorly or was preoccupied with matters other than work. It was the medical language that distracted her. More than the usual series of digits in a phone number, a house address, a social security number, or an insurance policy, the medical terms made the person seem more real. Greer maintained a list of medical conditions and occasionally spent a few minutes between calls researching the diagnoses on the internet. She knew some terms derived from Latin, and having learned some Latin prefixes and root forms during writing classes in college, could often grasp a term's meaning.

Until now, the satisfaction of doing a good job had been enough for her, but she no longer felt content or valuable. It was easy to understand what had changed her views. Exposed to the medical world because of her father's illness, the science of the human body now intrigued her. She saw the body as a compilation of anatomy, physiology, chemistry, and engineering. Her heart fluttered. For the first time in a year, she was excited about learning something new.

On her lunch break, Greer searched the internet for programs of study in the medical field. She ruled out medical school, but would consider a career in nursing. A few minutes later, she suddenly knew what career path she wanted to pursue. It was what Brian did that intrigued her the most. *I want to study physical therapy.*

The remainder of the work day passed without incident. After her shift ended, she sent a text to Brian. As she parked her bicycle at her apartment, her phone rang. It was Brian.

"Hi Greer. I'm glad to hear from you."

"Hi. Thank you for calling me. I want to talk to you about something. I told you I dropped out of school. That I wasn't certain I wanted to be a writer. And I've been working at the ambulance company. Well, today I realized I know what I want to do. What I want to study."

"Great! What did you decide?"

"How difficult is it to become a physical therapist?"

"Wow! That's wonderful! Do you really want to study physical therapy?" Brian chuckled. "I'm thrilled. I must have impressed you with my skills."

"You've done such a superb job with my dad. I never thought about the human body in terms of muscles and bones. I thought about body parts. Arms. Legs. Chest. But the medical terms have piqued my interest. I started researching them. The more I read, the more I want to learn."

"I'd be happy to talk to you more about what I do. The field is growing in popularity, and there's always a need for qualified people. Advances in the medical field have allowed people to survive illnesses they might not have before. And people are living longer. Anything we can do as a society to improve quality of life is a bonus. I mean, people in their eighties are active and do things expected of younger people. Like riding bicycles."

"Okay. You've convinced me—"

"Sorry. I know I can be too enthusiastic. Sometimes I have to take it down a notch."

"It's great that you love what you do. That's what I want. A career that I love. Everyone said I was a wonderful writer. But I didn't love to write. I couldn't see it as a way of life."

"I would be delighted to help you. I can give you some advice about schools." Greer opened her mouth to interject, but Brian continued. "Actually, hold on a second. I need to check something."

Through the phone, Greer heard Brian moving about. She opened the door to her apartment, retrieved her mail, and perused the advertisements and bills. After a few minutes, Brian returned to the phone.

"I'm back. Sorry it took me so long. I found what I was looking for. Your timing is perfect. Listen to this. I belong to an organization for therapists. The group is sponsoring an expo to promote the physical therapy field. There will be representatives from several schools there, and companies showcasing their new products and programs. Like biomedical technology. Prosthetic limbs made from 3-D printers. Devices that stimulate the muscles of people paralyzed by spinal cord injuries—"

"Okay. You've convinced me again."

Brian laughed. "Oops. There I go again. You don't have hours to listen to me. I'll send you the information about the expo. Let me know if you're interested. I'd be happy to go with you."

"That would be great. Thanks so much." Mickey was working late again, and as Greer heated soup on the stove, she heard whistling. Turning her head to determine its origin, she laughed with the realization that the sounds had come from her mouth.

Chapter 46

Paul had taken the first steps in the parallel bars with his prosthesis when the telephone rang. Brian quickly eased Paul into a chair.

"I'll be right back. I need to answer the phone. Our unit secretary is off today," said Brian, as his cell phone pinged with a text. "I'll answer this when I get back," he added, placing his phone on the chair beside Paul.

Paul wasn't one to intrude on others' privacy, but when the text message flashed in the corner of his field of vision, he turned his head slightly. To his surprise, he viewed messages between Brian and Greer.

Brian: "I'll see you tomorrow. At 12:00. I'll pick you up. Like we agreed."

Greer: "Sounds great. So excited."

Paul's brain barely had time to process the information before Brian returned.

"Sorry, Paul. It took me longer than I expected to find the

information the caller wanted. The therapists always flounder when the secretary is off. Now let's get started again."

Paul stood, then haltingly walked the length of the bars, as beads of perspiration gathered on his face and neck. During his lifetime, he estimated he had walked tens of thousands of miles without concentration or fanfare. Now, he could not believe that walking with one natural leg and one prosthesis required so much energy and focus.

Brian eased Paul into the chair at the edge of the bars. "You did great!" he exclaimed as he handed Paul a towel. "What a workout!"

Paul mopped the sweat from his face and neck. "Wow! I can't believe how hard that was. People with two good legs take walking for granted. I never thought about the process. Putting one foot in front of the other again and again. We don't think about it. We just do it."

"That's true. Most people never think about the mechanics of walking. Not until they have an injury or joint or circulatory problem."

"You're great at this. How did you decide you wanted to be a therapist?" inquired Paul.

"I was always interested in mechanical things. I loved to build things and take them apart. I was considering a career in engineering. It was my grandfather Walt's stroke when I was in high school that got me thinking about the mechanics of the body. The left side of his body was nearly paralyzed. I watched how hard he tried to move again. It amazed me how the therapists worked with him. He regained some strength and movement. It was then that I started thinking about a career as a physical therapist."

Paul sighed. "My son David knew in high school that he wanted to work with computers. He got his degree in computer science and is working for a company in California. He loves his work. But my daughter Greer—"

"We've met. She's a good person. Caring. Attentive."

"Yes. Greer is a wonderful daughter. And she's smart. She was studying to be a journalist. She was doing well in school. She has won awards for her writing. I thought for sure she'd follow in her mother's footsteps. Carly's a writer. I think I told you that."

"Yes, you did. But you mentioned Greer's journalism studies in the past. So are you saying she switched majors in school?"

Paul sighed. "Oh! I didn't realize I told you that. Carly and I haven't shared our disappointment with many others." He paused, unable to retract his admission of disappointment with his daughter's actions. "Well, actually, Greer didn't change her college major. She dropped out of school. Sprung it on us. Didn't bother to tell us before she did it. She said she wasn't happy with the coursework she needed for her journalism degree."

Brian brushed off his feelings of guilt over inquiring more about Greer. He had heard her side of the story. He respected her privacy and didn't plan to reveal their recent conversation to her father. *Besides, she may change her mind once she sees how much work it involves.* He struggled to maintain nonchalance.

"I'm sure she'll find something she wants to do. Something she loves. She'll find herself."

Paul sighed. "I hope so."

"Now let's try walking in the bars one more time before your session is over."

Chapter 47

C arly looked up from her computer as Paul entered the kitchen.

"I want to talk to you about something," he announced.

Carly refilled her coffee mug and added a teaspoonful of sugar. "Sure, honey. What is it?"

"I think Greer and Brian are a couple."

"Oh, I hope not!" Her hand shook violently; the coffee sloshed around the cup and spilled onto her cream-colored silk blouse.

"What do you mean by that?"

"Uh...I...just remembered...about a utility bill I forgot to pay," she stammered, breathing deeply to regain her composure. *This is the worst thing that could happen.*

"So we'll pay a late fee. Not a big deal." He glanced at his shortened limb. "Far worse things have happened."

"But Paul. How do you know they are a couple? Did you hear that from Greer or Brian?"

"No. But Greer came to the gym last week when I was there."

"Honey. She probably came to see how you were doing. Why would you think there's anything more to it?" Carly clutched her hands to steady them. *Just stay calm.*

"She's been texting Brian. It seems they've been communicating. Today I saw some texts they had been sending."

"Why are you looking at his phone? Are you sure it was her? Were you close enough to read his texts? And why wasn't Brian focused on your therapy session?"

Paul sighed. "Carly. I was resting after a walk. Brian got a text. He obviously thought he needed to answer it. Perhaps, with a different patient, he would have stepped away. But we're more like friends now. He doesn't have to be so formal. But I didn't look on purpose. He left his cell phone on the chair to answer a phone in the department. My eyes wandered to the phone. He and Greer made plans to be together. They agreed on a time to meet."

"Maybe you misinterpreted what you read. It was probably something totally different. Not at all what you thought. Besides, you shouldn't have looked at the texts. That was wrong." Carly's face was fixed and colorless.

"I'm sorry. Are you upset? I didn't think you would take it badly. Brian is a nice guy."

"Um. Yes. I agree. He's a good guy." Carly nearly choked on the words. "It's just that..."

"What is it? I thought you would be pleased. We always wished she'd find a professional guy."

"Their relationship will never work," she blurted. *I hoped this day would never come. I want so badly to tell Paul. But I can't. Not now.*

"Why not? I know he's older than Greer. But it could work. It's not like they're from different generations."

"No! He'll...ruin everything."

"Ruin everything? What do you mean? He's a great guy. Give the relationship a chance."

But Carly didn't respond to his last words. She had already left the room.

In the bedroom, Carly was frantic. *I have to tell Paul about Brian. If I'm wrong, if Brian isn't my son, I'll deal with the fallout. Perhaps we'll go to couples therapy. I think our marriage will survive, but damage is inevitable.*

If Paul was right, if Greer and Brian were romantically involved, the repercussions could be worse than simply being half-siblings. Carly placed a call to her daughter.

"Hi Greer. Honey, I want to talk to you about something."

"Okay. What's up?"

"Um...How are you and Mickey doing?"

"We're doing fine." Greer laughed. "Really? That's what you wanted to talk to me about? My relationship with Mickey?"

"Well, I'm just checking to make sure you're okay. That you're happy together. I...uh...had a dream that you two were having problems. "

"Mom. Honestly, we're a little stressed. Mickey's been working a lot of hours. We haven't seen each other much lately."

"But you live together. He comes home. I mean...you see him then. Right?" *I am a writer, so why is it so difficult for me to say what I mean?*

"Well, sure. But he's often exhausted. So he grabs a sandwich or leftovers for dinner, we say a few words to each other, he takes a shower, and falls right to sleep. So, yes. We're doing okay. But I suppose things could be better."

"I guess you're keeping busy. Especially with Mickey's schedule."

"I'm getting out a little. Seeing some friends." *Is Brian a friend?*

"I'm glad to hear you are both okay. Just a silly dream I had."

"Yeah. Okay, Mom." Greer chuckled. "But maybe you should have a dream about me winning the lottery. Or a rich benefactor who gives Mickey money to buy a business."

"Ha ha. I'll try."

"Okay, Mom. Sorry. I have to go."

"Okay, honey. Bye."

The conversation had done little to dispel Carly's guilt and anxiety. She would do everything she could to discourage a romantic relationship between Greer and Brian. Everything and anything. Except disclosing the truth.

Chapter 48

Mickey arrived home and dropped his oil-stained clothing on the bathroom floor. It had been an awful day at work. He had been certain he could rebuild the engine on the Porsche belonging to one of the garage's best customers. Once he owned the garage, he had planned to advertise foreign car repairs besides the domestic models that were the garage's specialty. But although he had memorized the auto repair manual and rehearsed the steps to dismantle and reconfigure the engine, he was met with failure when he slipped the key into the ignition and the car refused to start.

After showering, he dressed in clean jeans and a T-shirt and strolled into the kitchen to make a sandwich, to satisfy his hungry body until dinner. Opening the refrigerator, he could not find the ham and cheese he had expected. He glimpsed a cup of orange juice, two slices of pumpernickel bread, and a few eggs. Greer normally did the grocery shopping on Monday mornings and worked at the ambulance company in the after-noons. He looked at his phone and confirmed it was Monday, but it was obvious she had done no shopping. He really wasn't in the mood to cook, but he turned on the range and fried two eggs and toasted the bread. He wondered where Greer had gone. She hadn't told him she had plans, or left a note. If her boss called her into work early, she would have sent a text. He checked his phone again. There was no text. He wondered again where she would have gone.

He was working every extra minute he could to earn money for an engagement ring. Budgeting his money carefully, also putting aside hundreds of dollars a week to buy the garage where he worked. Greer knew he wanted his own place, but he hadn't told her that Marty, the owner of the shop, was planning to retire and move with his wife to Florida. He and Marty had agreed on a price for the business, and Mickey had already discussed the amount needed for a down payment with a customer who did business financing. Mickey wanted to keep the news about Marty a secret; he planned to tell Greer when he had the downpayment and the mortgage approval in hand.

Mickey's goal seemed within reach, but he worried about Greer's uncertainty about her career path. The job at the ambulance company was steady, but he knew she could do better. Becoming a supervisor was a step forward, but answering telephones, cleaning office buildings, and delivering food were jobs, not careers. Greer had the intellect and determination of a professional. He had expected her to return to school after a semester or two away. Perhaps not the same college or program, but one with a path to a vocation. But Greer was still undecided about what she wanted to do with her life. Now that they had moved in together and were sharing expenses, she could save a little money. But she deserved better than juggling three jobs for little reward.

Footsteps broke through his thoughts, the apartment door

flew open, and Greer entered the living room, clad in a knee-length black and white striped dress, black tights, and black boots.

"Hi, Greer. I was worried. I thought you'd be home. Or at the grocery store. It's Monday."

"Yeah. I know. Sorry. Something came up. I didn't get to the store."

"I noticed. I made myself some eggs."

"Sorry." Greer tossed her backpack on the counter.

"You're not wearing your work clothes. Where were you?" he stammered.

"I...got an offer to go out."

Mickey's face tightened as he approached Greer. "Go out where?" he implored.

"I...was planning to tell you. But now I don't want to. You're angry. Why are you so angry at me?"

Mickey clenched his fists. "Why don't you tell me where you were? You're all dressed up."

"These clothes? I'm not dressed up. It's not like I went to a party."

His voice rose. "Were you with another guy? Is that why you won't tell me where you went?" He searched her eyes, which had betrayed her again. "Oh, my God! You were with another guy!" He shook his fist a few inches from Greer's face.

"It's not what you think!" she proclaimed. "I can explain."

"I've been working extra hours almost every day. To save money. To buy a garage. I don't run around with other women. I don't smoke. I'm not a drinker. I don't do drugs. I found someone I want to share my life with. And now I find out you were with another guy!"

Greer had never seen Mickey so angry. His face was snarled and his neck veins bulged.

"Let me explain. Please," Greer pleaded.

"Not now!" he bellowed. "I don't want to hear any more lies. I'm exhausted. I just want to get some sleep. Don't bother me." Mickey slammed the door to the bedroom, leaving Greer with her mouth agape, wondering if their relationship was moving in the wrong direction.

Although Greer considered spending the night on the couch, two hours later she trod into the bedroom and hesitantly climbed into the bed she and Mickey shared. His lean body hugged the far side of the bed, so she clung to the edge of the mattress on the other side, away from the man with whom she had shared her hopes and dreams. Now she wondered if the guy snoring softly was the right one for her.

When Greer awoke, Mickey's side of the bed was empty. She retrieved the wrinkled sheets which spilled onto the floor, and removed two strands of hair stuck to his pillow. She tugged on the window shade and peered out of the tiny window to view the sunrise. Mickey had left for work earlier than usual. Greer trod to the kitchen and started the coffee maker. Seeing the sparse offerings in the refrigerator, she opened the small pantry and searched for breakfast food. In a corner of the cabinet she found a single pouch of plain instant oatmeal. It would have to do.

Greer mused over the previous evening's events. Mickey's anger had startled her. They had a few disagreements before, mostly under stress or fatigue, when harsh words were uttered and regretted within seconds; times they had been quick to apologize. But this argument was different. She had wanted to tell him where she had been, who she was with. But he had rebuffed her offers of explanation. *And why should I have to fight so hard to explain, when he had already decided that I had strayed. He thinks I betrayed him. Should I apologize? But perhaps he has already apologized.* She searched the tiny apartment for signs he regretted his anger and his actions. But there was no hand-written note with cutesy hearts on the table. She retrieved her cell phone, which lacked texts, words of apology, or strings of emojis proclaiming his remorse. It took just a few seconds to send a text. *Is he waiting for me to apologize?*

Greer knew that their relationship was worth saving, and she decided to take the first steps towards repairing it. Making his favorite meal would be a good start. She planned to stop at the grocery store on her way home from work. Once he was calm, Greer would tell him where she had been. She would show him the pamphlets, tell him about her plans for the future. When he saw her excitement, she was certain he would apologize for his anger. Greer scanned the apartment. It would be nice to have a bigger place, a spare room, perhaps an office. Once she was working in a professional environment and he owned a business, they could go far in life. Maybe they would buy a house with a driveway and a yard. Sighing, she dressed for work and climbed onto her bicycle for the short ride to the ambulance company. Hopefully she wouldn't be riding the bicycle for transportation much longer. Mickey had promised to look for a reputable car for her.

The future was promising: a career, a business, two cars, a bigger apartment, perhaps a house. Greer didn't want to let her imagination run wild, but she was certain things would get better.

Chapter 49

Working on automobiles usually calmed Mickey. Once he focused on diagnosing the problem with the engine or carburetor or alignment, he could block out other issues. But today he found it difficult to concentrate on mundane tasks like changing spark plugs or brake pads. He was so angry with Greer. He knew now that she had been with Brian. He saw the evidence on her cell phone. A few weeks before, Greer had told him her password, an easy combination of letters and numbers he had committed to memory. Arising from the bed after a restless sleep, his dreams littered with images of Greer kissing other men, he had carried her cell phone from the bedroom into the bathroom. After briefly questioning his morality, he entered her password into the phone and scrolled through her texts and messages. He had hoped he was wrong, that he would feel guilty for spying on her. But the thread of texts between Greer and Brian validated his suspicions.

Brian: "I'm glad you decided to join me. I think you'll enjoy it."

Greer: "Thanks for inviting me. I've arranged the time off."

Brian: "There are some decent restaurants nearby. We can get something to eat afterwards."

Greer: "Sounds great. I'm looking forward to it. And to talking with you."

Brian: "I'll see you tomorrow. At 12:00. I'll pick you up. Like we agreed."

Greer: "Sounds great. So excited."

Mickey was unable to identify their destination, but before him was proof that Greer and Brian had planned dinner afterwards. *Did they go some place that Greer asked me to take her? Did they go to a hotel? Would she cheat on me like that?* Their relationship had been affected by his extra hours working, returning home exhausted every day, eating whatever was available, dozing in front of the television. He was often too tired to have a meaningful conversation when he got home. He could blame himself for their rare intimacy. But he was working so many hours because he wanted her to be happy. She should have been pleased that he wanted to buy a garage. But while he was working, she had spent time with another guy.

Mickey was so angry, he wanted to call her and tell her their relationship was over. She had given up her apartment to move in with him. If they separated, she would need a place to live. He doubted she would go back to live with her parents. But maybe she would move into Brian's place. He was a professional guy who probably earned a good salary and could afford a nice home. He looked a good bit older than Greer; perhaps he was in his thirties, just at the age to settle down and raise a family. *Greer is an attractive, intelligent woman. Any man would be proud to be with her. I should fight for her. But if she wants to be with*

Brian, I will give her what she wants. I'll force her hand. I'll see how much she fights for our relationship.

During the half hour he normally set aside to eat his lunch, Mickey went home, packed Greer's belongings in two boxes he had carried from the garage, and set the cartons inside the front door of the apartment. He left a handwritten note, pouring out his anger, and added that she should think about whether they should be together. He asked her to leave her key on the table.

WHEN GREER RETURNED TO THE APARTMENT AFTER WORK, carrying bags of groceries purchased for Mickey's favorite dinner, she found her belongings piled by the door. Seated on the floor, she read Mickey's note and sobbed. She had never expected he would feel so threatened that he asked her to move out. Although he earned more money and the lease was in his name, she paid half the rent. *Now where can I go? I know my parents would let me come home. Especially if I said I'm moving back to help them. To help my father. But do I want to return?* Her parents would know that something happened with her relationship with Mickey, and Greer didn't want to subject herself to their questions and accusations. *If they know I went somewhere with Brian, will they also think Brian and I are more than friends?* Greer wondered where else she could go, who else she could contact. Then she knew. She sent a text, and when the response came, welcoming her, she knew her decision was right.

"I'll pick you up in ten minutes," came the reply.

Ten minutes later, Greer left her apartment key on the table, gathered the bag of groceries, her boxes of belongings, and her bicycle, and climbed into the car.

Chapter 50

Just when David thought things couldn't get any worse, Ben summoned him to his office. When David arrived, Ben's door was closed, but through the glass panel in the office door, David saw him clutching his phone's receiver, pacing on the carpet parallel to the window, and fingering a computer-shaped pewter paperweight on the corner of his desk. David heard Ben arguing with someone. Ben was red-faced and sweaty, his anger spewing forth.

"Okay! I told you I'll take care of it. And I'll do it!" he screamed into the phone, as he threw his body backwards into his chair. Ben slammed the receiver down and stared out of the window, waving his fists. David stepped away from Ben's door, counted to ten, then retraced his steps. He tapped lightly on the door. Ben turned in his chair and motioned for David to enter.

"David. Come in. Take a seat." The redness was fading from his face, but his expression was far from welcoming. David took a seat across from Ben.

"I asked you to come here...to tell you...you're being reassigned. To George's team."

"Huh? Why?"

"Stuart wants you to work with George."

"I...don't understand what happened. Did I do something wrong with the project? I took a few days off, but I had to see my father."

Ben shook his head. "No. It's not related to the visit to your father. I'm sorry. It's out of my hands."

"But...I was leading the project. Now I've been reassigned to another team. I think I deserve an explanation."

"I agree. Here's your explanation. Stuart told me to reassign you to George's team. I had no say."

"Ben! I thought we had a great relationship. We work well together. Didn't you fight for me?"

"Yes! I did! More than you know." Ben sighed. He stood suddenly and leaned his stocky body towards David, who was close enough to count the beads of sweat on Ben's cheeks. "But Stuart insisted on the transfer. If I put up more of a fight, I will jeopardize my job. I have two kids in college and a wife who loves to shop. I can't risk it."

David fought the urge to grab the paperweight from the desk and hurl it through the glass door. "I can't believe this. I mean, it's bad enough that Daphne replaced me as the lead. But it's as if I'm being punished. And I don't know why."

"I'm sorry. I don't know, either. I'll let you know if I hear anything. Anything reliable, that is. By the way, how is your father doing?"

"He's doing okay, but he has a long road ahead of him. It's fortunate he's a strong guy. And my mother is supportive." He lumbered to the doorway, then turned to face Ben. "I appreciate you asking."

Back in his office, David sat facing the doorway. His fingers clicked on the keyboard, and to a passerby, he looked engaged in his work. Hidden behind his desk monitor was his personal tablet. He couldn't say why he carried it with him every day to his job, because he had little free time to peruse the internet, and he often sent personal emails using his cell phone. Now, instead of engagement with his team—now his former team—he viewed social media accounts, hoping to find a reason for Stuart's decision. It wasn't his Facebook and Instagram and Twitter accounts he was viewing. It was Daphne's.

Daphne's social media accounts weren't under an alias or a cutesy name. She was easy to find: Daphne Wilkinson. Her postings did not address political or ethical or religious issues. She often asked for friends' opinions about her appearance, while posing in store dressing rooms wearing exotic and expensive clothing: a short black dress which accented her cleavage, red lingerie that left little to one's imagination, a skimpy leopard-print bikini. Clothing worn to please a man; not attire appropriate for the office. While David perused her Facebook page, George notified him about a meeting with his new team in five minutes. David closed his tablet and replaced it in his briefcase. If he had ample time to view the postings, David suspected that Daphne's photographs and captions would provide a clue to Stuart's or Ben's behavior.

Chapter 51

After several days of rain, the warm and cloudless day was an invitation for Carly and Paul to enjoy a meal on the screened patio overlooking their backyard. About an hour prior, they had discussed eating lunch outdoors. Carly had spent a half hour constructing a salad of fresh lettuce and vegetables. In previous years she and Paul had planted seeds in the vegetable beds in their backyard: tomatoes and peppers and peas and eggplant. But Paul's hospitalization and rehabilitation took priority this year, so Carly purchased fresh produce at a local farmers' market. The food was fresh, but nothing could replace retrieving vegetables and fruits from a garden minutes before ingestion.

Now, with the table set and her salivary glands awakened, Carly went in search of Paul. Ambling through the dining room, she heard sobbing. *Who is crying?* The only other person in the house was...Paul. Carly ran the remaining distance through the dining room and into the living room. There, lying on his side on the carpet, was Paul. His pylon had dislodged from his stump, but the straps remained fastened on his lower thigh. The sports section of the newspaper lay haphazardly next to the recliner where Paul had been seated. Paul's face was tear-stained and reddened, but he appeared unhurt. Carly rushed to his side.

"Oh my God! Paul! Are you okay? Did you get dizzy? How long have you been on the floor?"

Paul shook his head. "I'm not sure how long I've been on the floor. Perhaps five minutes. Or ten. I dropped the newspaper. When I reached to pick it up, I lost my balance. I called you when I fell. Didn't you hear me?" But to Paul's dismay, Carly appeared to ignore his question.

"Here. I'll help you up," she replied, straightening his prosthesis and aligning his walker.

Paul pushed her away. "I asked you a question. Didn't you hear me call you?"

"No, I didn't hear you! But I was two rooms away preparing our lunch. The water was running. Perhaps your voice wasn't loud enough. I'm sorry."

"I yelled as loud as I could," Paul stammered. "I could have been at a sporting event, as loud as my voice was. And I called you several times. Then I gave up. I figured you'd find me here."

Her face softened as she faced the reality of her problem. Paul had called for her—yelled for her—but she hadn't heard him. He wasn't seriously hurt. Not this time. But what about next time? What if he had fallen down a flight of stairs? What if his blood sugar was unstable, and he had lain there, unconscious? *Paul has medical problems, but there is no problem with his speech. He called for me. But I didn't hear his pleas for help. Is my hearing a problem?* Carly turned on the television. She turned off the closed captioning and raised the volume as high as it would go. Although she could hear the dialogue, she couldn't deny that her hearing had continued to deteriorate. The sound should have been blaring; instead, it varied between good and marginal. The realization that she needed hearing aids hit her hard. She had previously denied her hearing loss, but could no longer ignore the problem.

Then another thought struck her, and she sighed. *For months, I've been thinking that the worst problem Paul and I had was my hearing loss. I didn't want to admit it. My hearing has probably gotten worse. But this is a minor issue compared with Paul's medical problems. I can fix my problem by visiting an audiologist and getting a prescription for hearing aids. Even if I need one for each ear, this is not a big deal. It will take little time to insert them into my ears every day. It will cause minor discomfort. They may be barely noticeable; perhaps not at all if I change my hairstyle. I will have better hearing than I do now, and better than I have for many years. But Paul had a part of his body removed. He may always walk with a shuffle or a limp, and people will wonder what happened to him, why his gait isn't normal.*

"I'm so sorry, Paul. I realize now that my hearing is a problem. After lunch, I'll call for an appointment for a hearing test. And if I need hearing aids, I'll get them too."

Paul nodded. "I'm glad I wasn't hurt. Yes, I know it's hard to acknowledge a problem. I ignored my own medical problems. If I had listened to my body, I would have gone to see my doctor before my glucose was so high. Before it affected my circulation." He straightened his prosthesis. "Now let's have lunch. I'm starving."

Chapter 52

I t had been no surprise to Brian when Greer called him the previous day. He remembered her excitement at the expo. Seeing all the possibilities and meeting all the professionals, attendees, and presenters had left her as excited as a girl who received a sought-after birthday gift. She had ogled the posters featuring the body's anatomy, and engaged the presenters in conversation about their products, and what made their educational programs most appealing. It was obvious Greer was genuinely interested in entering the field; her eyes advertised her exuberance.

After leaving the expo, they had shared a casual dinner at a restaurant with a great selection of wonderful food. He and Greer had ordered an entrée each and shared an appetizer. He hadn't realized how young she looked until the server had asked her for ID when she ordered a beer. Luckily, her ID proved she was of legal drinking age; she had turned twenty-one a few months prior. Learning she was an adult had apparently triggered Brian's unexpected reaction. He remembered how happy he was that Greer couldn't see under the table—at the bulge in his pants.

Although the phone call wasn't a surprise, the purpose had shocked him. Without elaborating, she said she needed a place to stay temporarily, and didn't know if she and Mickey were still a couple. That sounded serious, but Brian knew firsthand that innuendoes and insinuations were often spewed during stressful moments and retracted with sincere apologies the next day. He sighed and reminisced about the break-up with Mimi. She had offered no apologies, reconciliation, or pleas for forgiveness. Removing her belongings from the bedroom and bathroom, she had walked out of the door, and his life. When she didn't respond to his calls and texts after a week, he stopped trying.

When Greer asked, Brian had immediately agreed that she could stay at his apartment. He offered his spare bedroom, furnished with a futon, with an adjoining bathroom. He hoped she patched things up with Mickey, who sounded like a decent guy who might have acted hastily. Greer had told him they had discussed marriage. That didn't sound like a relationship a man would throw away so quickly, especially with a woman as attractive and intelligent and ambitious as Greer.

Brian finished his breakfast, and placed his coffee cup in the dishwasher. He glanced at the clock on the microwave: 8:15. The door to the spare bedroom was closed; he remembered that Greer wasn't working until ten. Brian gathered his briefcase and his keys and left his apartment. Perhaps he would see Greer after he finished working. He wondered how long she would stay. They were friends now. Nothing more. He sighed. He knew more about the workings of the brain than most people did. His conscience wanted Greer and Mickey to reunite. The limbic system—the portion of the temporal lobe responsible for his emotions, sexual arousal, and behavioral responses, would be happier if they remained apart.

Chapter 53

Mickey was finishing a brake change when he noticed a car parked in the driveway. He had a photographic memory for cars he had serviced and did not remember working on this newer model sedan. But when the driver emerged, he wiped his grimy hands on a rag and went to greet her. "Ms. Casper. How are you?"

"Please, Mickey. Call me Carly."

Mickey didn't know if he was more embarrassed about using her first name or about having to explain his split from Greer. "Carly. What a surprise. Do you...need some work done on your car?" *I hope she needs my professional expertise. That she hasn't come looking for answers about our relationship, or offering advice.*

"Well, I think I need your help. I mean...there may be a problem with the car."

"Okay. What's wrong with it?" He exhaled. *So she may not know about our breakup.*

"Well...I'm sorry. Paul always did the car maintenance. The

diagnostic and easy stuff."

"I understand. It's no problem. Tell me what's the matter."

"I don't think the problem is the battery. But occasionally the car doesn't start right away. I'm not sure. This isn't my field of expertise." She laughed. "Well, you know that!"

"It's okay. It may be the starter. I'll look at it."

Carly scanned the surroundings. "There are several vehicles here. It seems like you're busy already. I can wait. I don't want any preferential treatment."

"Why not? You deserve it." Mickey opened the hood of the car and peered inside.

"Well, bringing my car to my daughter's boyfriend doesn't mean I'm special."

Mickey raised his head and his eyes met Carly's. He cleared his throat. "Um...I guess Greer didn't tell you. We're not together anymore."

Carly's lower lip fell, and she was momentarily speechless. "What do you mean...you're not together?"

"We broke up."

"No! No, she didn't tell me. She didn't say anything." *But I know things weren't rosy.*

"I'm sorry. I thought you knew." Mickey closed the hood. "Perhaps you don't want me to look at your car."

"Of course I do! What happened between you two? When did you break up?"

"About a week ago. Actually, it's been ten days. But I...really don't want to get into it."

"Where is Greer living? I assume she's not there with you."

"I don't know. I assumed she moved back home. With you and Mr. Brown...uh, Paul."

"No! She's not with us."

"Well, then she may be with a friend. Or her new guy."

Mickey hated to say the words aloud. But her mother needed to know there was someone else in her life.

"Greer said nothing about a new guy!" *What else is she not telling us?* Then Carly remembered Paul's proclamation that Greer and Brian were a couple. She had dismissed his utterance as a rumor without merit. It couldn't be. Carly opened her car door and turned the key. The car started.

"Mickey. Thank you. For looking at my car. Maybe I'll bring it back for you to check. Another day," she mumbled, hands shaking. Carly exited the lot, turned the corner, and stopped the car. Her body trembling, she feared an accident. *What have I done? Has my desire to hide my secret affected my entire family? Have I been so selfish in hiding my past that it threatens my family's future?*

She retrieved her cell phone from her handbag and placed a call to Greer. If what Mickey said was true, if Greer was staying with Brian and they were a couple, she would encourage Greer to end it. Brian was more than a decade older than Greer. Fourteen years and three months, with a few days thrown in. The age difference might be enough to make Greer reconsider. Carly knew she would do everything she could to discourage the relationship. She would put a stop to things before they got too serious. And before she had to reveal the truth.

Her plans forced her to question everything she believed in. By keeping her secret, she would shield her family from her past. But she also would deny herself a relationship with a great guy; a guy any mother would be proud to call her son. The son she had hidden from everyone. The son she now wanted to claim as her own.

Chapter 54

Heidi was growing exceedingly angry at David's lateness. Usually home for dinner before seven, for the third time this week he had sent a text that he was working late and wouldn't be home until eight. At home, he was often tense and quarrelsome. On the days David worked late, Matthew and Emily had dinner early, because it was unfair for them to wait until nearly their bedtime to eat dinner. Because Heidi hated to serve David reheated food—he could get that in a diner—she cooked dinner twice, which took up more of her time. Time she preferred to spend helping Matthew with homework or reading a story to Emily. Time better spent reviewing law school admission criteria or researching course work. Her body shook as she heard the foyer door slam. She cringed as David stomped into the kitchen. It promised to be an unpleasant evening.

"I can't believe George made me stay late again. I'm so angry I could spit!"

"I'm really sorry things are so bad." Heidi placed a bowl of tortellini and meatballs next to the salad on the table. "Please. Sit down and eat while it's fresh. Do you want a drink?"

"I want to drown my sorrows. That's what I want."

"I'm sorry it's been so rough for you. Have you learned anything about why they transferred you to George's team?"

"It has something to do with Daphne. I don't know what. But I'm sure it involves her."

"Why do you think she's involved?"

David sighed. "I have no proof right now. She does average work. At best. But she's well liked by everyone in the firm. Especially the men." He didn't want to revisit Daphne's physical attributes or her effects on the male gender.

"Well, anyone who looks like her would draw the eyes of all the men. A woman knows another woman is beautiful. I don't need you to point it out. I'm sure you enjoy looking at her."

"Oh. Okay. Yes. I admit it. She's a great-looking woman."

David hadn't planned to utter his private thoughts to his wife. He was not only fighting for his job, but suddenly, his marriage.

"You are beautiful, too. Please don't think I ever tried anything with her. I never came on to her. I wouldn't do that. Yes, she flirted with me. More than once. But I love you. I love our life," he stammered, hoping Heidi believed him.

"Relax, honey. I didn't think that. I trust you. But you might be right. Perhaps she is or was involved with someone in the company. Or made a pass that was rebuffed. That's possible."

"Thank you." David exhaled, grateful Heidi trusted him enough that he didn't need to defend himself. "And maybe she threatened to go to the top if she didn't get a project to lead. I think you might be onto something!" David hurriedly finished his dinner, then retrieved his laptop from his briefcase.

Although initially physically and emotionally exhausted, he now felt energized.

He logged onto Instagram and again found Daphne easily. Her Instagram page contained pictures of herself in various modeling poses, clad in dozens of outfits for varied social events. Some clothing he recognized from her Facebook posts. She posed alone in the pictures, and the commenters gaped at her clothing and her beauty. He clicked off of Instagram and onto Twitter. Although she had hundreds of followers and dozens of similar posts to those on Instagram, the photos and comments revealed no clues to link her to the men in the office.

His vision blurring from fatigue, David considered abandoning his search until the next day, but he knew attempts at sleep were futile if he didn't finish what he had set out to do. He logged onto Facebook and quickly found her account. David scrolled through her page and found photos not posted on Instagram and Twitter. More shots of her alone—some in bikinis and lacy nightwear. One photo had nearly a hundred comments, which he scrolled through quickly. The comments were similar to those on the other social media sites. One string of comments seemed to jump off the page. David read the thread three times to make sure his weary eyes weren't fooling him. But there was no mistake. It was a comment by a woman named Christy on a photo of Daphne wearing a skimpy dress that started it all.

Christy: "I bet if David from your office saw this, he could no longer ignore your charms."

Daphne: "I would have expected him to show some interest in me. I know he's married, but most men mess around. I thought I would have enticed him into a few hours of fun by now!"

Christy: "But what about Stuart? I mean...he's running the company!"

Daphne: "Yeah. He's rich and isn't afraid to show it. But I like my men younger. And David is much better looking. Sometimes when I'm with Stuart I pretend I'm with David!"

Christy: "Oh my! Does Stuart know you have the hots for David?"

Daphne: "Yeah. I made a mistake and called him *David* once. He was furious. I spent hours making it up to him!"

Although he was alone in the room, David felt heat rise in his face. Putting his ego aside, he recalled his interactions with Daphne. He remembered her flirtations and suggestive comments, and his refusal to stray. Like most men, he had opportunities, but he had never cheated on Heidi, and he didn't plan to. He loved her and his life, and he didn't plan to wreck it by giving in to another woman's charms. He knew that many of his friends had cheated on their women: long-term girlfriends, fiancees, wives—their status didn't seem to matter. The men often chided him for staying faithful to his wife, but some who strayed were now divorced or single, while most of the rest confessed to wanting out of unhappy marriages.

So now I know for certain that Daphne is in a relationship with Stuart. Since Stuart knows that Daphne really wants to be with me, he removed me from the project as punishment, and promoted Daphne, hoping her affection for him would grow. It all makes sense. But what can I do about it?

Chapter 55

C arly mustered the courage to call Greer, but she exhaled with relief when she reached her voicemail. It was easier than risking an argument by speaking with her directly.

"Hi honey. I'm...uh...checking in to see how things are going. I thought perhaps you could come for dinner. Maybe tonight. Or tomorrow. Or whatever fits with your schedule. Let me know. Okay...bye."

Two hours later, a text arrived from Greer: "I can come tomorrow. About five. I hope everything's okay. I want to talk with you and Dad about something. I need your advice. See you both tomorrow."

Carly froze. *What would Greer need advice about?* Perhaps she would finally tell them she had split with Mickey. Maybe Greer had given her a way to avoid the painful task of telling two lovers—she shuddered at the word, but realistically knew Greer and Brian might be lovers—that they needed to end their relationship.

. . .

ACROSS TOWN, GREER CHANGED INTO CLEAN JEANS AND A flowered T-shirt and thought about the dinner with her parents. She hadn't told them about her breakup with Mickey, but it was likely her mother knew, or she would not have extended a dinner invitation to Greer alone. She wondered now how her mother knew. Brian was still treating her father, but he agreed not to mention she was staying with him. Greer didn't want to announce she and Mickey were no longer together until she was certain it was a permanent situation. She also didn't want her parents to think she was cohabitating with Brian in the same way she had been living with Mickey. Brian was a perfect gentleman; occupying a spare bedroom in his comfortable apartment never threatened her privacy. He made extra coffee in the morning and left a handwritten note on the counter if the refrigerator contained leftovers. *I wonder why he is still single. Any woman would be thrilled to have him as a partner.* Brian had acknowledged his recent split from Mimi, largely because she disagreed with his attempts to locate his birth parents. Greer couldn't imagine growing up knowing you were adopted, wondering who your birth parents were or why they had relinquished you for adoption. Brian might even have siblings or half-siblings, unaware their mother or father had more children.

I wonder what it would be like to have children of my own. Greer wasn't ready yet, but two of her high school classmates had married a year after graduation, and both had given birth in the past year. Greer couldn't imagine having to care for another human being every day, especially an infant. She assumed the desire to procreate got stronger as one aged. If she was in her mid-thirties and childless, she was fairly certain she would be eager to have a family.

· · ·

GREER ARRIVED AT HER PARENTS' HOUSE AND STROLLED INTO THE foyer. She heard their voices in the kitchen and moved with trepidation to greet them.

"Hi, honey," said Paul as she approached and planted a kiss on his cheek.

"Hi, Dad. You're looking good."

Carly wiped her hands on a towel and hugged her daughter. "I'm glad you could come. We have hardly seen you lately."

"I've...been busy."

"Yes. I'm sure," replied Carly, her back to Greer. "It will be good to catch up."

Feeling her insides churn, Greer tried to maintain a poker face. *I hope I'm not on the receiving end of an inquisition.* If the situation soured, she would leave the house.

While Greer poured iced tea into glasses, Carly decided to address the issue before they had dinner. It was senseless to eat a nice meal with tension hanging in the air.

"Greer. Sit down. I didn't invite you here to ask a million questions. But I wanted to tell you I saw Mickey yesterday."

Greer nearly choked on the iced tea. "You saw Mickey! Where?" she sputtered.

"I've had a problem with our car. Well...I guess I still may have the problem. I went to the garage where he works. Your father has always taken care of our cars. But I don't know any other mechanics. Even if I did, I probably would have taken the car to Mickey." Carly articulated so well in writing; now she wondered why she couldn't say the words she wanted.

Paul came to his wife's rescue. "What your mom is trying to say is that Mickey said you two aren't together anymore. And we know you moved out of the apartment."

"Okay...that's true." *I don't like where this conversation is going.* "Yes. I moved out. Actually, Mickey packed my things in boxes

235

and left them for me when I came home from work. So I guess you could say he told me to leave."

"I'm sorry that happened," sighed Carly. "Regardless of the situation, I'm sure it hurts to leave. Not that we are saying you are to blame. But, it's often a two-way street."

"He's angry at me. But he won't let me tell him the whole story. He just blew up."

"I haven't seen Mickey angry, but you see a different side of a person when you live together," replied Paul.

"I had never seen Mickey get this angry before," admitted Greer. "He accused me of cheating on him. But I didn't cheat on him. He wouldn't let me explain."

"Oh, Greer. I'm so sorry. But why would he think you cheated on him?" asked Carly.

"Okay. Mickey thinks I cheated on him with Brian. He might have seen our texts. And I went somewhere with Brian about two weeks ago. But we're friends. That's all it is."

Paul exhaled. *So my suspicions have been correct. She has been spending time with Brian.* "So...is that where you have been staying? With Brian?"

"He was kind to let me stay at his place. He has an extra bedroom and bathroom. But we're not living together the way you think. Not like when I was with Mickey. Brian and I are friends. He is a perfect gentleman."

"I hate to ask. It's probably none of my business where you went with him. What got Mickey so upset," said Carly. *I may be the only one in the room rooting for Mickey.*

"Mom! I really didn't want to get into this! I considered not coming to dinner today. I was afraid that you would question me about everything." Greer rose and started towards the living room. "Maybe I'll leave now. Then you and Dad can eat in peace. And you can think of all the reasons I don't want to discuss every aspect of my life with you. This is why most people my age leave home and live on their own. It's why I left last year."

Carly raised her hand. "Okay. Stop. Please. I'm sorry I asked. I shouldn't have pried. Your life...and your relationships...are your business. We just don't want you to make a mistake."

"How do you know I am making a mistake?"

Wracked with guilt over not telling her daughter the truth, Carly opened her mouth to ease her conscience, but her brain saved her before the words flew from her mouth. When the reality of the situation hit her head on, she nearly fell over. *I can't tell Greer the truth and not tell Brian. Or Paul. I can't reveal to Brian that I am probably his birth mother without telling my husband the secret I've kept since college. How can I accuse Greer of hiding details from us, and from Mickey, if I have closeted my own indiscretions?*

"I don't know that it's a mistake. You are right. I'm sorry. You're not a child. You are an adult. An adult entitled to privacy," answered Carly. "I shouldn't have pried."

The trio ate the dinner Carly had prepared: roast pork, scalloped potatoes, and a green salad. After a few minutes of silence, they spoke about the forthcoming change in weather, movies they had streamed, how well the area sports teams were doing. They didn't speak of relationships, or betrayal, or omissions, or lies.

Chapter 56

Ben observed David standing at his office doorway and waved him in.

David started speaking before he lost his nerve. "Hi, Ben. I need to ask you something. I think you owe me the courtesy of an answer. I can't force you to answer, but if you don't, I'll assume my suspicions are correct."

Ben sighed. "Okay. I'm all ears."

"I have substantial evidence that Daphne and Stuart are a couple."

If David expected his superior's face to betray him, he was disappointed, for Ben's expression was unrevealing.

"Okay. Thanks. Then I'll assume I'm correct. So I suppose Stuart asked you to assign Daphne to manage the project. Instead of me."

Ben's eyes flickered almost imperceptibly, but just enough that David assumed he was correct.

"Thanks, Ben. Don't worry. I'll never reveal my source."

"I didn't tell you anything."

"No. You didn't."

HE KNEW BETTER THAN TO ACT ON IMPULSE, BUT IT WAS THE straw that broke the proverbial camel's back that led David to approach Stuart. Later, looking back at the events, he could have simply picked up his briefcase and gone home after George insisted he stay late again. Instead, heart pounding in his chest and unable to tamp down his anger, he marched into Stuart's office without knocking. The situation was rapidly deteriorating, and he needed to take immediate action.

"Stuart," David bellowed as he barged through the doorway, "I need to speak with you. Now!"

Stuart rose from his chair, as he lowered a crystal tumbler from his mouth. He quickly removed a whiskey decanter perched on his desk. "David! You can't come crashing into my office like this. That's no way to act. What is wrong with you?"

"What's wrong with me? What's wrong with you? Ordering my removal from the project I designed! Replacing me with Daphne. Your...your mistress!"

"What? How dare you make an accusation like that!"

"It's more than an accusation. I believe it's a fact."

"You have no proof," replied Stuart, brushing a stray hair into position.

It was all the confirmation David needed. Stuart hadn't refuted David's actions; he had simply denied there was proof of them.

"It's public knowledge that Daphne really wants to be with me. Although I'm not interested in an affair or a rendezvous of any kind. I'm happily married. I've never cheated on my wife and I don't intend to."

Stuart rose from his desk, straightened his silk tie, and

tucked his shirttails into his suit pants. "So, you're an honest man. A saint. What does that have to do with Daphne? Or me? And what public knowledge?"

"Facebook. Over two-and-a-half billion users worldwide. Ever hear of it?"

"Of course I've heard of it! I keep up with the younger generation. But I'm proud to say I don't use the site myself. So much garbage on there."

"Okay. Let me show you something." David removed his phone from his pocket and opened his Facebook app. He found the page he had bookmarked, moved his fingers to enlarge the post, and handed the device to Stuart.

"Read this post. See it? Right there."

Although Stuart reached for his reading glasses, he didn't need them to read the thread attached to Daphne's photo. David watched embarrassment spread from Stuart's face and onto his neck and scalp.

"I...don't know...who this woman Christy is. I've never heard of her. Could be...a spammer," he stammered. "That's what they call them, I believe. A person who puts inappropriate and erroneous information on another person's website."

"This isn't a spammer. Look at Daphne's response."

Stuart ignored David's request. "What does any of this have to do with me?"

"It's obvious that you're jealous. Although you're sleeping with her, she obviously has a thing for me. But I haven't done anything to encourage her, and you want to punish me anyway."

"Punish you? What are you talking about? That's bizarre."

David flipped to another post from Daphne. *This one is more damning. Stuart can't wiggle out of this one.*

Daphne: "I had the raciest dream last night. David and I were in a posh hotel."

Christy: "Ooh. Do tell."

Daphne: "Let's just say he couldn't keep his mouth or hands off of me. I woke up in a sweat!"

Minuscule beads of perspiration collected on Stuart's face and neck. Awkwardly brushing them away with his tie, he pointed to a chair. "Please, have a seat."

"Thank you, but I prefer to stand," replied David.

Stuart gulped the whiskey remaining in his glass. He held the decanter towards David. "Would you like some?"

David pounded his fist on the desk. "No! I don't want your whiskey. I want answers."

"Okay. I know Daphne really wants you. You're much younger. And better looking. But I removed you from the team because I want to go in a different direction. That's all."

David pondered his response. "A different direction from the one you verbally approved a few days before. So why didn't you have me lead the team in the new project?"

"I...figured you wouldn't want to. The other project was your idea. Your baby."

"So you changed the project and removed me. And you replaced me with Daphne."

"Daphne. Yes. I assigned her to lead the team in the new project."

"And you reassigned me to George's team. Basically, a demotion."

"No. Your salary is the same. And your title didn't change."

"That's true. But I went to the bottom of the pack. George gives me the scut work to do. Work far below my capabilities."

"Take it up with him if you don't like the work he assigns to you."

"I have. He responded by giving me assignments in the late afternoon that are due by close of business. He's forced my hand. I've had to stay late several days."

"That's not my problem."

"Just so we're clear. It's obvious you assigned Daphne to lead the team to earn some Brownie points with her. And by moving me to George's team, Daphne no longer has to interact with me. Or see me. So it's a win-win for you. Ironically, because I have refused to cheat on my wife I came out the loser. In my job. Certainly not in my life. If I had seduced Daphne, or agreed to her flirtations, she probably wouldn't be with you. You have her. But she apparently wants me. And that drives you crazy. So feeding your ego, you gave her what amounts to a promotion, even though she hasn't proven she can handle a project on her own. All to elevate your status in her eyes."

"If that's what you think."

David stared at Stuart. Their conversation had done nothing to ease David's anger. He picked up his briefcase and left the office.

Chapter 57

My Life and Yours- by Carly Casper

To my valued readers: Thank you for your words of kindness and inspiration. I never expected so many of you to empathize with our struggle, and to offer words of wisdom and encouragement.

Paul has been improving every week. Since he has learned how to manage the stairs outside of our house, he is receiving physical therapy as an outpatient. The highlight of his rehabilitation was the delivery of his temporary prosthesis—a pylon—a metal rod with a synthetic foot attached. Paul said it was possibly the ugliest and most wonderful gift he has received. Now he practices walking with his prosthetic leg in parallel bars—two metal bars secured in long blocks of wood, enabling Paul to hold each one as he walks five to ten feet. He needs to improve his balance, his strength, and his endurance before he can advance onto a walker or a cane. We hope that Paul will be ready for a permanent prosthesis later this year. This week, we learned that Paul will undergo testing to see if he will be able to resume driving. Getting behind the wheel of the automobile he has driven for several years will be a huge step towards regaining his independence.

We have learned so much from our journey to this point. I have written about individuals and families enduring hardships and disasters, experiencing grief. I have researched and written about the five stages of grief: denial, anger, bargaining, depression, and acceptance. Until Paul's illness, they were simply words I added to my articles. As a society, we think of grief as an emotion we experience after the death of a loved one. Paul and I were fortunate that we lived more than half a century without experiencing a significant loss. Although we grieved when our parents died, we had expected to outlive them. What we did not realize was that grieving can occur for other losses: our homes, our livelihood, removal or dysfunction of a body part, and loss of independence. Fortunately, when Paul hurled a coffee cup at a nurse, she realized he was displacing his anger, that he was really grieving the loss of part of his body and his independence.

I have taken some steps forward, too. I experienced a breakthrough of my own. We have been concentrating on Paul's struggles and our acceptance of his limitations, but I failed to address my own impediment. Since before Paul's illness, I have experienced a problem with my hearing. Of course, I initially denied that it impacted our lives. I blamed my misinterpretation of the dialogue on television shows and movies on the actors mumbling and whispering their lines. We turned on the television's closed captioning, and I thought my problem was solved. It was when my husband really needed my help—and I wasn't there to provide it—that I was finally able to admit my hearing difficulties. An audiologist diagnosed me with a bilateral moderate hearing loss. I am awaiting delivery of hearing aids. I have been assured they will be much smaller and less obtrusive than the boxes and wires worn by my mother's and grandmother's generations. It no longer really matters to me what they will look like. Placing them into my ears every morning will become normal, just as Paul applying his prosthesis will be routine.

I thank you for traveling with us, as we continue along our journey to our new state of normal. Paul and I do not yet know how much further we have to travel, but we will do it together.

Chapter 58

Carly drove the sedan into the parking lot and parked it next to the office door. She exited her car and surveyed the area. Finally, she saw Mickey emerge from a bay.

"Hi Carly," he called. "This is a surprise."

"Hi. Mickey. You're here alone again. It looks like you're running the place."

"Kind of. I mean...I'm here all the time. A couple of guys work part-time. It's just me much of the time. But hopefully it will be my place soon. I'm keeping my fingers crossed. So what can I do for you?"

"Well...I want to get my car checked out thoroughly. Paul will be tested to see if he is safe to drive. I want to make sure everything is working as it should. Can you check my car? Do you have time? I will understand if you can't do it. Or if you would prefer not to."

Mickey nodded. "Of course. You can count on me. Just because Greer and I aren't together anymore doesn't mean I should stop being your mechanic."

Carly exhaled. "Thank you. That's a relief. I didn't want to look for another mechanic. I trust you. Regardless of what happened between you and Greer, I'd like to continue to bring our car here."

"Yes, I would like that. Let me check my schedule." Mickey walked to the office and opened an appointment book containing handwritten entries. He saw a look of surprise envelop her face. He smiled. "Yes, I still do things by hand. I'm planning to upgrade our appointment system once I own this place. I have so many plans." He scanned the entries in the ledger. "I can get to your car tomorrow afternoon. Will that be okay?"

Carly opened her mouth to respond, but before her thoughts became words, Mickey added, "I'll tell you what. If you bring the car here in the morning, I can drive it back to your house tomorrow after I'm finished with it. I'm going to my brother's house for dinner. He lives about a half mile from you. I can drop off your car and walk to his house. He can drive me back to my place afterwards."

"Mickey, that's really nice. Are you sure it's not a problem? I can come to get the car."

"It's no problem at all. Assuming everything checks out on your car, I can bring it by."

"That would be wonderful. Thank you so much."

During the drive home, an idea formed in her brain. Carly wasn't one to interfere, but she decided to risk the consequences if her plan backfired. Once she arrived at the house, she sent a text, and awaited a response.

THE FOLLOWING MORNING, CARLY WOKE TO A CLOUDLESS SKY, and the local meteorologist promised sunshine and a light breeze with temperatures in the seventies. After leaving her car with Mickey, she started the mile-long walk to her home. It was the perfect time to stop at a farmers' market she loved but rarely patronized. Now, she perused the food items arrayed on pallets and aligned in baskets of various sizes and shapes. Carly purchased several pounds of tomatoes, ropes of sausage links, and packages of fresh linguine. She added a bottle of Zinfandel and two bottles of Cabernet Sauvignon to her shopping bag and exited the market. Carly wasn't certain if dinnertime would be fabulous or a failure. But if her plan was successful, one problem would disappear.

Chapter 59

A week had passed since his altercation with Stuart, and David was still miserable. His position on George's team felt increasingly like a demotion. Ben had given him a much wider berth in choosing his assignments. George was a micromanager; he gave his employees little freedom in the workplace. David crept out of the office at five before George could assign a last-minute assignment that couldn't possibly wait until the morning.

He arrived home to the aroma of garlic and onions, and found Heidi stirring a pot of chili on the stove. He kissed her on the cheek and wrapped his arms around her.

"Yum. It smells great."

"Thank you. I know how much you love chili. But dinner won't be ready for an hour. I wasn't sure what time you would be home. "

"That's fine. It's great to relax a little. I haven't done much of that lately."

"How was your day?"

"No huge disasters. I kept to myself most of the day. That's how George likes it. Minimal team interaction. Everyone gets their job. If a team member asks for help, people pitch in. But otherwise, we all work solo." David opened the refrigerator and retrieved a bottle of beer. He waved it in Heidi's direction. "Do you want me to open one for you?"

"No, honey. But thanks."

David took a sizable guzzle from the bottle. "I'm trying to make this work, but I'm growing more frustrated every day."

"I'm sorry things haven't improved. Um...I hate to ask. Have you heard anything about how Daphne is doing? Perhaps she'll fail miserably and you'll go back to leading the team."

"I'm grateful for your optimism. I've heard nothing, although I haven't asked around. The last thing I want to hear is that she's doing well. Sometimes I want to tell everyone about Stuart and Daphne. But I suspect many people know already."

David strolled to the wicker basket on the counter containing the day's mail. He perused the pile—mostly advertisements and bills and renewal notices for magazines and journals they had no intention of continuing. There, among the flyers and envelopes, was a brochure addressed to Heidi from a company specializing in LSAT study guides.

"Are you going to use this company to study for the LSAT?" he asked.

"I'm considering it. Their reviews are wonderful. I understand they're one of the best."

"I'm so happy you want to further your career. You'll be a brilliant lawyer."

"Thank you. But first I have to do well on the LSAT. Then get accepted to a decent law school. I'll have a lot of studying to do. So perhaps in four or five years..." Heidi sighed. "I know you will help, but I don't know how we can manage. I'm not sure I trust anyone with our children."

"We can hire someone else. Someone older. Not a college student with studying on her mind. Perhaps someone who is retired. And trustworthy. I can ask around at work and see if there are recommendations."

Heidi shook her head. "You weren't at the accident scene. I spoke with Matthew and Emily right after it happened. I was a wreck. It was hard for me to hold my emotions in check. I didn't want them to get more upset than they were. But I don't want to go through that again. Having them involved in an accident when I'm not there to comfort them. Last night I had a dream that Emily called me and I couldn't reach her. That's the third time this week I've had a dream involving the children. I don't know if I can leave their wellbeing in someone else's hands."

"Okay. I know the accident upset Matthew and Emily. And it's not just you. I also hugged them a little tighter that night. I still do. But we can't upend our lives because of this. We'll find someone else to help us. We'll do interviews. And background checks. The kids will be okay."

"No! I don't think so! I don't want to find anyone else. I can't imagine letting someone else be in charge of our children. We'll have to find another way."

"What other way? We have to work to pay our expenses. Have you forgotten that our monthly mortgage payment is more than what many people earn? And we have the car payments...and the cable...and the food...and our entertainment."

"David! Stop! I know all about our bills. I just think we have to find another way. Perhaps we should let Matthew and Emily ride the school bus. It might be better than telling them to walk home."

"Then they won't be able to do their other activities. We'd be asking them to give up the things they love. That's not fair."

Heidi was pensive. "Perhaps they can go with their friends."

"How are they going to get there? Are you planning to ask the parents of their friends to drive them? Isn't that the same? Asking someone else to assume responsibility for our children? That's the thing you are most worried about, isn't it? Another person driving them around. Someone else getting into an accident."

"Yes. You're right. I'm not thinking clearly." Heidi was sullen. "Perhaps I'll quit my job."

"No! You cannot quit your job! You have that backwards. We have to work more! Not less! We are barely treading water now." His face was crimson and contorted. "If you quit your job, then we'll have to give up something. Do you want to move to a smaller place?"

Over the years, Heidi had heard David rant and occasionally utter profanity, but she had rarely seen the physical characteristics of his ire. She trembled. *Have I touched upon something that's been brewing inside of him?* She willed herself to maintain calm.

"David, I know I need to work to maintain what we have. But I don't know if that's the best thing now. I think we should consider other options. That's all I'm trying to say."

"Really? You would give up our lifestyle? Is that what you're saying?"

"I always said I wouldn't give up any of this. But now I'm not so sure. I'm torn. I like my job. But if I'm going to go to law school, I can't see how I can do it all. I could walk away from my job, but then we'd have less income. Plus the cost of law school."

"It doesn't look like I'm on track for a promotion in the near future," David mumbled.

"I think we should look at the situation realistically," said Heidi. "Maybe I can go to school and work part-time. Perhaps I can do some work from home."

"Okay. That's not a great solution, but it may be the only one we have. Take the review class and the LSAT. If things haven't changed with my job by then, we should consider your idea."

Heidi wasn't certain she wanted David to agree, but she was happy his anger had abated and peace could prevail during their dinner.

Chapter 60

S he had set the dining room table for three, but Carly hoped there were four for dinner. Paul was reading a book, and the house was fairly tidy, although she couldn't guarantee there weren't specks of dust on the polished tabletops and in the corners of the rooms. Once she had children and a job outside the home, Carly had given up her goal of a perfectly clean house. She reasoned that no one really lived like that, except those with a daily cleaning service, which she and Paul could not afford and did not desire. The laundry was done and folded, the bathrooms cleaned, and the walkway to the house cleared of debris. The cleaning spree Carly had undertaken that day had tidied the house and tamed her anxiety.

Carly was relieved that Greer had agreed to have dinner with them. She hoped there was no repeat of the scene from their previous meal, and that their dinner was more relaxing, although she worried the conversation would sour if Mickey arrived at the house while Greer was present. Carly wasn't concerned about the cause of the estrangement, although it pained her to encourage Greer to reconcile with Mickey if he had caused the breakup. She shuddered to think Mickey might have been unfaithful or aggressive towards Greer. He didn't seem the type, although the guilty didn't usually wear shirts announcing their misdeeds. Carly had one goal for the evening —to disrupt the relationship between Greer and Brian, without compromising her secret.

Greer arrived at five o'clock, just as Carly began to prepare dinner. Carly heard her husband and daughter in the living room, laughing at something Paul had said. She hoped for a continuation of the peace and pleasantries. After a few minutes, Greer entered the kitchen and planted a kiss on her mother's cheek.

"How are you, honey?"

"I'm good. I wasn't sure you were here. The car is gone."

"I forgot to tell you. It's getting checked out. Your dad has a driving test scheduled. I want to make sure the car is in perfect working order. "

"That makes sense. It will be great if he can drive. He'll be more independent."

"It would be wonderful. He's looking forward to being able to leave the house on his own. He's not up to being out for long stretches, but if he wants to go out for a bit, it would be great to do that."

"I'm glad you're on top of things. And you're organized."

"Well, you know that I can't stand disorganization. What about you? Did you have a good day at work?" asked Carly, desperate to steer the conversation away from the car.

Greer smiled. "It was fine. Uneventful. But yesterday, a guy who reports to me really messed up the information about an ambulance trip. He never asked how much the patient weighed. I sent two women to take the patient from the hospital to a nursing facility. One of the women weighs about ninety pounds. But the patient being transported weighed about four hundred pounds. The women couldn't move him. And the gurney couldn't support that much weight. The other crews were busy. I estimated it would be a couple of hours before another crew was available. The hospital social worker called the nursing facility and said the patient would be late, but the facility wouldn't accept the patient after four o'clock. I had to plead with them to take the patient later than they wanted. I sent them a fruit basket as a thank you."

"Wow! Good job! It seems like they picked the right person to supervise."

"Thanks Mom. I like my job. It's interesting work. I get a little taste of the medical stuff, too."

"That's great, honey." Carly piled the dinner onto a serving platter. "Please tell your father we are ready to eat."

When Greer left the kitchen, Carly glanced at the clock: 5:30. She hoped Mickey arrived soon. Perhaps not too soon, as she wanted to enjoy dinner before the arguments or animosity spoiled the ambiance.

THE CONVERSATION WAS LIGHT AND THERE WAS AMPLE LAUGHTER and murmurs of reminiscence about family vacations and Greer's childhood antics. Then the doorbell rang.

"I wonder who that is," said Paul, turning to Carly. "Are you expecting anyone?"

Carly sped to the living room and tried to act surprised when she opened the door.

"Oh! Hi, Mickey! Thank you so much for bringing my car back. You have great timing. We are just finishing dinner. Would you like something to eat?"

Greer was already on her feet when Mickey and Carly entered the dining room. Carly hoped her daughter's sour expression was annoyance, but the words that spilled from her mouth reeked of anger.

"Mom! I can't believe you! So Mickey is the mechanic who was checking out the car! I can forgive you for that. But it's obvious you planned to have him bring the car back today. While I'm here. How could you?" Greer snarled and pushed past her mother. It surprised Carly that Greer didn't address her anger at Mickey. She seemed to ignore him completely.

"Greer! I'm so sorry. Okay. I won't deny it. I admit I planned this!" Carly cried. "But I just wanted to get you and Mickey in the same room." She had never seen Greer so angry; her face was flaming and contorted, and her hands trembled. Mickey clenched his fists, his gaze alternating between Carly and Greer. Finally, he faced Greer and broke the silence.

"I think I'd better leave. Greer, I'm sorry about what happened between us. I had no idea you would be here when I agreed to bring the car back. Perhaps I should have suspected something."

To Carly's delight, Mickey's apology caused Greer's face to relax immediately. *Perhaps there is hope for this encounter. Maybe if I keep quiet, Mickey and Greer will have a civilized conversation. Maybe more.*

As if Greer could sense her mother's thoughts, she faced Mickey and spoke. "I believe you. I know you better than that." She touched his arm. "You're not the type to be part of a scheme."

Mickey smiled. "Thank you, Greer. Uh...Perhaps we could have a few words in private." He turned towards the living room. "Can we talk in here?"

. . .

HOURS LATER, GREER LAY AWAKE, AWAY FROM THE BED WHERE SHE had spent the last month. Mickey was snoring softly beside her. She wanted to stay angry at her mother, but the ploy to reunite Mickey and her had worked. It was premeditated, but not pretty. Once out of her parents' prying ears and eyes, Mickey had tearily apologized for acting in haste. He said he understood Greer was now in a relationship with another man, and although he could accept it, the thought of her being in another man's arms tore him apart. Greer recalled how shocked Mickey looked when she told him Brian was just a friend, that she was sleeping in a spare bedroom. When she revealed to Mickey that she and Brian had spent their day together at an exposition for physical therapists, he kneeled, begged for forgiveness, and pleaded with her to take him back, confessing his stupidity for making assumptions about her cheating and professing his love for her. Normally eschewing public displays of affection, Greer didn't know and didn't care whether her parents had seen the spectacle.

After they said goodbye to her parents, she and Mickey had gone to a coffee shop and talked about the exposition and her job promotion. Mickey sent a text to his brother that he wasn't coming for dinner as planned. They talked for hours over two cups of coffee and a piece of carrot cake. He told her how close he was to being the owner of the garage. Then Mickey asked Greer to come back with him, to share the apartment, to be a couple again. Greer had agreed, and they had left the coffee shop and walked the mile to the garage, arm in arm, then climbed into his car for the drive to the apartment. Their apartment. The apartment cluttered with his belongings, the possessions she had left behind, the furniture and accessories and kitchen appliances they had bought together.

Greer smiled. They had barely made it through the

entryway of the apartment before they fell amidst the living room clutter of empty takeout food containers and plastic grocery bags and unopened mail piled atop the coffee table and spilling onto the couch. It was there that they rekindled their connection. There had been no one else for either of them. They cemented the relationship that had almost gotten away.

ACROSS TOWN, HOURS AFTER THE ANGER AND TEARS HAD subsided, Carly lay in bed awake. Although she wasn't happy with the way she had handled the situation with Mickey and Greer, the results were as she had hoped. If Greer and Brian had been a couple, they were no more. Carly had avoided spying on Mickey and Greer in the living room, but her mood had brightened when the pair spoke no angry words and came to an understanding that their relationship was worth salvaging. She surmised Greer would be appropriately angry with the interference in her life, but Carly had done what many mothers would do to protect their child's interests. She had hatched and executed a plan to get two young people back together. It had been successful, and her daughter was back in the arms of the man she loved.

Of course, the biggest beneficiary of Greer and Mickey's reconciliation was Carly. But no one else knew that.

Chapter 61

The light from Brian's laptop cast a glow over the corner of the living room he had arranged as an office. Although the apartment contained two bedrooms and two bathrooms and there was ample kitchen space for seating and cabinets, the main living area was smaller than he would have liked, but overall, he had more space than a single man living alone required. The furniture was basic but well-made; his belongings were organized and free of clutter. Mimi had nearly convinced him to convert the extra bedroom into an office, but she was gone now, and with it his thoughts of redecorating. He glanced at the navy sweatpants and T-shirt he had retrieved from the bottom of his closet the evening before; they were leftovers from his college days. The two days of stubble on his cheeks and chin were an anomaly, too. He usually cared more about his appearance, even if he was home alone and without expectations of leaving his apartment or welcoming visitors.

The melancholy had enveloped him two evenings before, when Greer had texted him to say she and Mickey had reconciled, and she was moving back to the apartment they had shared. She thanked him for letting her stay in his apartment, and for respecting her privacy by not asking about the events surrounding the split from Mickey. Brian responded that he was happy for their reconciliation, so the gloom that descended upon him the next morning was uncharacteristic and unexpected. At first he surmised that the lethargy blanketing his body was a virus or a case of exhaustion, and the previous day he had called out sick from work—something he had done only once in four years of employment. But today his body felt no worse, and he had ridden his bicycle ten miles on a trail near his home. He felt stronger after the ride, but his mood was worse. Upon his return home, Brian opened the hall closet for a towel, but the shelf was empty. It was then that he recalled the two extra bath towels in the other bathroom—the one Greer had used. The barrage of tears that began when he stepped onto the tiled floor shook him to his core. He dropped to the floor and sobbed, realizing what he didn't have. An intelligent and decent-looking guy—he'd heard some women describe him as handsome, but he didn't want to assume everyone thought so—in his mid-thirties, and in a marvelous profession, earning a decent salary. He had a wonderful family—an adoptive family—parents who had raised him well, a sister he adored. *I should be happy.* Mimi was the first woman he had considered marrying. He had secretly looked at engagement rings and had set some money aside for a purchase. But she had broken off their relationship, and in removing her belongings from his apartment had withdrawn his best hopes for a family of his own. Perhaps a small part of him had hoped that Greer would become his partner, his soul mate, the mother of his children. He could deny that he had thought of her that way, but he felt the heat rise in his face; he had wondered more than once what would happen if she abandoned the bed across the hallway and climbed into his. If he was honest, perhaps he had hoped it would happen. She was an attractive woman, although younger than he usually liked, and he was a man, and he doubted he would have refused her advances.

But finding a woman to marry and bear his children was only part of the equation. *I am likely near the middle of my life. If I am fortunate, I will remain healthy and live into my eighties.* Although he was looking for someone with whom to share the second half of his life, he recognized it was the unknown beginning causing him angst. He desperately wanted to learn the circumstances of his birth and the reasons for the adoption.

Brian showered, and armed with a growing determination and direction, he retrieved the copy of his birth certificate from the papers piled next to his laptop. He entered his mother's name in the search engine, as he had done dozens of times in the previous weeks. *Carlotta Casperella.* The search returned thousands of names that included Carlotta or Casperella, or variations of both. But in the hundreds of links he had clicked on since his search began, he had found no one with the name matching his birth certificate. Although he hated to think his mother had died at a young age, he had checked death notices, but that search also turned up nothing. At least he knew she was likely alive. He was more determined than ever to leave no stone uncovered in the search for his mother.

After more than a hundred clicks on links that provided no answers, Brian found an entry that caused him to sit a little straighter in his chair, rub his eyes, and peer again at the computer screen. A three-paragraph article from a college newspaper, *The Word*, identified the author as Carlotta Casperella. Brian thought his eyes and brain were playing tricks on his weary body. But the school was real—Northern Virginia

College—and the date of the article was seven months before his birth. Brian scoured the college's website and alumni listings for any additional information about this woman, but there was none. Her name did not appear on other newspaper articles, and she was not among the lists of alumni.

Aided by several cups of coffee, an array of snacks and finger foods, and a glimmer of hope, Brian spent the rest of the morning and the entire afternoon searching the internet. He rose from his chair only to use the toilet, refill his mug with coffee, or stretch his stiffened muscles. He had neglected to open the shades that covered the large window, the focal point of the space, so he missed the sunshine casting shadows on the winter day, and the beginning of the sunset that plunged the area into semi-darkness before many had finished their commute from work. His eyes grew weary, and his resolve threatened to break. Still, he soldiered on.

With his brain foggy and his sanity in question, the words blurred on the computer screen. He rose from the chair, buried his face in his hands, and sobbed. It was a catharsis of the disappointments that had shattered his peaceful existence— not only his inability to locate his mother, but the breakup of his relationship with Mimi, which he had never fully addressed. The tears cleansed his soul and cleared his mind. The fogginess lifted, and he returned to his seat to continue his search.

A thought appeared, and he leaned forward in the chair, excited to explore a new angle. Since Carlotta hadn't graduated from Northern Virginia College, he wondered why she had given him up for adoption. It would make sense if she had dropped out of school to raise him, but that had not happened. It seemed she left college before he was born, and did not return. *Why would she have done that?* He stood again and trod back and forth along the short-pile beige carpet that covered the living area. He tried to think like a detective, wondering how Sherlock Holmes, Jacques Clouseau, and Sam Spade would solve this case. *A young woman attending college was pregnant. The woman had a baby. The woman did not return to college.* Then a thought came to mind. She had not returned to this college, but perhaps she transferred to another college.

Brian searched the internet for other colleges in the area with degrees in writing or journalism, although it was certainly possible that she might have transferred to another college or university and changed her field of study. Perhaps Carlotta chose not to continue in the literary field. *But if she transferred to another college, why wasn't she listed elsewhere on the internet?* He stopped again to contemplate this. He thought of his sister's friend Allison, who became pregnant after a drunken one-night stand. Although she was committed to having the baby and surrendering it for adoption, Allison had been distraught about being drunk and having minimal recall of the guy who had fathered her child at a party.

So distraught that she moved to another city. And changed her name.

His pulse quickening, Brian compiled a list of colleges with degrees in a literary field that were within 150 miles of Northern Virginia College. He tried to calm his nerves. If she had changed her name, there was no guarantee the new name bore any relationship to her birth name. Brian glanced at the clock on the computer screen: 9:30. Nearly eleven hours had passed since his search began that morning. Exhausted a few hours before, his body and mind now infused with fresh energy, he wouldn't quit and couldn't stop.

Brian identified the colleges in the radius he sought, then eliminated those without degrees in writing or journalism.

Although it was possible the young woman who birthed him had changed her field of study, he would assume she had not. Brian searched the archives of school newspapers, yearbooks, and magazines. He perused lists of alumni and their reunions and donations. He examined pictures of every female who would have attended the schools in the few years after his birth.

It was a writer's name on an article on the front page of *The Pulse*, a newspaper published by Central Virginia University, that caught his attention. His mouth spewed the words before his brain reconciled what he had seen. "Carly Casper."

Blanketed in chills, his body trembled, and he dropped his head between his knees to stop the room from spinning. Although he was certain he was staring at proof of his heritage, he searched the list of graduates. The grainy black-and-white photograph was not clear or flattering enough to use in a byline or as a headshot, but it was all the proof he needed. The name change made perfect sense. *I would have made a terrible detective. I can't believe I missed the clues.* Emotions flooded his body. He wanted to cry with relief and with anger. His search was complete. There was no need to look for a current address or search social media accounts. The picture was clearly his mother. And he knew where to find her.

Carly Casper. She was a journalist. And Paul's wife.

Chapter 62

It was likely their new normal, a state Carly had not understood until now. Paul could climb stairs to their second floor, although his trips upstairs occurred less often and required exquisite care and Carly's supervision. But he and Carly were sharing a bedroom again. Sleeping together again should have brought comfort. Carly was sure it was that way for Paul. Thrilled to regain some independence and intimacy, he reached for her frequently when they lay together in their king-sized bed. Carly hadn't expected bliss. That was for new relationships or newlyweds. She had anticipated comfort, and perhaps serenity. But it was anxiety that filled her body when she lay beside her husband now. The trembling she felt when his body brushed hers was not of a familiar sexual nature—it was fear that he would learn of her betrayal. The panic and apprehension overwhelmed her. *If he knew the truth, he would no longer choose to be close to me.*

Unable to sleep, heart racing, she stood from the bed. Paul was snoring softly. She didn't want to wake him; he deserved a restful sleep. Carly retrieved her tablet from the top of the dresser. Normally feeling relaxed and peaceful sitting in the flowered Queen Anne chair that had belonged to her mother, now she was powerless to extinguish the raging turbulence in her body and mind. Carly located a novel she had been reading, but was unable to immerse herself in the story. She abandoned the novel for a magazine. Perhaps she could concentrate on the short stories. But that didn't work either. As a journalist, she had learned to decipher passages quickly and thoroughly, but if questioned about what she had read in the previous ten minutes, she would have failed. She rose from the chair and trod lightly past Paul to the doorway.

Just then, Paul fell with a thump onto the floor.

"Paul! Oh my God! Are you hurt?" Carly cried, as she scurried around the bottom of the bed to where Paul lay on the floor.

He looked at Carly and sighed. "I was dreaming. It was so realistic. You and I were walking along the beach, hand in hand. I saw the waves rippling through the ocean. I felt the cool water spilling on my toes. We ran into the waves, giggling like teenagers. We must have been newlyweds. Not middle-aged like now. Then I said I had to use the bathroom. I stepped from the water onto the sand." Paul studied his aging body and missing limb. "I guess I forgot I couldn't just stand up and walk, like before." He grasped the bed frame, and with Carly's help, stood and pivoted onto the bed.

"In your dream you were walking on two legs. I can understand why you forgot you couldn't. Dreams are often unrealistic," murmured Carly. She handed him his walker, watched him saunter to the bathroom, and waited for his return. When he was safely in bed, Carly reached for her robe from the back of the door and grabbed her tablet from the table.

"If you're okay, I'm going to head downstairs and read a bit."

Paul glanced at the clock illuminating his bedside. "Carly, it's only five o'clock. Why are you up so early? Are you having trouble sleeping?"

"Yes, honey. I'm sorry. I can't sleep. Before you fell, I was heading downstairs."

"You've been up early a lot. It seems like it's happening more often."

"I didn't realize you had noticed. I've tried to be quiet."

"You have been quiet. But I can sense your movements. My hearing is better than yours, too. I hear even slight activity."

"I'm sorry. I certainly didn't want to wake you. You need your rest."

Paul positioned himself upright in bed. "What's the matter? You don't usually lose sleep over something trivial. There's obviously something eating at you. Do you want to talk about it?"

"Uh...I don't know."

"You don't know if you want to tell me what's bothering you? That sounds like you're hiding something."

Carly trembled with the realization that denial of her problem was no longer acceptable or appropriate. *I have to tell him!* Her mouth opened, but no words came forth.

"Carly, honey. What is it? You can tell me anything. We have been through so much together. You have been a rock. I don't know what I would have done without your support. So tell me. What is bothering you? What has kept you from sleeping?" he implored.

Carly inhaled, hoping the increased oxygenation would strengthen her entire body. "I need to ask you something. I know you and Brian are really close now. Do you...?" She paused, hoping for the power to continue.

"Do I what?"

"You said Brian was adopted and that he has his birth certificate with his mother's name."

"Yes. But you can't possibly be losing sleep worrying about Brian's mother's name!"

Paul peered into Carly's eyes, barely visible in the clock's glow. But the dim light showed him enough. He could easily read her expression. "Carly. What are you trying to tell me? Do you know who his mother is?"

The reality of her expression collided with the recollection of what Brian had told him. Paul grasped the side of the mattress to keep from falling. "Oh, my God! Brian said his mother's name was Carlotta. We wondered if her friends called her Carly."

Carly had a sudden urge to run, but dizziness and nausea blanketed her, and she took several deep breaths to ward off the feelings.

"I remember now. You said your birth name was Carlotta," Paul whispered.

He turned towards Carly, hoping and expecting she would deny the connection, but her look of dismay confirmed he was correct. Then the sobbing began, and a gush of tears flooded her face.

"I'm...so...sorry. It was his eyes. His eyes told me."

"But his eyes aren't the same color as yours. Yours are different. So they must be..."

"Brian has his father's eyes," Carly blurted. The voice that spoke the words couldn't be hers; it seemed to come from elsewhere. Grappling with her tremulous and tortured body, Carly stood and faced Paul, whose face was unreadable. "I'm...so sorry. I was young. And in college. I made a mistake. I never wanted you to know."

"You never wanted me to know that you had a baby by another man? That you gave up a son?" he bellowed.

"No! I tried so hard to forget what happened. To forget I had a baby before I met you!"

Tension hung in the air and threatened to suffocate Carly. With her heart racing and bile rising to her throat, she gasped for breath.

"Who else knows?" stammered Paul. "How many people have kept a secret for you?"

"Just one. My friend Amy. Brian's father knew I was pregnant. But I never contacted him after the birth."

"What about your mother? She must have known."

Painstakingly, Carly chronicled the details of her relationship with Nathaniel, the discovery of her pregnancy, Nathaniel's betrayal, and her decision to hide the truth from her mother. Her name change. The real reason she transferred colleges. The details spilled from her mouth, as if a dam had burst, the contents rushing in a flourish. She held nothing back. She told Paul all of her heartbreak and fears held inside for decades. When Carly had exhausted her body and soul, she stood from the bed and locked eyes with Paul.

"I won't blame you if you are disappointed. Or if you hate me. After all, I pretended that the pregnancy with David was my first. I didn't lie to you. But I omitted a major part of my life. I should have told you. I wanted to tell you. But I was so afraid to mess things up between us. You were so different from my previous relationship. You are kind and caring. As our relationship grew, I realized what love really was. I hadn't been in love before. I pretended I was. After all, what eighteen-year-old female wouldn't pretend to love her college professor, especially when he said he'd leave his fiancee for her? You showed me what love really is. And how good marriage could be."

Paul was silent. Carly started towards the bedroom door. Her secret was out. She had told him everything. Unlike a movie where one could rewind and replay the scene, or fast forward through undesirable parts, she would have to live with the repercussions. Even if it meant the end of her marriage and estrangement from her children.

"Carly." Paul grasped her arm. "We've spent years building a wonderful life for ourselves. So I guess I can understand why you didn't tell me. But I wish you had."

As the first glimmers of sun rose over the horizon, Carly spoke. "When we first met...I was afraid to tell you. I worried you would run. I couldn't risk it. Later, I thought you would be angry that I had kept it from you. It was easier to keep the information to myself. I didn't want you to hate me. I didn't want to lose what I had."

"I could never hate you. I admit I am disappointed. I wish you had told me years ago about your son. About Brian. I wouldn't have thought less of you. I would have thought you were remarkably brave for an eighteen-year-old. To have a professor treat you like that. He's the one I might hate. But never you."

Tears flooded Carly's cheeks and spilled onto her robe. But unlike the torrent of tears minutes before, this cascade was born of relief. Her secret was out. Paul didn't plan to end their marriage. He understood.

"Oh, Paul," she cried. "I am so sorry I kept this from you. I wanted to tell you so many times. But I couldn't find the words. After a while it was easier to keep my secret."

"I understand. But it must have been so difficult. Like on his birthday."

"You have no idea how hard it was. Every year his birthday... August third...was a day I would have liked to celebrate. Instead it was a day I dreaded. I wished him a happy birthday but couldn't celebrate with him. I wondered if he was happy. If he had a good life. If he knew of his adoption."

"I can't imagine what that was like for you."

"I took comfort in my wonderful life. With you and David and Greer. Our marriage. My career. That's what I focused on."

"So your mother never knew? You never told her she had another grandchild?"

Carly sighed. "I regret withholding the information from her almost as much as I regret hiding it from you. But I couldn't handle the disappointment I expected to receive from her. Pregnant at eighteen. Knocked up by a college professor. She would have been so ashamed to tell her friends. I couldn't do that to her."

"I'm sorry. But perhaps you were wrong. Maybe once she saw her grandson, she would have tried to convince you to keep him. Did you consider doing that? Raising him on your own?"

"I considered it. But it was obvious I would not get any support from...his father. Not without going through the courts. I didn't want to put myself through that. Even after what he did, I remained idealistic. But more than that was the realization that I would have to give up my dream of being a writer. Well... being an educated writer. I didn't want to raise my child in a tiny apartment making minimum wage in a job I hated. It wouldn't have been fair to him."

"It seems like he has had a good life. And he's a wonderful man."

"Yes, that he is. I have wondered how he was doing for all of these years. But now I know. I'm happy now. I know I made the right decision."

"Now I understand why you were avoiding him. And why

you went on an errand every time he was here for my therapy. But is his eye color so rare that you knew he was yours?"

"The eye color is rare. I thought he probably was my son. But I couldn't be certain. Perhaps he was a distant relative. Not Nathaniel's son. Not my son. But Nathaniel was an only child. I hoped the whole thing was a mistake. A small part of me wanted Brian's mother's name to be Lucy or Mary or Veronica. Anything but Carlotta."

"I understand. So now that you know he's yours, you can tell him."

Carly trembled. "Yes. Now I can tell him. Now that I know he has been looking for me. We can put an end to my agony. And his."

"When do you want to do that? I suppose you want to do it in person. Don't you?"

"I hadn't thought that far. My biggest concern was telling you. I couldn't go any further until you knew."

"Okay. Now I know. And even more...I forgive you for not telling me sooner about him."

"Oh, Paul. You don't know how much that means to me. I was a mess inside. I couldn't sleep."

"I knew that you weren't sleeping well. But now I know why. Just think about how you want to tell Brian. Do you want to invite him here? I can call him and ask him to come over. I'll tell him it's related to my therapy. I can fabricate a story."

"Let me think about that." Carly rose from the bed and took Paul's hands in hers. "Paul, I don't know why I doubted you. I love you."

Remembering their beginnings as a couple, Paul smiled. "I have loved you since our first date. If I remember correctly, it took me some time to tell you. I finally realized how special you were, and that I didn't want to lose you. We've been through a lot together. I have no regrets."

"Me neither. I love our life together."

"Obviously, we will never know what your life would have been like if you had raised Brian yourself. But we probably would never have met. We wouldn't have this life together."

"I've thought about that so many times over the years. It's often what kept me going. Knowing that if I had kept Brian, I might not have had you. Or David and Greer."

Paul smiled and kissed Carly's hand. "Let's talk more downstairs. Let's have breakfast. I'm suddenly starving."

Chapter 63

G reer couldn't keep from smiling. It seemed as if her life had turned around in an instant. She and Mickey had reconciled, and their relationship was better than it had ever been. He was more attentive, and had surprised her with roses the previous evening. Greer had opened her mouth to protest the expenditure—he had nearly enough money for a down payment on the garage and she didn't want him to splurge on flowers—but Mickey had covered her mouth with a passionate kiss that ended her attempts to argue.

He had told her how proud he was of her job promotion, especially since she had been working there barely a year. Greer said she liked the increased job responsibilities, but she really wanted to study physical therapy. She showed him the pamphlets from the expo, and Mickey again apologized for thinking she was cheating on him. Since he had worked sixty hours that week, Greer had expected him to go to sleep after dinner, but Mickey sat beside her as she compared the programs: the application process, the types of degrees conferred, the credits given, the costs, the distance from home, the prerequisites. Then Greer showed him information from Human Resources confirming that she would be eligible for a grant to defray the tuition costs. She did not realize how excited she was about her career choice until Mickey stopped while chewing his food and stared at her.

"What's the matter?" she had inquired.

"I've never seen you this excited. Not even when I brought you flowers."

"I love the flowers. Although I want you to save your money for bigger and better things."

"Greer. Your smile is a mile wide. You're smart and detail oriented. You care about people. I know you'll make a great therapist."

A ring from her desk phone brought Greer back to the present. She spoke with Nolan, a new employee who needed help to arrange ambulance transports to a physician's office on a recurring basis. She showed Nolan how to schedule the transports and returned to her desk.

The rest of the day passed uneventfully. Greer left work and headed for home. She planned a quick meal of soup and a sandwich for dinner, as Mickey was working late again, so when she arrived home, she was astonished to see Mickey's car in his designated parking spot. He rarely left work early; Greer wondered if he was sick or had sustained an injury at work. After securing her bicycle, she hurried into their apartment, expecting to see Mickey reclined on the couch holding a heating pad or ice pack against his body. Instead, he stood in the kitchen wearing a navy suit, white shirt, and striped tie, clutching a bottle of white wine in one hand and a corkscrew in the other. He strode to the table, adorned with a white linen tablecloth and napkins, and two matching place settings, complete with wine glasses. Greer's mouth was agape.

"What...is going on? What's all this? Why are you home so early?"

Mickey placed the bottle of wine in a makeshift ice bucket on the table. He took Greer's hands in his.

"This, my dear, is to celebrate the beginning of the rest of our lives." Then he handed her an envelope. Hands trembling, she broke the seal and removed the single sheet of paper that lay within.

Greer's eyes widened as she perused the words on the paper. "Oh, my God! You got approval for the mortgage for the garage! You can buy it! It will be yours!"

As they danced throughout the tiny kitchen and into the living area, Mickey held her hand as she twirled on her tiptoes, reminiscent of her childhood days practicing ballet moves with the other five-year-olds in dance class.

"I love you so much," Mickey murmured into her ear. "I wish it could be like this forever."

"You look so handsome in that suit." Greer beamed. "Just wait. Don't move. I'll be right back," she announced, as she headed towards the bedroom. It took only a minute or two to find what she wanted from her closet, and when she returned wearing a black mini-dress and heels, Mickey nodded his approval.

"You look even more beautiful than usual," he whispered. "As if that's even possible."

Then, though Greer would have claimed the day couldn't get any better, it did. Mickey pulled a small box from his jacket pocket and kneeled beside her.

"Will you marry me?" he asked, his eyes glistening and his smile larger than ever.

"I don't believe it! Yes! Yes! Of course I will marry you!" Greer cried, as Mickey opened the box and removed a ring with a basic gold band and a round diamond in the center. He placed it on the fourth finger of her left hand as she cried tears of joy.

"It's beautiful!"

"It's only half a carat. I wish it was bigger. I wanted to buy a full carat, but I needed the money for the down payment. I wanted to get the mortgage approval now. I heard rates are rising and didn't want to wait."

"How were you able to do all of this? Save money for the ring and qualify for a mortgage?"

"I've been working a lot. When you left, I was barely here. I slept at the garage some nights. And I saved as much as I could."

Greer draped her arms around Mickey's shoulders and nuzzled his neck. "I'm so lucky to have you," she murmured.

"It's me who is lucky. I was such an idiot. I nearly threw this all away. I jumped to conclusions. And I almost lost you. If it hadn't been for your mother—"

But Greer didn't let him finish. She smothered his mouth with kisses.

They sat together, drinking wine and dining on perfectly cooked and seasoned ahi tuna and rice pilaf, planning the next chapter of their lives. Not until much later did Greer realize that Mickey was right. She had always hated when her mother meddled in her life. But this time, her mother had interfered at exactly the right time.

Chapter 64

Although exhausted, Brian couldn't sleep, his emotions wavering from ecstasy and exuberance to agony and anguish. Overnight, he had spent hours exploring the reasons for his ambivalence. *I should be elated to realize my mother has been living less than an hour's drive from me for several years.* For most of the night he had fought the urge to drive to her house, to the home she shared with his patient. He imagined running through the front door and past the powder room, ignoring Paul, who was likely on the couch in the living room, and throwing his arms around Carly, showering her with hugs and kisses. It would be the beginning of the rest of their lives. No longer would she be the wife of his patient—they would be mother and son. But each time this impulse came, the logical part of his psyche, the fragment that kept him organized and grounded, warned him the behavior could cause more grief.

Carly had changed her name and switched colleges after he was born. Logic told him she had wanted to forget that part of her life. She had married and had two more children. She wrote articles for the newspaper. He had paid little attention to her newspaper work before meeting her, but during the night hours, sitting at his computer, he had read several years' worth of her articles. Her work was good, and she had quite a following. He agonized over whether he should approach her. *Does she want to know I am her son? I suspect Greer and David don't know they have a half-sibling. I wonder whether Paul knows.* Paul had told Brian that he and Carly had met in their twenties. According to his birth certificate, Carly was barely nineteen when he was born. *Has she ever told Paul she had another child, one she had given up for adoption in her teens?*

Even if Paul was privy to Carly's secret, it seemed likely that he did not know Brian was the son she had relinquished. *I wonder if Carly knows.* Perhaps that was the reason she had avoided him. He had heard that a mother always knew her baby's cry or her child's voice, even in a crowded playground or store. But he was a few days old the last time she had laid eyes on him, when he had left the hospital in the arms of his adoptive parents. They had told him the story so many times that he could visualize the lawyer and the social worker collecting the official paperwork in a manila folder as his mother dressed him in an outfit purchased in the infants department minutes before the department store closed the previous evening. According to his parents, the phone call announcing they had a son came at 7:13, just after dinner. They left the food-caked dishes and utensils in the sink and drove to the mall for the necessities: a bassinet, changing table, infant bathtub, diapers, bottles, and enough clothing to last a week. It wasn't until his mother reviewed the hospital paperwork two weeks later that she noticed he had weighed seven pounds thirteen ounces at birth. An omen for sure, she had thought.

Does my desire for a relationship with my birth mother overrule her desire for privacy and confidentiality? What if she doesn't know I am her son? What if Paul knows little about Carly's life before he met her? Will I destroy her life in an attempt to make mine whole? Brian shook his head. He was a peacemaker. He could never intentionally hurt her, or act selfishly and cause her unhappiness or harm.

Minutes later, he realized that it was he who would suffer if he didn't act, if he didn't claim Carly as his mother. *I have to reach out to her. If she doesn't want to maintain a relationship with me, I'll have to live with that. At least I'll know.* Brian decided to speak directly with Carly without involving Paul. He scrolled through the names and numbers in his cell phone contacts. He had Carly's number in a note under Paul's contact information.

Now that he planned to reach out to her, Brian just had to gather the courage to do so.

Chapter 65

After several days of gray skies and cool temperatures, Heidi and David were seated on their porch enjoying the sunshine and warm breezes, when a phone call interrupted their lunch. When David's phone rang, to Heidi's surprise, he glanced at the display, mouthed an apology to her, and left the room with the phone to his ear. He returned about ten minutes later, as Heidi was clearing the lunch dishes from the table.

"Sorry for the interruption," he murmured. "But I'm glad I answered the phone. I had a feeling I should. I can't explain it."

"Okay. It's unusual that you take a call during a meal. So tell me. Who was on the phone?"

"It was Aaron. One of my friends from college. You may remember him."

"I think so. Tall. Dark curly hair. Very personable."

David recalled Aaron had always been a hit with the ladies, who considered the combination of height and curls and personality irresistible. "Yes. That's him."

"Does he still live on the east coast?"

"Yes. In Delaware. He works for a big firm there. Well, it started as a small firm. They manage the technology for several medical practices. He was one of the first employees. The company has taken on dozens of new clients in the past few years. Since most practices use electronic medical records, they've been at the forefront of new technology for quite a while."

"If he's been there so long, he must be happy there."

"Aaron says it's a really good firm." David paused, planning his next words. "He called to tell me the company is expanding again. They're on a hiring binge. He basically offered me a job. As a supervisor."

"Really? A supervisor? Without an interview?"

"The offer is contingent upon a satisfactory interview. But with my education and background, Aaron assumes I'll wow them. He apparently has been singing my praises for years. Now his bosses are listening."

Heidi tried to process what she was hearing. *Is David really considering a job change and a move to the east coast?* "What did you tell him?" she asked tentatively, afraid of getting her hopes up.

"Heidi. Honey. Look, honestly...he's tried to get me to move back there for years. I always cut him off without hearing the entire pitch. But this time I let him tell me more about the company. And I have to tell you, it sounds like an interesting job."

"Wow. I see a glint in your eyes that hasn't been there for months. Delaware. That's near your family. Right?"

"Well, kind of. It's not in their backyard. But within a couple of hours' drive. Certainly much easier than flying across the country and dealing with a three-hour time change. We've talked about how the cost of living is much lower. Housing is much cheaper. And gasoline." David chuckled. "Of course, almost every place is less expensive than here. Delaware is close to Philadelphia. So there are a lot of cultural opportunities. And many excellent schools. And there's no sales tax in Delaware."

"Really? That's a bonus. But did you discuss salary?"

David sighed. "Well, not specifically. But Aaron said he lives well and has saved quite a bit. His wife works part-time at a non-profit, so it's likely she doesn't earn much. But if they can live well and still save money."

Heidi grinned. "It sounds like an opportunity worth exploring."

"Really? So you would consider moving? You're okay with packing up our stuff and moving across the country? Leaving our friends here? We've talked about it before. We always said we wouldn't do it."

"David. Yes. I would consider it. Neither of us wanted to move before. We were happy here. I love our house. We have wonderful friends. Matthew and Emily are doing well in school. But you are miserable in your job. And I want to go to school. I still don't know how I would work and go to law school. If I'm fortunate enough to get into one. I thought there was no way I could give up my salary and pay for law school. And there's still the issue with transportation for Matthew's and Emily's activities. I've been searching social media sites but have found no one that I'd consider interviewing. I looked at after-school programs. But that would mean an end to their outside activities. At least the afternoon ones. Perhaps I'm just anxious now. But if the cost of living is so much lower there, perhaps I can quit my job. We can sell our house here for a nice profit. That can pay for law school."

"It might work. We can be near my family, too. My mom and dad will love it. Greer too."

"I'm sure they would love it if we live closer. It will be good for Matthew and Emily, too. They can bond with their grandparents and aunt a little better."

"Okay." David removed the cell phone from his pocket. "It's settled. I'll send a text to Aaron. I'll let him know I'm interested in the position. I'll set up an interview. If I'm offered the job, we'll decide whether to move."

Chapter 66

B rian awoke early, after the best night's sleep in days. Although he hadn't yet confronted Carly, just knowing he had located his birth mother, and that she lived so close to him, had resulted in better sleep than the Melatonin tablets he had taken the previous few nights. He had a scheduled day off of work, and he knew exactly how he wanted to spend it. After coffee, a banana, and a bagel, he dressed and grabbed his car keys from the hook by the front door. He strolled down the steps to the driveway and entered his car. Hands trembling, it took several attempts to insert the key into the ignition. He thought of the words he told his clients when anticipating an anxiety-producing situation: *Take a few deep breaths. Clear your mind of everything else. You can do this.*

After about five minutes, with his hands steady and his mind clear, he drove out of the parking space and started for his destination. Despite his decision the previous evening to speak with Carly via phone, he had decided to confront her in person. It was risky, but he would pour his energy into everything he could in a single attempt. If he failed, he could destroy her happiness, her family's, and his own. Paul might request a different therapist, and Greer could decide to abandon her aspirations of becoming a physical therapist. However, Brian considered that the potential rewards—a relationship with his birth mother and her family—far outweighed the risk.

Brian parked his car on the street, in front of a neighbor's house, and walked the length of two houses to his destination. His heart pounding furiously in his chest and his breathing rapid, he ducked behind a car in the driveway to calm himself. He chuckled. *It'll be just my luck that someone calls the police because they think I'm going to rob the house.* Counting to ten, he emerged from his hiding place and crisscrossed the property to the front door. He rang the bell and heard footsteps approaching. He couldn't see his reflection, but imagined his face was devoid of color. And then the door opened, and he was looking into his birth mother's eyes.

"Brian! How are you? What brings you here today?" Carly smiled and opened the door to greet him.

Brian was happy for the warm welcome. He wasn't certain, but he thought she looked at him differently. At least she hadn't turned away this time.

"Carly," Brian sputtered, "how are you? I...uh...wanted to see how Paul is doing."

Carly motioned for Brian to enter the house. "Please. Come in. Paul is doing fine. Do you have a concern about something? Did he miss an appointment? He said he's not scheduled to see you until tomorrow."

Brian entered the foyer and scanned the room. "Is Paul here?"

"Yes. He's on the back porch reading the newspaper. We just

finished our breakfast. Would you like a muffin or some coffee?"

As Brian opened his mouth to decline the extra calories and caffeine, Paul meandered into the room, with his cane, prosthesis in place. He strolled across the living room and greeted Brian in a bear hug.

"This is a surprise! Good to see you. Nice of you to stop by," he bellowed.

Brian stared at Carly, then at Paul. He had practiced exactly what he would say once he had a captive audience. But he hadn't expected the lump in his throat or the precipitous production from his tear ducts. Embarrassed for his overt display of emotion, he reached for the couch behind him, hoping to steady himself.

"Are you sick? Do you need a doctor?" cried Carly, removing the decorative pillows from the sofa to give him more room.

"I...uh...I'm so sorry," he cried, wiping the tears from his cheeks with the back of his hand. "I'm so embarrassed. Forgive me."

"Forgive you? For what? Tell us what's wrong!" pleaded Carly. "Let us help you."

Brian stood from the couch. He opened his mouth to speak the words he had written on his laptop and practiced and committed to memory. But he was suddenly mute, his lips and tongue and larynx unable to collaborate to produce the words and sentences his brain had designed. He contemplated running out of the house, like a child avoiding a punishment. But that would involve rapid muscle movement, and in his state of panic, his limbs might as well have been paralyzed. Carly and Paul stood before him, concern visible on their faces, their eyes wide.

In desperation, Brian removed his cell phone from his

pocket, and with his trembling index finger opened an app on the screen, then scrolled the images until he found what he wanted. He pressed his thumb and index finger to enlarge the image, then thrust the phone in their direction. He willed himself to raise his eyes from the floor, to look at their faces. He peered at Carly's face and saw her cheeks fall and her lower jaw tremble. She emitted a loud gasp and covered her mouth with her hand. Brian braced himself for the fallout: surprise, denial, anger, outrage. He took a few steps back, an instinctive strategy to protect himself. But the action didn't matter.

"Oh my God!" cried Carly as she enveloped him in a hug. "You figured it out! I knew you had a copy of your birth certificate. Paul told me you did. I was trying to figure out how to tell you I knew. That I never stopped thinking about you. That I've always loved you."

"Wait! You knew it was me? Then why—?" Brian glared at Paul. "You obviously knew. And you didn't tell me?"

"Brian! Calm down. Carly just told me. I found out yesterday. She kept the secret from all of us. Our children don't know yet."

"I'm so sorry, Brian," sobbed Carly. "I'll tell you everything you want to know. Everything that I can. I was young and in college. I knew I couldn't care for you. Not the way you deserved. So I did what I thought was best. Only one friend was aware of my pregnancy. My mother died without knowing of your existence. I regret that almost as much as not telling Paul the truth."

The separation of mother and son had spanned decades; now, only three feet divided their bodies. Carly reached across the gap and gingerly brushed the face of her first-born with her fingertips. She stared into his eyes—those blue eyes—and hoped her son saw the regret and remorse that had ravaged her body. Now that she could touch him, she hoped her actions didn't push him away. To find, then lose him, would be devastating. Brian's blue eyes flickered, a smile broke on his handsome face, and he grabbed onto Carly as a drowning man clutches a life preserver. Although his frame towered over hers by at least half a foot, their faces touched and bodies meshed in near perfection.

"I can't believe it's you," cried Brian, caressing Carly's cheeks. "To think that we have been living so close to each other. Our paths may have crossed before. Perhaps we were at the same restaurant. Or the same movie theater. But it was Paul who brought us together."

From a seat on the periphery of the room, Paul beamed. "I'm happy to take credit for this reunion, but I don't think I deserve it. What did I do?" Glancing at his prosthesis, he added, "Okay, Brian. But if I hadn't lost my leg, you still could have found each other. It might have taken a bit more research, but you would have found Carly."

"I suppose you're right, Paul," replied Brian. "I would have found Carly. Eventually. It's been a very emotional process. There's something I didn't tell you. After the break-up with Mimi, I considered giving up my search. Mimi was adamant that I needed to focus my attention on her and on our future. That future didn't include looking for the woman who gave birth to me. I loved Mimi and didn't realize how selfish her request was. I thought I would give up everything else for a lifetime with her. I convinced myself that she would complement me, cement my future, carry my children. My birth mother couldn't do that. I was exhausted, and ready to plead with Mimi to take me back. But Paul, when you reached out to me, I decided to continue my search."

"I remember how tired you looked. Then we started talking," declared Paul. "I just gave you a bit of encouragement."

"I rarely share my personal issues with others," replied Brian. "When you reached out to me that day, I couldn't believe that I told you my story. To know I could talk with you, man to man, was more of a relief than you know. You gave me the fortitude to carry on." He beamed. "I don't know what to expect from the rest of my life, but I have found the woman who made my life possible. I thought that finding my birth mother would be the best thing to happen to me. But I was wrong. Finding that both of you are in my life is better than anything I could have hoped for."

Chapter 67

The plane carrying David to Philadelphia touched down a few minutes later than expected, but David didn't care. Advanced Engineering Solutions had arranged for a driver to transport him from the airport to the company office in Delaware. The ride from Philadelphia International Airport would take less than half an hour; perhaps a bit more in traffic. Soon he would meet with the CEO of the company. Aaron had assured David the interview was a formality, that the job was his to lose. David had researched the company and prepared for the interview as if he was simply another candidate. He refused to make assumptions or let down his guard, so he had worn his freshly cleaned black suit paired with a white shirt and a decorative, but subtle, tie. It was fortuitous that the seat next to him on the plane was vacant; he had placed his suit jacket in the empty seat, along with his briefcase. Now, he donned the suit jacket, retrieved his briefcase, and checked his phone for the email with the driver's name.

Sitting in the bench seat in the back of the spacious

company car, he was grateful the driver Marco didn't force him to make idle conversation. David was happy to let his mind wander during the short drive. He recalled his last visit to the area, when his father was seriously ill. His relationship with his parents had improved considerably since his father's illness, although most of their conversations via phone or video chatting centered on how his father was progressing. He and Heidi had told their children that the removal of their grandfather's leg below the knee was caused by an infection. It sounded better than having to explain his compromised circulation. They breathed a sigh of relief that Matthew and Emily posed few tough questions about Paul's condition or recovery. So when Emily skinned her knee in a fall from her bicycle and was nearly hysterical the next day, terrified that the redness and bruising accompanying the minor skin abrasion meant a leg infection that would lead to an amputation, they realized that Paul's medical problems had affected them all.

Although it was a two-hour drive to his parents' home, David hadn't told them he would be in the area, and had scheduled a return flight for late afternoon. With the time change to the west coast, he would get home in the late evening. Although he had left home at five that morning, flown across the country, and would fly home after the job interview, David thought it best to concentrate the travel into one day. He expected to be weary the next day, but he could craft an excuse about not sleeping well. David suddenly felt guilty about not stopping to see his parents, but if he did well at the interview, and the salary and benefits were favorable, they would be overjoyed to hear that he and his family were moving to the east coast. As Marco drove the car into a sprawling business complex near the waterfront, David's thoughts returned to the reason for the trip—his interview.

. . .

DAVID WOWED RICHARD, THE CEO OF AES, AND LEONARD, supervisor of the department, and to David's delight, the men offered him the position within an hour. David was pleased with the salary and benefits package presented to him. It was less money than his current job, but when he factored in the lower cost of living, his net income would be comparable. After he and Heidi had reviewed and discussed the specifics, he expected he would accept the position. David had promised Richard and Leonard an answer within three days.

Now, David sat in the front seat of the sedan as Marco drove to the airport. The men compared stories about the sports their children played. When they arrived at the airport, Marco refused the tip David placed in his hand, but he relented when David designated the money for a new baseball glove for his son.

Inside the airport, David rode the escalator to the second floor and proceeded to the gate. But when he arrived at Gate 48, David was dismayed to see a sign showing the airline had canceled his flight because of mechanical problems. *A cancellation? Perhaps I can eke out a flight as a standby passenger.* After a wait that seemed more like hours rather than ten minutes, Maggie, a ticket agent, appeared at the desk, and reiterated that David's expected flight home had been canceled.

"But Ma'am, I need to get home tonight." David knew the best way to receive kindness was to give it. He also was a proponent of commiseration. "Here's the thing." David moved closer to Maggie and whispered, as if sharing a secret. "I came for a job interview today. I took a personal day, but I'll need to invent a great excuse if I don't show up for work tomorrow." David saw the woman's face soften. "I would really appreciate it if there's anything you can do."

"Sir, let me see what I can do," she responded, turning her attention to the computer in front of her. David thought his personal tale had worked; Maggie was humming to the music streaming from the overhead speakers. After a few minutes, she spoke.

"Mr. Brown, I'm sorry, but there are no flights this evening with extra seats. Here's what I can do. There's an early morning flight. It leaves at 5:10. With the time change, the expected landing time is a little after 8:00. Will that work for you?"

"Oh, my gosh! That's wonderful. I should be able to get to my office at a reasonable time. I can justify being a little late." David flashed his finest smile. "Thank you so much! I really appreciate it."

Boarding for the new flight would begin at 4:45. Over twelve hours until he could step into the plane. *I need to eat and sleep. A shower would be nice, too.* He pondered his options. *I could pay for a hotel. There are several nearby, with shuttle buses for transport to and from the airport. I can justify the expense, because I'll probably accept the position AES offered me.* David took a seat in an empty terminal and called Heidi.

"Hi, honey," he said, when she answered.

"David! Sweetheart. I've been waiting for your call. How was the interview?"

"It went fine. I liked them. And I was offered a nice package. We can talk about it when I get home, but I'm seriously considering it."

"That's great! Are you boarding your flight soon?"

"Unfortunately, I can't get home tonight. The airline canceled my flight. I am booked on the first available flight. A little after five. Tomorrow morning. I'll pick up my car and go directly to work." David sighed. "I had to sweet talk a ticket agent to get on that plane. So I guess I'll get a hotel room near here. I can take a shuttle from the hotel back here in the morning."

"Well, you could rent a car and visit your parents."

"I didn't consider that option. But it's a long drive for a few hours' visit." As the words left his mouth, David realized his mistake. "Actually, I think you're right. It's a great idea. A chance to see my parents. To see how my father has progressed. I'll get a little sleep there, and I can sleep on the plane. I'll call them. But I won't say anything about the job offer. We'll discuss it when I get home. I don't want to disappoint my parents by telling them we're moving back here if I'm not positive yet."

Fifteen minutes later, David sat behind the wheel of a black Mustang convertible. His parents were thrilled he was in town and would hold dinner until his arrival. David fabricated a story that his company had sent him to AES to evaluate their software. He replayed the story in his mind several times until he was sure he could repeat it with a poker face—something he often found difficult to do.

Chapter 68

C arly and Brian sat side-by-side on the couch while he scrolled through the pictures on his phone and told her stories about his childhood and adolescence. Paul had slipped from the room as quietly and gingerly as he could, to allow his wife and her firstborn the opportunity to reconnect privately. The photographs which chronicled Brian's life produced bitter-sweet moments and torrents of tears. Carly cried for the lost days and months and years, for the birthdays and holidays and graduations she had missed, but also tears of happiness for the good life her son had experienced, for the knowledge that as a nineteen-year-old single mother, she could not have given him as much as the man and woman who adopted him, the couple who carried him from the hospital the day she relinquished her legal and maternal rights.

While David's call had interrupted their reunion, it had set in place a more urgent timetable. Carly had not expected to tell Greer and David about Brian so soon. Being a writer, she had hoped to craft a few passages, starting with her college life and her pregnancy, followed by her decision to relinquish her baby for adoption. Gradually she would announce that she and her firstborn had reunited, and when they asked to meet him—as she was certain they would—she would introduce Brian as her son.

Perhaps Greer would understand why Carly had interfered with her relationship with Brian, why she had staged the scene to reunite her and Mickey. David was different. He had never met Brian, and she did not think Greer had mentioned her relationship with him in the occasional conversation with her brother. At this moment, perhaps serendipitously, while Brian was beside her, David was on route to see them. She could not —and would not—concoct a story, or introduce him simply as Paul's therapist. It was time to gather her courage and tell David the truth. Today. *But if I'm going to pour out my heart and soul to David, I should include Greer in the news.*

"Is this too much for you?" she asked Brian. "For me to tell David and Greer today? For you to face them?"

Brian grinned. "I admit I wasn't expecting to be introduced as your son today. To call them my sister and brother. I was concerned that you would throw me out of the house when you heard what I came to say. But why wait? David is on his way. Of course we should include Greer. I can't wait to tell her we're more than friends!"

Carly silently said thanks that Greer and Mickey were back together. Learning that they were half siblings could strengthen a friendship between Greer and Brian, but the knowledge might have led to catastrophic consequences if they were romantically involved. "Okay. I'll contact Greer." Carly retrieved her phone and sent a text to Greer.

Carly: "Can you come over in about an hour?"

Greer: "I had a busy day. So tired. Can I come tomorrow?"

Carly: "I'd like to see you today. Is Mickey home? Can he come too?"

Greer: "OMG! Are you okay? Are you sick? We'll come now!"

Carly: "No! It's nothing like that. I just want to talk to you."

Greer: "Okay. I want to talk to you too. Be there soon."

I wonder what Greer wants to tell me. But I won't focus on that now. Whatever Greer has to say, I'm certain it pales when compared to my announcement.

"Greer and Mickey will be here soon. Greer said she's exhausted. But I'm sure our news will energize her. When she learns that the two of you are more than friends." Carly inched towards Brian, onto the same couch cushion. *Oh! Is my physical closeness overpowering him?* "Brian, forgive me if I'm too close! After all these years, I want to feel your body next to mine. I only held you once before I handed you over for adoption. I guess I'm trying to make up for all the years I missed."

"Carly." A sudden thought hung in the air. "Should I still call you Carly? Is that okay?" Brian asked. "You're my mother, but..."

It was an innocent question posed by a man to his mother. An inquiry decades in the making, music to the ears of the woman who had relinquished her claim to him. She wanted to answer, but her sobs would have drowned out the words. Brian, sensing Carly's response, clutched her tighter.

"It's okay," he whispered. "I'll take that as a yes."

TEN MINUTES LATER, THE SOUND OF A CAR ENTERING THE driveway broke the silence. Carly released her grip on Brian and loped to the window, and as Greer and Mickey exited the car, Carly threw open the front door.

"Mom! Are you okay? Your face is so red. You look like you've been crying! What's wrong?" inquired Greer.

"Come in the house," replied Carly, embracing Greer and Mickey. "There's someone else here too. And David is on his way."

"Really? David traveled from California for your announcement?" Greer grabbed onto Carly's shoulders and shook them forcefully. "This must be serious. Don't make us wait any longer! I want to know now!" she demanded.

Carly was determined to delay her announcement until David was present. She checked the time. *How much time does it take to rent a car? How much longer until he is here?*

"No! David had a business trip to a company in Delaware. His return flight was canceled. So he'll be spending a few hours with us. Please come into the living room. Brian is here too."

Brian stood by the couch, an arm's length away from the woman who was unaware they were closer than friends. His face was puffy and tear-stained.

"Mom! Why is Brian here?" Greer froze, overwhelmed by a new possibility. "Oh, my God! It's not you, Mom! It's Dad! Where is he? Is this bad news about him? It must be. Why else would Brian be here? And he's been crying too!"

Mickey saw the color rush from her face, and afraid Greer would collapse, rushed to her side.

"Stop!" demanded Carly. "Your father is fine. I'm surprised he hasn't heard the commotion!"

"I heard the ruckus. And I'm here," Paul cried as he plodded down the stairs. "Nothing about my health has changed." After reaching the living room, he pointed to his prosthesis and exclaimed, "I'm the same perfect physical specimen I have always been!"

Carly smiled at Paul's humor, but Greer spurned the frivolity. Stoically, she hugged her father.

"You're close to perfect. And I'm thrilled you're able to use the stairs so well. But Mom didn't demand I get off the couch and rush over here so Mickey and I could see that."

Carly wasn't certain how much longer she could delay. She retrieved her cell phone from the table, walked into the kitchen, and phoned David.

"David! How much longer until you're here?" she cried when he answered, omitting the usual greetings.

"Hi, Mom! I lost some time because of construction. But I'm close. Perhaps ten minutes."

Carly brightened. "Okay. Come right in. I have something to tell you."

It took all of Carly's restraint to remain in the kitchen. *I can hold out another ten minutes.* To keep her hands busy and pass the time, Carly gathered six glasses from the cupboard and piled them on a wooden tray, then added ice cubes to a pitcher of cold water. Satisfied she had squandered five minutes, she carried the tray into the living room.

The scene before her was reminiscent of the sterile and gloomy atmosphere in the hospital lounge. Greer and Mickey were huddled on the loveseat, across from Brian, who was seated in the rocking chair that had belonged to Carly's mother. Brian's face was expressionless. As Carly peered out the front window, she thought how difficult the wait must be for him. Then, suddenly, an unfamiliar car stopped in front of their house, and David sprinted from the driver's seat, up the walkway, and into the foyer.

"Thank goodness you're here," bellowed Greer, bounding from Mickey's arms and hugging her brother. "David, this is Mickey. Mickey, this is David. David, meet Brian. Brian, meet

David. Mom, now that the introductions are complete, tell us why you called us here."

Five sets of eyes turned to Carly, who was suddenly overcome with fear. *What if David and Greer can't forgive what I've done? What if they refuse to acknowledge Brian as my son?* Her eyes locked with Brian's, and he smiled and nodded. She could sense his message: *It will be okay.* She stood and exhaled deeply. Then she started from the beginning.

"Greer and David, I was once a young woman. A college student. I was idealistic. And like all young people, I did some things that I'm not proud of." Carly paused, and was met with silence.

"When I was eighteen and a college freshman, I entered into a relationship with a professor there. He promised me the world. And I believed him." Carly's hands trembled and she fought the urge to cry, but she forced herself to continue. "I became pregnant. The professor refused to marry me. He left me little choice. I didn't believe in abortion. You know that I still don't. I gave birth to a son the month before I began my sophomore year. I gave him up for adoption." Her eyes wandered to Brian. "I never forgot about him. I spent the years since then wondering what he was like as a boy, and what type of man he had become. Now I know. And after more than thirty-five years, I found him."

A smile broke the tension in her face and in the surrounding room. "Actually, we found each other." Carly nodded to Brian, and he stood and linked his hands with hers.

"Brian is my son."

A PHOTOGRAPH CAPTURES EXPERIENCES AND EXPRESSIONS AS A reminder of an event, but years later, Carly didn't need a photograph to recall the exhilaration and euphoria that permeated the room. Although David and Brian had not met before the announcement, David knew that much of his father's recovery and rehabilitation had been because of Brian. As cries of joy replaced those of anguish, Paul stood on the periphery of the scene and thought about how life had changed. Carly had given birth to Brian, but it was Brian who had rejuvenated Paul. *A rebirth of sorts.*

Suddenly, Greer cried, "I didn't tell you my news!" Releasing Mickey's hand, she announced, "Mickey proposed to me! We're getting married!"

"That's wonderful!" exclaimed Carly. "I was so preoccupied with my news that I forgot you had something to tell us!" She embraced Mickey. "Congratulations! Today we added Brian. And we're adding Mickey to our family, too! What a day it has been!"

Mickey graciously accepted the hugs, back slaps, and high fives. He wanted to interject, but couldn't break through the din of voices that filled the room. Growing frustrated, he finally interrupted.

"Excuse me!" he cried, waving his hands above his head. "Thank you for your congratulations. But Greer told you only part of our news. The rest actually involves Brian. Let me say that I was a fool to think that Greer cheated on me. I now know where she and Brian went the afternoon I accused her of cheating. They went to an exposition about physical therapy." Mickey's eyes met Brian's, as Brian nodded in agreement. "Greer was floundering. She didn't know what she wanted to do with her life." Mickey gazed lovingly at her. "Well...besides becoming my wife. But the work Brian has been doing with Paul piqued Greer's interest. Her father's illness stirred her desire to learn more about his condition. Working at the ambulance company exposed her to medical terms every day. But it wasn't until she saw Brian with Paul that she realized what she wanted to do with her life. What she wanted to study in school. Going to the exposition sealed her decision." Mickey paused, but no one spoke.

"So I'm proud to say that my future wife intends to become a physical therapist! She wants to help others gain independence, as Brian has done for Paul."

"That's wonderful," cried Carly, as she embraced Greer. "I'm so happy for you!"

"Honey, I'm thrilled!" Paul bellowed. "Another therapist in the family!"

"Good choice, Sis!" exclaimed David. "I can't wait to tell Heidi."

Greer locked eyes with Brian, who was beaming.

"Greer. At first I was happy to call you my friend," he declared. "Then I was delighted that you wanted to enter the same field as me. But I am so thrilled to call you my sister."

The last words broke through Brian's strangled sobs. As he reached for Greer, Brian searched Mickey's face for approval, and as Mickey smiled and nodded, Brian clutched Greer to his chest and planted kisses on her face. They stood together, as friends, siblings, and peers, as the others watched through eyes blurred by tears.

Suddenly, Greer parted from Brian, and she cried, "There's more! Mickey is going to own the garage! He saved enough money for the down payment! And he got approved for a mortgage! So he will be a business owner!"

The celebrations began anew. It appeared that everyone had something to celebrate. Almost everyone. Greer turned to David and chuckled.

"I don't suppose you have news to tell us. Something for us to celebrate."

Five pairs of eyes locked with David's.

Greer laughed. "It's your turn, David. Come on. You must have something to tell us. Perhaps there's a new baby coming," she teased.

David thought of the pledge he had made to Heidi to withhold the true reason for his trip to Delaware. She would have to forgive him for breaking his promise. He paused, surveyed the room, and began his announcement.

Chapter 69

My Life and Yours- by Carly Casper

To my valued readers: This is the final chapter in my story, and as much as it may be startling for you to read this column, it is a catharsis for me. I have written many words, all carefully chosen and necessary to finish my story.

As we travel through life, we traverse hills and valleys. It is not always a smooth journey. We trudge up the hills, a foot or two at a time, sometimes missing a step, falling backwards, and starting the climb again. Sometimes we sprint through the valleys, only to reach another hill. My family and I have climbed many hills and run through many valleys. Our plans were threatened and thwarted. But we have thrived, and our cast of characters has expanded along the journey. I have often wondered if it would have been better to have a crystal ball, what we would have done if we had known about all the changes that would occur. I suspect I would have cried out and demanded our lives not move forward. After all, who thinks they should have to endure a leg amputation and a fight to regain independence?

Paul and I were blessed with good lives and good health. As you may recall, the most troublesome health issue we faced previously—and which for a long time I denied and then ignored—was my gradual hearing loss. I am happy to report that I have received my hearing aids, a pair of earbuds that resemble wireless technology such as Bluetooth. They are nearly invisible, and I am amazed what a difference they have made in my life. Sometimes I sit on our porch and listen to the birds sing. I thought their sounds were all alike, but I was mistaken. I have learned to distinguish the tones in their voices. The difference in my hearing amazes me. I am sorry I did not acknowledge my problem earlier.

Now, I need to share a secret—something I didn't even tell my husband for thirty-five years. Something that occurred in my late teens, a few years before Paul and I met. At first it was difficult, but once I learned to conceal it, to lock it away in a corner of my brain, I did not think much about what I was hiding. But I never forgot. I just tried not to remember.

During my freshman year in college, I had an affair with someone who I looked up to. I was young and in love; I suppose he was in lust. The man was older than me and more powerful, and while I cannot excuse what I did, neither should he. His name does not matter. We conceived a child. When he refused to marry me, or to have anything more to do with me, or with his child, I was distraught and ashamed. I did not realize he had taken advantage of my innocence. He risked his career and his reputation and bet I wouldn't reveal what he had done. And I didn't. I gave birth to a son and signed adoption papers. My widowed mother never knew I had relinquished custody of her first grandchild. I changed my name, and although I told my mother that *Carly Casper* was much better suited for the journalist I aspired to be, it was only a partial truth. I wanted to sever ties with my previous life. I transferred to another university and tried to erase that block of time from my life.

I met Paul about two years later. As our relationship grew, I considered telling him of my affair and the child I had borne. But I couldn't find the words to describe my indiscretions, and I wouldn't chance a blemish on our relationship, even though I realize now that my wonderful husband would have understood and forgiven me. As the years passed, the decision to hide my past from Paul and our two children haunted me, but telling them grew more difficult. I never forgot my firstborn. I remembered him on his birthdays, but I celebrated silently and alone. I hoped he was happy and successful. Although I wondered about him nearly every day, I never tried to find him. What I did not know was that he would try to find me.

Some people believe in coincidences or luck or the power of a higher being. Others believe in fate or Tarot cards or crystal balls or horoscopes, or the alignment of the stars and planets and moons. But whatever the force, my son found me. In the end, we found each other.

In a previous column, I introduced you to Brian, Paul's physical therapist. I told you what a wonderful man he was, and how much he helped Paul in his recovery. What we did not know until a few months ago was that Brian is my son, the baby I gave up for adoption more than half a lifetime ago. The man who is Brian's birth father passed down his hair color to his son. A common shade of brown, no one would identify Brian as his son based solely on the hue. But Brian also inherited an unusual feature from his father—his eye color. The same eyes that I was drawn to decades ago. When I saw those eyes on Brian, I knew the truth. But I couldn't face my family. Or my fears. I tried to deny what I knew was the truth. But serendipitously, or perhaps due to a higher power or an outside force, Brian had begun his search for me. His birth certificate bore my birth name. A name not much different from the name I have used since shortly after his birth—just more ethnic-sounding.

I've also told you about my son David and his family, who were living in California. They were happy there—or so he and his wife, Heidi, thought. David and Paul and I experienced the minor estrangement common in so many families. Because we didn't argue, we would have denied a schism, and we scheduled occasional video chats with David and Heidi and our grandson and granddaughter, and sent gifts for birthdays and holidays. But we didn't really talk about things that mattered.

David and Heidi reevaluated what was important to them, what they really wanted in life. Armed with his new job offer, they elected to move to this area, where David will continue to work in website development. He is transitioning from a firm on the west coast to become a supervisor in an expanding company in Delaware. Their new home is about an hour from ours. We were accustomed to scheduling our trips to California, making airline and hotel reservations, adjusting our bodies to the three-hour time change. We now travel by car to their home, often to visit for an afternoon or to share a meal. Heidi, who worked for many years as a paralegal, had recently considered applying to law school. She did well in the LSAT, and in the past week has received acceptances to two schools in this area. She will start law school in the fall. We know she will make a wonderful attorney. Now, our grandchildren use Zoom to chat with their California friends. Although unhappy to move across the country, they are thriving in school and have forged new friendships here.

Our daughter Greer disappointed Paul and me—especially me—when she dropped out of college, where she was studying writing and journalism. She is a gifted writer, and I expected she would follow in my footsteps and earn a living in a related field. But although she was doing well in school, she was unhappy. She left school, and the comfort of our home, and took some time to find herself, to discover what she wanted in life. Because of her father's illness and recovery, Greer found her calling. She decided to pursue a career as a physical therapist, and we are proud to say she has received a partial scholarship and acceptance into a wonderful program. She is currently taking prerequisite courses at a local college. Watching her father fight so hard during his recovery fueled her interest in rehabilitation. But it was Brian who fed the flames, spending hours discussing the intricacies of the human body, and advising her on academic programs. We are also elated with Greer's recent engagement to Mickey, a great guy and gifted mechanic who has worked very hard, and very long hours, to save sufficient money to purchase an automobile repair shop, the garage where he has worked for a few years. He will rename the business *Mechanics by Mickey* after the official change in ownership later this month. Paul and I are proud of Mickey, and delighted that he will marry our daughter. Of course, our automobiles will always be in excellent condition!

After Greer's birth, our marriage hit a rough spot. We initially considered counseling, but instead, I went to see a crystal ball gazer, who looked into the future and proclaimed that our marital discord was short-term. But when the fortune-teller announced that I had three children, I denied the existence of my firstborn and asserted I had two children and planned no more. The woman insisted I had three children, and I finally acknowledged I had relinquished a son for adoption. She told me he wasn't lost to me, that he would return unexpectedly. I wasn't sure whether I believed her, or whether I wanted to. I continued on with the life that Paul and I had created. Our marriage strengthened, and I rarely thought again of the psychic or her predictions.

Being a writer, I possess a greater than average attention to detail. I can be quite methodical. Many writers sit at a computer and let their fingers tell a story, the words pouring forth without an organized plan. That is not me. I prepare extensive outlines, and I usually follow them religiously. Rarely do I waver from my plan. I have said more than once that if I only knew what would happen next in my life, I could prepare. I have even joked about wanting a crystal ball, so I could plan my life like I plan the words I write. We can embellish our financial futures by saving money for emergencies and retirement, calculating our expenses, and constructing budgets. But life has a way of surprising us. It doesn't always follow the outline we have prepared, or the budget we have made. We can use our seatbelts every time we ride in a car and still get injured in an accident. Looking both ways before crossing an intersection does not always prevent getting hit by a speeding car. We can do exemplary work at a job and still lose it because of a company restructuring. We can find ourselves hungry or homeless with a few turns of bad luck.

Sometimes good things result from bad ones. Paul's illness and amputation were so terrible that we couldn't imagine an emergence of happiness. We did not think Paul would travel through the stages of grief and accept what had happened. Of course, the journey through the stages is fraught with movements forwards and backwards—the backwards travel occurring suddenly, like potholes in a stretch of smooth road. We have learned that no matter how long we travel on the road, staying within the painted lines and obeying the rules, there is an occasional bump that reminds us we cannot let down our guard, that we have to pay attention. Sometimes it is a minor obstacle—such as an able-bodied person claiming the last parking space in front of a store—that causes Paul to move from acceptance to anger. He continues to work with a wonderful therapist who has taught him how to maneuver around life's obstacles.

I initially hoped that Paul would acknowledge his body changes and become independent enough to not be a burden. I knew he wouldn't want to rely on me or on other family or outsiders for physical help. Then I raised the bar. I hoped he could ambulate, even short distances, with a walker or a cane, and hopefully with a prosthesis. Brian helped him to achieve and surpass those goals. Under Brian's guidance and skills, Paul grew from a man emasculated by loss of part of his body and a sudden decline in his medical and physical condition. He required physical help to move to the toilet or chair or to stand and was restricted to the first floor of our home upon discharge from the hospital. Paul is now completely independent with all activities, ambulates with a prosthesis with a slight limp, and passed testing to safely drive an automobile. Next month, he will return to his job in the insurance industry, part-time, training others in the field. A year ago, we were planning a trip to Scotland, to explore the birthplace of Paul's parents. Sitting by Paul's bedside in the hospital, I thought our future travel would be restricted to day trips to wheelchair-accessible destinations. Fortunately, I was wrong. Paul and I are exploring a trip to Scotland next year. Although he may need a wheelchair for longer distances, he can walk and climb and dance.

I would have been happy enough to write this column detailing Paul's journey of hardship, perseverance, and success. But our family got so much more along the way.

Brian had already begun his search for his birth mother before he met Paul. He had a copy of his birth certificate, which bore my given name. It would not have been a stretch for him to find me with the information he had. Interestingly, like many younger people, he does not read a physical newspaper, preferring to sift through the myriad of articles available online. Although I have written articles for this paper at least twice a week for many years, Brian claims he never read them. He didn't recognize my name. It was pure coincidence that we have lived less than an hour apart for a half dozen years. But regardless of my address, Brian said he never would have stopped looking for me.

Shortly after Greer and Mickey announced their engagement, Brian traveled to see Greer at the ambulance company where she works as a supervisor. While he waited to see her, he chatted with Morgan, a manager at the company, who is also training as a paramedic. Their conversation—and relationship—has continued. Now, a few months after their initial meeting, they are officially a couple. I won't ask someone to peer into a crystal ball to tell us what the future holds for them. It will be more fun to see for ourselves.

Our family has received another gift—a relationship with the wonderful man and woman who adopted Brian: Ed and Lisa Snyder. I could not have found a better couple to raise my son if I had chosen them myself. We share gratitude. They are grateful that I relinquished my newborn for adoption, and I will forever be thankful that they raised him to be the man he is today.

If we had consulted a crystal ball along the way, would we

have believed its forewarnings? If we had known what would happen to Paul, to Greer, to David, and to me, would we have changed anything? I always thought I would want to know what the future held. Now I disagree. I would not have wanted a crystal ball. I liked our life the way it was and would not have asked to know what changes would befall us. We can spend endless hours wondering about the what-ifs and thinking about how our lives might have been different, if we had known in advance what paths our lives would take.

If we all knew what would happen tomorrow or next week, would we change how we are behaving today? Perhaps many people would. I posed this question to my family. I reached deep inside myself as well. My family answered unanimously. "No." If I had not allowed Brian to be adopted, I probably would never have met Paul. Without Paul, I would not have given birth to David and Greer. If Greer had been happy studying writing, she wouldn't have left school—and would not be engaged to Mickey. If David never went to California, he would not have met Heidi, would not have fathered Matthew and Emily.

Paul's illness and hospitalization changed our lives in so many ways. We came from the depths of catastrophe to the cusp of exuberance. When he rode through the hospital doors on a stretcher, we had no indication that our lives would change so dramatically. In the ensuing months we traveled from the depths of despair to the peak of elation. It has been a ride that we never expected.

If I had known I would be reunited with my firstborn thirty-five years after his birth, I cannot say I would have welcomed that intrusion into my life.

I thought I was living a good life. But it is so much better now.

Acknowledgments

I wrote "If We Had Known" because of the wonderful support and feedback of readers of my debut novel "Beneath A Blanket Of Snow."

As readers of my first novel are aware, my journey as an author followed a career of more than forty years in health care. After a coworker remarked a week prior to my retirement in 2019 that I should start on my bucket list, to my surprise, I responded that I would write a novel.

When I released "Beneath A Blanket Of Snow" in July 2020, I did not know how it would be received. After all, I was in my sixties and had not thought about writing a book since my adolescence. I dipped my toe in the waters of the world of writers. Now, I have taken a plunge with my second novel.

A huge thank you to the readers who encouraged me to write another book. I am so grateful for your comments, reviews, and messages. Every author dreams of the ratings and reviews I have received.

I owe enormous gratitude to Eve Lefkowitz, a fellow nurse,

former coworker, bicycling buddy, and dear friend, who accepted the role of beta reader, editor, and proofreader. As expected, your input and insight were invaluable, and much appreciated.

Of course, none of this would be possible without the support of my husband Gerry, my first beta reader; my cheerleader, sounding board, assistant, and partner of more than twenty-five years, who has grown accustomed to me sitting at my computer for hours at a time. We are so fortunate to be able to pursue our passions in retirement.

Author's Notes

Please visit my website at **www.arlenelomazoffmarron.com** to sign up for my newsletter and follow my journey as an author.

All authors appreciate their readers' feedback, and I am no exception. Consumers read product reviews before deciding whether to purchase the product, and readers of books do the same. I would appreciate your ratings and comments on Amazon and, if possible, on Goodreads.

Find "Beneath A Blanket Of Snow" amazon.com/dp/B08DH91FMM

Made in the USA
Middletown, DE
30 April 2021

38748507R00191